THE PRYCE *OF* DECEIT

KARI BOVÉE

THE
PRYCE
OF
DECEIT

KARI BOVEE

VINCI
BOOKS

By Kari Bovée

The Pryce of Murder

Vinci Books

vinci-books.com

Published by Vinci Books Ltd in 2025

1

Chapter One

SEPTEMBER 1885

I hesitated, my fist motionless in the air as I stopped myself from knocking on the door. Everyone knew it was bad luck for the groom to see his bride before the ceremony on their wedding day, but there was definitely a male voice coming from Eliza Swindon's room. And whoever he was didn't sound happy.

"This isn't right!" the man shouted. I thought I detected a hint of admonishment in his tone, or perhaps even a threat, but it was all I could make out. I could tell that it wasn't Eliza's fiancé's voice, though. The timber of the voice emanating from behind the door was much deeper—and angrier—than Rupert Townsend's.

My brow furrowed with concern at this highly irregular turn of events. "Who is in there with her?" I whispered to Bijou, my little Havanese dog, who stood faithfully at my feet. She looked up at me with her big brown eyes and cocked her head, clearly as confused as I was.

I knocked on the door. "Eliza, it's Arabella. May I come in?"

The voices ceased. In a few seconds, which seemed like minutes, the door opened, and I stood staring into the handsome, dark-skinned face of Bob Parkhurst, the town blacksmith and farrier.

Highly irregular, indeed! I had not been aware the two even were acquainted, let alone close enough that she'd allow him in her room.

"Mr. Parkhurst!" I couldn't hold back my surprise. "What are you doing here?"

Tall, muscular, and broad shouldered from forging iron all day, he gave me a nod of greeting, but I dare say his usually friendly smile seemed forced.

"Mrs. Pryce." He gave me a nod. "Just stoppin' by to wish the bride good luck." He planted his hat back on his head and made his way to the staircase, nearly tripping on Bijou and causing her to let out a tiny yelp of surprise.

I watched him jog down the stairs to the next landing, still a little perplexed as to why he would have been in Eliza's room and what exactly he meant when he'd said, "This isn't right."

Eliza waved me toward her. A small woman with large brown eyes and a head of thick auburn hair, she looked like a fragile being from a fairy wonderland. "Come in, Arabella."

I entered, Bijou on my heels, and closed the door behind me. "Is everything okay?"

"Of course!" She beamed. Bijou raised herself on her hind legs and set her front paws on the skirt of Eliza's dress.

"Bijou, no!" I scolded, worried she'd get the gleaming white wedding dress dirty. The little imp lowered herself and looked up at me with pitiful eyes.

"Oh, don't worry, Bijou." Eliza bent down and gave her a pat on the head. "You've caused no harm."

"Mr. Parkhurst seemed . . . perturbed," I said.

"Oh dear, I'm afraid so." Eliza straightened and then batted a dismissive hand in the air. "That's my fault. Last week, I used one of the horses at the livery and didn't have my handbag with me, so I couldn't pay him. He let me take the horse anyway. Then I forgot to take him the money as I'd promised. He was a little annoyed with me, but I've paid him and all is well."

"I see." I mulled over what she had just said. Bob Parkhurst was nothing if not a perfect gentleman. In fact, I had never seen him upset. He was always quick with that easy smile, and although he was big as a barn, he had an extremely gentle nature. Before today, I couldn't imagine him even raising his voice—especially over something as petty as a few cents to rent a horse—but from what I'd heard through the door, *annoyed* was putting it mildly.

I itched to press her for more, but it really was none of my business.

"Are you sure you're all right?" I ventured.

She gave me a reassuring smile. "Don't look so worried, Arabella. Everything is fine. In fact, everything is wonderful! I'm getting married today." She held out her left hand to admire the three-stoned, sapphire-and-diamond, gold fili-gree engagement ring.

She seemed positively giddy, excited for her big day, and it put me at ease. So I set aside my confusion at the situation and joined her at the mirror, standing slightly behind her so I wouldn't block her view of herself.

"So, how are you feeling, Eliza?" I straightened her veil, which was slightly mussed.

Her ensemble, a high-necked affair, consisted of a

cream satin jacket, which hugged her envy-provoking tiny waist, fitted over a matching skirt overlayed with lace that was dotted with artificial pearls. The modest bodice emphasized her diminutive yet womanly figure. The veil, equal in length to the dress's train, was made of tulle and tiny, colorful embroidered butterflies graced the netting. The entire look added to Eliza's otherworldly quality.

"I'm so nervous." She placed a hand on her chest. "My heart is racing like a runaway coach."

"That's understandable." I smiled. "It's not every day a woman gets married."

A former actress like myself—but with much less acclaim—Eliza Swindon had arrived in La Plata Springs after corresponding with Rupert Townsend, the former manager of the local general store, Archer's Dry Goods. Recently, he had come into money after staking a claim—the Cougar—in the silver mines that had produced some of the valuable ore in these southern Colorado mountains. Now financially secure, the man had been in want of a wife and had put an ad in nearby Denver's most popular newspaper.

"Oh, Arabella." She turned to face me. "I don't know what I'd do without you. You've been such a good friend since I arrived. You've treated me like a princess. These rooms are lovely, as is your hotel. I've so enjoyed staying here at the Arabella these last six weeks."

"Your fiancé would spare no expense," I said.

I had inherited the Arabella—yes, the hotel was named for me—from my late husband, an occurrence that had upended my life in ways I'd never thought imaginable. Suffice it to say, I was still reeling, and that was just a few months ago.

Mr. Townsend had rented one of the suites of rooms on

the third floor for Eliza, and they were the finest in the hotel
—second to mine, of course.

The Arabella, although a bit tired on the inside, something I was trying to remedy, was grand in stature, the largest structure in the town, and had been built in the American Victorian design, complete with red bricks and embellished with carved white stone. The interior was opulent for these parts, with furnishings in the popular Queen Anne and Victorian styles, yet it had a homey feel. I had seen to most of the leaky roof, peeling paint, and buckling wallpaper, but the refurbishing of the hotel to its former glory was still underway and not without its challenges, namely financial in nature.

"Yes, Rupert is such a dear man." Her cheeks blushed pink. "I aim to be a good wife to him. Even though, I'll admit, living in such a provincial place as La Plata Springs is not as stimulating as a big city, I'm ready to settle down. Establish some roots."

"Yes," I agreed with her assessment of La Plata Springs, almost too quickly. As a newcomer to the town myself, I'd found adapting to my new surroundings a bit more difficult than what Eliza expressed.

The little settlement, nestled in a valley below the La Plata mountains, was organized by the railroad some years ago and then developed primarily by a man named Archibald Archer who, after discovering a lode of silver, copper, and gold, opened the first mine. He left the railroad but retained a vested interest in it. One of the wealthiest men in the American West, his sole aim was to put La Plata Springs on the map as one of the most popular spots for tourism in the region.

On account of the fact that he owned a vast majority of the businesses in town, the locals around here called him

"Boss," but I simply couldn't bring myself to do the same. It seemed so undignified and, well, subservient, which I could not abide.

My late husband, William, also a visionary and equally enterprising—and just as wealthy—had heard of the treasures found in these rugged parts and, like Mr. Archer, had purchased some land in this little burg from the railroad.

Knowing that many others out to seek fortune would soon venture to this area, William, with the help of an architect named Percival Blank, had built the Arabella, a hotel equal in splendor to any in Colorado and, I daresay, the entire Western frontier.

"I will miss Denver." Eliza looked up at me with a wistful expression. "But I am so glad we have become friends. We will adjust to small-town living together."

I took her hands in mine. "I look forward to it."

I had only been in La Plata Springs for a mere three months, and though it may seem grand that I had inherited such an establishment, it had not come as welcome news. In his will, William had stipulated that I leave my wonderful life and my beloved theater in New York to come oversee the operation of the Arabella—one of his prized possessions —for a year's time in order to obtain my *full* inheritance, which was quite substantial.

Apparently, he'd felt I had immersed myself too deeply in the world of the theater and my celebrity, and he wanted me to have a more well-rounded perspective of life. I know he'd made this demand with no ill intent in his heart, but still, I couldn't help but feel hurt by it.

As a woman and a widow, and someone who had known all too well the bone-deep ache of poverty in my youth, I could scarcely afford to refuse. To do so would mean losing everything. And I couldn't lose my theater or my adoring public. They were my lifeblood.

So, while I did not want to be here, it was necessary for my future.

Meeting Eliza had been like a balm to me. We had much in common with our experiences in the theater, and we had come from similar backgrounds of painstaking struggle. We differed in how we were reared: me, an English rose and an only child who had started acting in London at the age of ten to support myself and my mother, and Eliza, an American who had been raised by a neglectful drunkard of a father. She had a sister, but the two had been long estranged.

Both of us had grown up feeling unloved and alone in the world, and our only solace had been our art. Our new friendship had been forged by many an hour spent over tea and freshly baked biscuits in recent weeks.

Movement in the mirror shook me out of my reverie, and I gasped. Bijou, sensing my alarm, let out a bark.

"Arabella?" Eliza took hold of my hand. "Are you all right?"

"Yes, yes," I assured her, trying to keep my voice in check.

"You look like you've seen a ghost."

I pulled my attention from the mirror and did my best to arrange my face in a way that would belie my irritation. For indeed, I *had* seen one.

Chapter Two

I tried my best not to glare at the man—well, the ghost—the aforementioned architect, Percival Blank, who had died here at his beloved creation. He had popped up out of nowhere in the mirror, which he was annoyingly wont to do. He'd made a habit of surprising me at the most inopportune times.

He pulled his pipe from his velvet smoking jacket, then flicked his fingers and the bowl of it glowed orange, coming aflame. Instantly, the aroma of spicy tobacco filled the room. He bounced his eyebrows up and down at me, and I bit back my irritation.

"Do you smell that?" Eliza asked. She was about to turn toward the mirror again, and I took her by the elbows.

"It must be coming from outside." I nodded toward an open window. "Now, shall we get you to the church?"

She picked up the small watch pendant from the chain I wore around my neck and looked at the time.

"Won't we be too early? I don't want anyone to see me until I walk down the aisle."

She did have a point. We would be early by fifteen minutes. But I needed to distract her from turning toward the mirror again, as Percival was now leaning against the bureau, his legs casually crossed at the ankles. It seemed he was not about to budge.

I was familiar enough with ghosts to know that not everyone was as keenly aware of them as I was, but I also knew that should he choose to do so, he could make himself seen. Especially by those who were even the slightest bit sensitive, whether they realized it or not, to the phenomenon, a fact that could have repercussions for the reputation of my hotel—worse yet, my own, should anyone find out about my particular gift of seeing the dead—and I could not have that.

When in the mirror, Percival's form was solid, and he looked to be as alive as any earthly being. As long as he was in the mirror, he could move objects about, which he was also fond of doing to scare certain guests he disliked. While looking at his reflection, one could also feel his touch, should he be in the mind to lay a comforting hand on one's shoulder, as he'd done with me a time or two. However, once he stepped out of the mirror, he was as translucent as a firefly's wings and with his presence came an icy coolness that sank into one's bones.

"You're right," I said to Eliza, trying to ignore him. "It is a little early to show up to the church. I don't know what I was thinking. I guess I'm nervous, too. Your wedding reception will be the first event I have hosted here at the hotel."

She let out a tinkling laugh. "Nervous? You? But what about all those lavish parties you hosted in New York? Surely, you aren't worried about such a small affair here in this sleepy little town."

It was true. I shouldn't have been anxious about it, but

in New York I had lived in a mansion on Fifth Avenue. I had a cook—nay, an Italian chef —and a large staff, all of whom had come with excellent résumés and had grown accustomed to my tastes and my requirements. Here, I had Mrs. Betty Gilroy, on temporary loan, whom I had borrowed from the bakery down the street for the occasion. I had put out an advertisement for a cook but had not had luck in securing one who'd had a repertoire of more than rice, beans, roast beef, and chili stew.

It had taken some doing, but I'd managed to sweet-talk William's estate lawyer into extending the stipend left for the management of the hotel to pay for more employees. Unfortunately, that meant I had to endure the Colorado mountain town for two months more than I'd planned to make up the difference. Eager as I was to get back to New York and my theater, I had to make a living in La Plata Springs. I also wanted to make running the hotel as bearable as possible.

In New York, I had been the toast of the town. Admired. Sought after. An invitation to one of my parties or events was a privilege people clamored to obtain. Here, I had been welcomed with a somewhat neglected hotel and, most horrifying of all, an accusation of murder. Two murders, in fact. I, of course, did not commit these crimes and eventually cleared my name by sussing out the killer, but the whole experience had left a bad taste in my mouth.

The people of the town had, in truth, been warm and welcoming in the end, but I still felt they looked at me askance and quite as if I'd fallen from the moon. As much as I hated to admit it, I wanted to be liked, valued, and most importantly, worthy of those honors. At a mature thirty-six years of age, I should have been less concerned about such things, and I was working on my insecurities, but at times like this, the fear of failure pressed down on me like a dark cloud.

I shook the unpleasant memory from my thoughts. "Why don't you go into the bedroom and get your reticule and anything else you might need for the ceremony," I suggested, hoping to otherwise occupy Eliza while I dealt with Percival.

Luckily, she complied.

I approached the mirror and fixed him with a glare. "What are you doing here?" I whispered. "She might see you, and I don't want her upset on her wedding day."

He heaved a sigh. "I was bored and wanted to talk to you. And besides, you know as well as I do, that not everyone can see us spiritual entities, at least not without some effort on our part."

"Well, I don't want to take the chance, and as you can see, I'm quite busy and will be for most of the day."

"Right. The wedding reception. The staff and guests are all abuzz about it." He frowned. He looked like a recalcitrant child who wasn't getting his way. I would never tell him, but I thought he was quite handsome when vexed, or moody, which was more common for him. He had a romantic and Byronic quality about him that was at times trying but nevertheless strangely attractive.

"We can talk later, all right?" I glanced behind me to make sure Eliza hadn't reappeared.

"Very well," he said, the stem of his pipe clenched between his teeth. He vanished from the mirror, and I let out a sigh of relief.

"Arabella?" Eliza came back into the parlor. "Which one do you think looks best with the dress?" She held up two small, beaded handbags, one with a pink floral design and the other with a monogram of her initials in blue.

"I think the blue," I said. "In England, we have a saying that applies to every bride and what she needs on her wedding day. It goes like this: *Something old, something new, something borrowed, something blue, and a sixpence in her shoe.*"

Eliza let out a pleasant tinkling of laughter. "Oh my. Well, this takes care of the something blue." She held up the monogramed reticule. "And this necklace"—she pulled a thin chain of gold out from under her collar—"is all I have left of my mother, so that suffices for old."

"Your dress is new," I added.

"I borrowed these shoes from sweet Cordelia." She held up the hem of her dress to reveal buff-colored lace-up boots. They were Cordelia's finest pair, and she only wore them on special occasions. "The boots I had purchased pinched my toes. It was so kind of her to lend me these."

Cordelia was my assistant, my companion, and my best friend. She had been with me for over a decade, and I don't know what I'd do without her. Right now, she was tending to the preparations for the party downstairs in the Bella Saloon.

"That's Cordelia," I agreed. "Shy, too intelligent for her own good, and yes, very kind."

"But what about the sixpence?" Eliza asked.

"Hmm," I tapped my lower lip with my index finger. "I haven't had one of those for a long time; however . . ." I reached into my own reticule, which was lying on the bureau, and pulled out a silver dime. "I had a friend in New York," I started.

She was actually still my friend, a ghostly friend— Leticia Crookshank, an elderly actress who had come to her end in the theater I owned in New York City. Her death had occurred before my husband had purchased it for me. Until Percival, she and a childhood playmate, Oliver Shrewsbury, had been the only spiritual entities I'd encountered. When my mother had found out about my "friendship" with Oliver, she had marched me off to a spiritualist who had taught me how to close myself off from such sensitivities. They had only recently been reawakened.

"Who told me," I continued, "that silver dimes are very lucky. I'm sure it can serve as your sixpence."

She grinned and then placed it in her boot. She straightened and beamed at me. "There. That's it, then. I think I'm ready."

I went to the window to look down onto the street below. "Ah, the coach is here. Let's get you married."

Chapter Three

"You may kiss the bride." Reverend Stills beamed at the couple, and my heart swelled with happiness for Eliza. I did not have many close female friendships, aside from the one I shared with Cordelia, and it was nice to feel such joy for someone else's happiness.

A loud snuffling to my left broke my reverie. Constance Chatterley, the owner and editor of the local newspaper—if you could call it that—pressed a handkerchief to her nose and blew loudly. I flinched with embarrassment for her.

"Oh, I just love weddings," she blubbered.

Always flamboyant in every way, including her taste for ostentatious attire, today Constance wore a black-and-white-striped silk jacket, which was fitted so tightly over an enormous, and dare I say *outdated*, bustled skirt in the same bold fabric. Her ensemble fit so snugly it seemed that her corset was pushing all the blood in her body up into her red face. I wondered at how she could breathe, much less emote with such fervor.

Her hat, equally overbearing and garish, threatened to

take off my head with every twist of her body. The entire outfit had large red silk roses dotting it. She looked like an oversized and squeezed jail bird with the measles.

To the contrary, at my right, sat the more modestly attired Cordelia who, true to her nature, wore a simple ensemble in ochre, a color that was difficult to wear but suited her warm-toned complexion, strawberry-blond hair, and hazel eyes.

Like me, Cordelia had little tolerance for such emotional displays. A bookish and introspective soul, she was innately mystified by them. As a woman of learning and logic, Cordelia relied on her intellect. Also, she couldn't understand why someone should so publicly display their feelings, preferring to deal with hers alone.

I, on the other hand, while sympathetic to the reasons behind those displays, was uncomfortable with such a show of open vulnerability. I know it seems strange, but I never allowed myself such indulgences—only on the rare occasion did I succumb—and I tried my best to understand why others could not show the same restraint.

The bride and groom, having performed the traditional kiss, made their way down the aisle to a resounding round of applause.

The groom, Mr. Townsend, a man of thirty-some years, who had the evergreen look of youth with his pencil-thin neck, large Adam's apple, boyish face, and large ears, shined with pure joy. Only briefly acquainted with him, I considered him a decent enough man, from what I knew of him. Our interactions had always been pleasant, and he was quick with a smile and exceedingly polite. He was liked by everyone.

"We should get back to the hotel." Cordelia leaned closer to me to speak over the voices of the crowd. "I need to check on Mrs. Gilroy in the kitchen and see that all is in order for the reception."

"You go ahead," I told her. "I'll be right behind you. I want to see the happy couple into their coach."

I had offered them the coach owned by the hotel. Mr. Townsend had come in his own, of course, but he had left it at the livery, as his horse had pulled a shoe on the way into town. Eliza had arrived at the church in the Arabella's coach, which I'd had the staff decorate with paper streamers and flowers. She had honored me with a request that I accompany her to the church, for which I gladly obliged her.

"But how will you get back to the hotel, dear?" Cordelia asked, concern written on her features.

"Same as you, silly. I'll walk. It's only down the street."

"But your new dress . . ."

I batted a hand in the air, unconcerned. "It's of no matter. A little dirt won't hurt it."

"Very well," she said with a shrug of her shoulders.

We filed down the aisle with the other wedding guests. Several of the townspeople, including Cynthia Mayes, the dressmaker—who had made both Eliza's beautiful dress and mine—and her cousin, Mr. Archer, nodded a greeting to us as we passed.

My heart lurched as Sheriff Marshall stepped out from the back row of the church and sidled up next to me. I shouldn't like to admit it, but Clayton Marshall had an effect on me that I found quite discomfiting yet stimulating at the same time.

"Mrs. Pryce," he said with a smile. His cobalt-blue eyes danced, making my stomach flutter. Really, but it was both-ersome that I should feel like a mooning schoolgirl around him. Only three months ago, the man had put me under house arrest for murder. Granted, there had been several factors that had made me seem guilty, but I had not committed the grievous deeds and had proven it.

In the end, Sheriff Marshall, with whom I'd had several uncomfortable yet annoyingly heart-melting encounters, had claimed he hadn't really thought me responsible for the murders, but he'd had to do his due diligence until the real culprit had been found.

"Hello, Sheriff," I returned the greeting stiffly, ignoring the heat that had suddenly blossomed in my cheeks.

"Fine day for a wedding. The weather is finally cooling off."

"Indeed," I agreed. The late-August heat had given way to the crisp mornings and evenings of September, and the leaves of the aspens dotting the mountainsides flickered like gold coins in the breeze.

As we started down the steps leading out of the church, I turned my face to the warmth of the sun. Reaching up to keep my hat from coming askew, I suddenly found myself falling forward, and I let out a little yelp of panic.

To my surprise and utter relief, strong hands grasped me around the waist and upper arm, saving me from a tumble. The relief was soon followed by embarrassment when I realized the sheriff had come to my rescue. Again.

"Looks like you might have missed a step," he said, his sapphire eyes flashing with amusement.

I swallowed my chagrin, as I always seemed to become an instant klutz in the presence of the good sheriff. He must think me a complete twit. I reminded myself that I should care less what he thought of me, but annoyingly, I did not.

"Are you coming to the reception?" I asked in an attempt to divert his attention from what had just happened.

He shook his head, still smiling at me. Heat rose again into my cheeks, and I cursed my silly emotions.

"I wasn't planning on it," he said. "I've got some business in Addison later this afternoon."

"Oh, I see." My embarrassment was instantly replaced with disappointment, which was even more vexing. *How much later?* I wanted to ask. Could he not come for just a short while? It was maddening that I felt let down.

If I was completely honest with myself, I found Clayton Marshall exceeding handsome with his finely defined jawline and a physique that belied his middle age. But it behooved me not to have feelings for him. We had nothing in common, and in a year's time, I would leave La Plata Springs forever to return to the city I so missed.

"My loss," he said with a click of his tongue and then gave me that dazzling smile of his again. "But I'm sure you will do a grand job for the couple. You are certainly a capable woman."

Capable woman? I fought another wave of disappointment. Was that all he thought of me? Capable? In New York, I was seen as far more than capable. The words *brilliant*, *talented*, *incomparable*, and *luminescent* had often been used to describe me. I reminded myself, yet one more time, that I shouldn't care what Sheriff Marshall thought of me.

He leaned his head closer to mine, and I was immediately enveloped by the scent of something wonderfully woodsy and fresh. Why did he always have to smell so good, too?

"Did you give any more thought to those riding lessons?" he asked.

He was referring to my clumsiness on a horse, as I had become injured from a fall from one not too long ago—again, in his presence. Recently, he'd offered to teach me to ride. I wasn't quite sure about the whole matter. While knowing how to ride would certainly come in handy out here in the godforsaken West, it would serve me little in New York.

"I haven't really had time to think about it," I said by way of excuse, his closeness making me want to lean in and run away all at the same time.

"Well, when you're ready, you know where to find me." He graced me with a wink, and I suddenly found it hard to swallow. And I had become increasingly warm throughout our conversation. Must have been the cloister of the church, I reasoned.

"Gather round, everyone!" Constance Chatterley's voice rose above the din of the enthusiastic crowd. "We need a photograph for the paper." She gestured wildly with her pudgy hands for people to surround the couple and then took individuals by the arms, setting them in place.

Andrew Archer, Archibald Archer's nephew, stood behind the wooden tripod upon which the box camera sat. He was a quiet yet enterprising young man who had an artistic bent. A skilled portraitist and painter, it was not at all surprising that photography would also be in his repertoire of talents.

"That's my cue to head out," Sheriff Marshall said with a chuckle. "You have a good afternoon, Mrs. Pryce." He put his hat back on his head, and his face broke into that knee-weakening smile again. I wished he would quit doing that.

I gave him a nod farewell and was about to join the group for the photo when Archibald Archer approached me.

"Lovely wedding," he said. He was a tall man, stout and barrel-chested, with a head of silver hair and a well-groomed frosty beard. His very presence commanded respect.

"Yes, it was," I agreed.

He set his arms behind his back. "I'd like to speak with you. At your convenience, of course."

"Oh? What about?"

"About the Arabella."

"The Arabella? What about her?"

"I realize that things have been . . . well, *difficult* for you since you've arrived in town. With the recent murders and all the problems at the hotel . . ."

I gave him a tight-lipped smile. "Yes, you could say that." I would have chosen the word *nightmare*, but I refrained.

"Well, my dear lady—" he fixed me with a most charming smile "—I'm prepared to offer my help."

I raised my eyebrows. "Oh? In what way?"

"Financial, of course."

"I see." I wasn't sure what he was getting at, but it sounded intriguing, despite the fact that something in his tone made the hairs on the back of my neck stand up.

"Come see me at the General."

The General was the rival hotel to the Arabella and was owned by Mr. Archer. It did not have nearly the amenities, nor grandeur, of my hotel and served to house many of the miners who worked for Mr. Archer. Mr. Archer was making strides to gentrify the boarding house in his efforts to increase tourism in the area, which put his hotel in direct competition with the Arabella.

I nodded. "Perhaps. Once things settle down after the wedding."

"I look forward to it."

"Arabella!" Eliza waved me over. "Come stand by me."

Pleased with her request, I complied, and Mr. Archer joined a group of some of the wedding guests who'd declined having their picture taken. After a few blinding rounds of gunpowder flash, the crowd grew restless and Andrew dismissed us, stating he'd gotten what he needed.

I gathered my skirts to step away from the group when I noticed Mr. Everett Emerson walk by with a scowl on his face. He was the new manager of Archer's Dry Goods, Mr. Townsend's replacement.

I had spoken to him a few times, about things we needed at the hotel. Although he was pleasant enough, his scowl seemed to be a permanent fixture. Perhaps that was his normal expression? He tipped his hat to Mr. Archer and continued walking.

"Thank you, all," Miss Chatterley's thin yet shrill singsong voice rang out. "It's time for the reception. Please make your way to the Bella!"

In her usual busybody fashion, it seemed she had just appointed herself in charge of getting everyone to the event, which rankled a bit. She had done nothing to help with the preparations but write about them in the one-page chit she called a newspaper.

I let out a sigh. I supposed it didn't really matter that she felt she had to marshal the guests. We did need people to make their way over to the hotel's saloon.

"You'll come with us?" Eliza asked, pointing to the coach.

I was about to protest when Mr. Townsend spoke up. "Yes, Mrs. Pryce. Please accompany Eliza back to the hotel. I'm going to go over to the livery to check on my horse. He pulled that shoe when we hit a patch of mud and was favoring that leg after. I need to see if it's still bothering him, because if it is, I'll need to send for the veterinarian in Addison. I'll meet you two at the reception."

"Of course," I agreed. "But I could have Clarence check on him for you." I was referring to one of the two bellhops in my employ who often ran errands for me.

"That's quite all right, Mrs. Pryce. I'd like to check on him myself."

I was a bit surprised that the groom should not want to arrive at the party with his bride, but I guess it made sense that he should check on his horse. It would be needed for Eliza and him to make it back to his home for their wedding night.

"He's just crazy about that horse," Eliza said. "I tease him that he cares about that horse more than he cares about me." She chuckled and then took my arm. "Come on, then. I want to know what you thought of the ceremony."

Chapter Four

Back at the Bella, I glanced at the watch locket I wore around my neck. It had been more than forty-five minutes since Mr. Townsend left us at the church, and some of the guests were beginning to ask of his whereabouts. What could be keeping him?

I drummed my fingers against the well-worn wooden surface of the bar, thinking. Perhaps he had gone to the postal office to send a telegram to the veterinarian in Addison. Bijou let out a small yip from her spot at my feet and stood on her hind legs, wanting me to pick her up. Absently, I complied, and she rewarded me with several kisses on my chin.

The wedding guests had been slowly filtering into the Bella Saloon through its grand, wrought-iron-embellished glass and wooden doors. My eyes traveled to the landscape painting that hung above them. A refreshing replacement for the garish nude that had been there before. I cringed at the remembrance, and the very preposterous idea the locals seemed to have that *I* had sat for the awful portrait.

The Arabella, which housed the drinking parlor, was the heart of the town, despite her problematic interior issues. It was my aim to fix those problems so I might sell the grand dame at the end of my tenure.

And those issues were not the only problems at the Arabella. Its very reputation was at stake due to the fact that there had been four mysterious deaths at the hotel, including the aforementioned murder I had been accused of. The other two deaths were that of a Mr. Valdez, a contentious drinker and gambler who had supposedly died in his sleep, and that of Mr. Percival Blank who had allegedly succumbed to illness. He, however, claimed he had recovered from his illness, so how he had come to his demise was a mystery to him. This was something that I found curious, as both Oliver Shrewsbury and Leticia Crookshank had been privy to the reasons for their earthly departures. At any rate, I needed to ensure that any guest of the Arabella would indeed come to no harm.

My thoughts again returned to the absence of Mr. Townsend as Bijou raised her nose in the air, sniffing.

"What is it, girl?" I asked her, and suddenly, I knew. The faint odor of smoke wafted into the room . . . and not tobacco smoke. Something a bit more acrid.

"Arabella," Cordelia said as she approached me with a ramakin in her hands. Her small, pert nose, which had become freckled from exposure to the intense Colorado sun, wrinkled. "We have a problem in the kitchen."

I met her eyes. She had been much transformed since our arrival in La Plata Springs. Once pale and fragile, with no stamina to speak of and subject to migraine headaches, she now had a robustness about her that suited her. I had never seen someone take so well to an environment completely foreign to them, but the woman was thriving in the small mountain town. Her adaptation to it had far surpassed my own. A few months in and I still struggled with the thin, brittle air.

Cordelia presented me with the ramakin that held something that looked like a pale, crumpled pork-pie hat. Bijou strained in my arms to get a whiff of it.

"Oh dear." I sighed. "Is that the cheese soufflé?"

She nodded. "I think we may have overestimated Betty's culinary expertise."

I eyed the fallen, eggy mess. "Are they all like that?"

I had procured the recipe from one of my dear friends in New York, a French chef who ran a fine dining room there. Although Betty Gilroy's husband did the lion's share of the baking at their bakery, Betty was quite a skilled cook, but perhaps the soufflé had been a bit ambitious on my part.

"I'm afraid so." She bit her lip. "And there's more. Something is wrong with the stove. The kitchen is filling with smoke."

"What? Oh no! What about the rest of the food?" My stomach tightened. Since this was the first extravaganza I was hosting at the hotel, I wanted to make a good impression. Though I hated to admit it, the thought of failing—at anything—struck terror in me.

Someone at my elbow startled me.

"Arabella, have you seen Rupert? He's been gone so long." Eliza blinked up at me with her wide brown eyes.

I laid a hand on her arm. "Don't worry, darling. I'm sure he'll be here soon."

"Should I go look for him?" She worried her bottom lip.

"No, dear. You stay here. I'll send Clarence to fetch him."

I caught the eye of the young bellhop, a boy of nearly

thirteen with gangly features and a sweet demeanor. I waved him over.

He swiped his cap off his head when he approached. "Yes, Mrs. Pryce?"

"It seems Mr. Townsend has been detained at the livery, and Eliza is getting worried. Would you go see what is keeping him?"

"Yes, ma'am."

"Oh, and would you take Bijou? She needs to . . . well, you know, tend to her business." I handed him the dog, and the boy turned on his heel and hurried out to the street.

"I'll go mingle with some of the guests," Eliza said. "I don't want to be rude."

I gave her an assuring nod. "I'm sure he'll be here any minute."

She turned to a group of people standing next to us and engaged in polite small talk.

I took Cordelia by the arm, and we made our way to the kitchen. When we walked through the door, we were greeted with a billowing cloud of gray smoke. The door leading outside to the annex—a large, grassy courtyard area off the side of the hotel with two rows of small houses, all part of the Arabella—had been opened. With the help of two of the new maids, Betty was attempting to fan the putrid cloud out of the kitchen.

"What happened?" I asked and then choked, regretting that I had opened my mouth. I grabbed a hand cloth and held it over my nose and mouth.

"I'm not sure," Betty said, coughing, a frantic tone in her voice. She was a heavyset woman with kind eyes, a ruddy complexion, and hands that had been no stranger to years of hard work in this harsh climate. Her cheeks were red as a beet, and perspiration dotted her forehead and nose. "Everything was going well at first. I baked the soufflés and set them on the table over there." She pointed to a long wooden table. "I left the kitchen to use the . . . well, to use the outhouse, and when I came back, smoke was pouring from the holes in the cooking plates."

A man appeared in the smoke-filled doorway and greeted us with a cough. "You called for me?" Mr. Johns, the other bellhop, straightened his uniform.

"There is something wrong with the stove," Betty said. "It is belching smoke like a raging dragon. You must fix it right away."

"Let's see what we've got here." Mr. Johns puffed out his chest, obviously pleased at being asked to save the day.

Betty handed him a thickly crocheted hot pad. Kneeling down, he used it to open the door of the firebox where the wood and coals burned, heating the two side ovens and the eight cooking plates on top. He took the poker that had been resting against the stove and used it to rummage around in the coals.

"Well, here's your problem." He pulled the poker out and held it up for us. It was full of soot, but beneath the soot, there was something shiny. "It's wet in there. Someone doused the fire." He stood and then moved some of the pots around on the cooking plates. He opened the small trap door that was used to tend the fire from above and stopped short. "Ah. And here's the other problem."

"What is it?" I asked.

Using the hot pad, he stuck his hand down into the trapdoor and then reached toward the back of the stove, near the ventilation pipe. He pulled his hand, and the now completely black hot pad, out of the trapdoor. A smooth river rock rested in his palm.

"This was blocking the smoke from going out the stovepipe. It had nowhere to go."

"How in the world did that get in there?" Betty asked, her hands on her plump hips.

Immediately, I thought of Percival, but that wasn't possible. There was no mirror in the vicinity, and he could not move objects unless they were in the mirror.

"Someone must have deliberately put it there," Cordelia said.

"Why on earth . . . ?" I wondered out loud, but then a thought crossed my mind. Someone wanted to sabotage the reception.

"Is there a problem in here?" came a woman's voice.

Kitty Carlisle walked into the kitchen and immediately started coughing, waving her hand in front of her face. A daunting figure of considerable largess with raven hair, piercing dark eyes, and the stern demeanor of a school-marm, Kitty managed the saloon and owned a brothel, which, much to my chagrin and out of my control at the moment, operated out of two of the small houses in the annex. "Kitty's girls" lived there, along with some of the miners and their families. Some of the young women in her employ worked in the saloon as well.

"More than one." I sighed, tilting my head toward the pile of congealed egg in Cordelia's hands. "Someone put water on the fire in the stove and then blocked the ensuing smoke with that." I nodded toward the stone in Mr. Johns's hand.

"Land sakes. Who would have done that?" she asked.

"We don't know," said Cordelia.

"Well, the troops are getting restless in the saloon," Kitty said. "Will there be a delay in the meal?"

"Maybe," Betty said. "I'll need to get that wet wood and

ash out of there. The stove and the oven are still hot, so if I hurry, we might be able to retain the heat." She rolled up her sleeves.

"I'll fetch more wood," Mr. Johns offered.

"Thank you kindly," Betty said. "I'd best get to it." She pulled a bucket toward the firebox door and started removing the partially burned logs and ash with a small shovel.

I tilted my head for Kitty and Cordelia to follow me out of the kitchen. At the door Kitty stopped Cordelia who still had one of the soufflés in her hands.

"What is that?" she asked. "And why are you bringing it with you?"

"Shh." I rolled my eyes toward Betty, who was stoking the fire.

"Oh!" Cordelia said. "I'd forgotten I was still holding it."

We stepped through the door and back into the lobby area.

"It's supposed to be a cheese soufflé," I said.

"Right." Kitty lifted her eyebrows. "That looks like something a horse stomped on."

Cordelia pinched off a bit of the custardy edge and put it in her mouth. "But it tastes good."

"You don't really expect people to eat that do you?" Kitty asked. "What's it made out of?"

I explained the art of soufflé making, and Kitty looked at me with a dubious expression on her face. "Well, lucky for you, I bet more than half the folks here have never heard of it, so they won't know the difference."

"You think so?" I asked.

She gave me a confident bob of her head. "I guarantee it. It's a good thing you got some smoked ham and beef from the butcher to add to the menu. These people have hearty appetites."

"Well, I'd better get this back to the kitchen." Cordelia left us with a smile and took the yellow pile with her.

"What's the other problem?" Kitty placed her fists on her hips. "Anything I can do to help?"

"Mr. Townsend has not yet arrived, and Eliza is a bit anxious about it, as am I. The guests are expecting a meal, and I don't want to serve it until the groom is with his bride. I've sent Clarence to look for him. Could you give Betty a hand in the kitchen? I think she is rather over her head with this party to begin with, and now with the problem with the stove . . . I can't imagine who would do such a thing."

She shook her head. "It was right unneighborly, but we can't think about that at the moment. I'll get in there and give Betty a hand." She reached out and gave my elbow a squeeze. "It's going to be a fine party. Don't you worry."

My heart warmed at her gesture. "Thank you, Kitty."

She gave me a wink and was off.

It had taken me a while to get used to Kitty's serious demeanor, but over the last couple of months, she had been quite helpful to me in dealing with other matters at the hotel. She had run her brothel for several years, and she had a keen business sense. While it was true that I had my own theater back in New York, I had a manager who ran things for me. He handled all the administrative and business dealings, giving me room to pursue my art, which left little time, or the inclination, to learn matters of commerce.

I was indeed growing fond of the matronly woman. Her girls adored her, and she took good care of them. I was quite conflicted about her running her business out of the Arabella, though, as it really wasn't in keeping with my or my late husband's vision for the establishment. I had been flummoxed that William had allowed it. Daniel Bledsoe, the former manager of the hotel, had thought it would bring in more business, and while he was likely correct, it wasn't at all appropriate for the kind of hotel to which I wanted my name attached. The brothel would have to go . . . eventually.

From behind me, Bijou's familiar bark snapped me out of my musings, and someone tapped me on the shoulder. I turned around to see Clarence, white-faced and wide-eyed, standing there. Bijou was panting furiously at his feet.

"Clarence, what's wrong?"

He opened his mouth to speak, but nothing came out. Bijou danced on her hind legs barking furiously.

"What is it, Clarence? Did you find Mr. Townsend?"

He swallowed hard and then took in a gulp of air and croaked out. "You need to come."

"Come where?"

Bijou, still on her hind legs and barking, pawed at my skirt. Clarence turned around and headed for the hallway that flanked the row of lower level rooms. It ended at the back entrance of the hotel, Mystified by his behavior, I followed, Bijou at my heels. He walked fast down the hallway, and looked as if he might break into a run. Bijou sprinted ahead of me and then him on her short little legs.

"Bijou, come back! Clarence, where are you going?" I called after them. "Slow down!"

Ignoring me, Clarence continued down the long hallway. Bijou, having reached the back entrance first, let out another round of anxious barking.

I broke into a jog to catch up with them, but they fled out the door. I followed as they headed toward the river. Bijou was running so fast in front of him, her little paws created a cloud of dust in their wake.

I hurried behind, annoyed that I'd had to leave the hotel, Eliza, and the guests but also fighting a sickening feeling in my stomach. Up ahead, on the bank of the river, I spied a horse and carriage, but there was no driver. The horse was happily munching on some grass.

Bijou, having reached the carriage, continued her barking while waiting for us. Clarence got there next and bent over, his hands on his knees, catching his breath.

"What on earth—" I finally caught them, winded and a bit light-headed. Bijou jumped up onto my skirts, wanting my attention, but I was too busy fighting for breath, as I'd had Cordelia pull my corset strings a bit tighter than usual that morning. I had wanted to look my best for the festivities.

Clarence straightened, his face the color of paste. He pointed to the open door of the carriage. I peered in and gasped.

Rupert Townsend, his eyes wide and staring, was sitting at an unnatural angle, his legs akimbo and his torso tilted over onto the seat. A stain of thick, inky blood had spilled down his fine morning suit.

Unable to believe my eyes, I blinked rapidly, taking in the horrid scene. My heart slammed against my ribs, and the air in my lungs froze, causing a powerful and over-whelming tingling that permeated through my limbs. My gaze traveled to his chest, and I sucked in a deep breath. Sitting right below the cheery white mum on his left lapel was what resembled a calling card with the image of a small bouquet of flowers wrapped in a pink bow.

Chapter Five

"Mrs. Pryce? What are you doing out here? I thought you were throwing a party at the hotel."

Still in a state of shock, I hadn't noticed that Sheriff Marshall had ridden up on his horse, Queenie. I tried to speak, but the words wouldn't come out of my mouth.

"He's dead, Sheriff," Clarence croaked, pointing to the interior of the carriage. "Mr. Townsend is dead."

A wave of consternation flitted across the sheriff's face. He dismounted from the horse and came over to join us. He peered inside the carriage.

"Good Lord," he whispered. "It looks like he's been shot."

"Or stabbed." I finally managed to speak. "He was late for the reception. He'd gone to the livery to check on his horse. Eliza was becoming distressed, so I sent Clarence out to look for him and—"

"I saw his coach here by the river," Clarence finished.

"Did you see anyone nearby?" the sheriff asked.

"No, sir. Just the horse, the coach, and . . ." The boy pointed to Mr. Townsend's lapel.

"What's this?" The sheriff reached in and took the card.

"It looks like a calling card, but why is it there?" I asked.

Peering over his shoulder, I looked at the card. The bouquet consisted of one white lily, one red rose, and a sprig of lily of the valley entwined with a pink ribbon that was tied in a neat bow around the little bundle.

"The culprit is either sending some kind of message or leaving a clue," he said. "Which leads me to believe this was not just a random killing. This was planned."

"How awful! How am I going to tell Eliza?" My voice wavered as I looked into the sheriff's brilliant blue eyes. "It's her wedding day. She's waiting for him. This is just terrible."

He reached out, took me by the arms, and quietly said, "You don't have to do it alone." His steadfast gaze and soothing voice settled me. He turned to the boy. "Clarence, go fetch Doc Tate. Run as fast as you can."

"Yes, sir."

Suddenly, my head grew light and a violent shaking overcame me. My knees went watery and threatened to give out. I faltered and swayed.

"You need to sit down." The sheriff led me to one of the boulders along the water's edge.

"I need to get back to the hotel. To the guests. To Eliza." I tried to pull away from him, my body a jumble of nerves. How could I possibly sit?

"And you will," he said, gently encouraging me to lower myself onto the rock. "It will only be a few minutes."

"Someone tried to sabotage the reception," I said, looking up at him.

"Pardon?"

"The stove. Someone put a river rock in the stove, blocking the ventilation. The kitchen was full of smoke. Everything is going wrong."

He rubbed his chin. "That's odd."

"Someone wanted to ruin this day for the couple," I added.

"Well, someone succeeded." He looked over at the carriage.

"Unless whoever tampered with the stove wanted to ruin me." A different kind of anxiety filtered through me. Memories of being set up and accused of murder surfaced, causing a painful ache in my chest.

"I doubt that's the case. Please, Arabella. Sit down. You need to catch your breath."

I obeyed, my breathing as rapid as Bijou's on a hot day. Feeling my distress, she jumped onto my lap and pressed herself against my chest. Immediately calmed by her warm little body, my breathing slowed.

"Who could have done this?" I asked after a few minutes. "First the stove . . . and now this."

"What happened with the stove could have been a prank," he said.

"But this isn't a prank," I added, pointing to the carriage.

"No." The sheriff set his hands on his slim hips and shook his head. "I can't imagine anyone wanting to do Rupert harm. He was such a happy sort, and as far as I could tell, everyone around here liked him. Or that's what I thought."

"Yes," I agreed. "He was always so kind."

In the distance, Clarence came running toward us. The

doctor followed further behind, carrying his leather satchel under his arm. Dr. Tate was an older man and had trouble keeping up with the boy's swift legs.

Finally, he arrived on the scene, slightly winded. The thinning fringe of hair at his forehead was blown back by the effort. He took a handkerchief from his pocket, removed his spectacles, and gave them a good cleaning.

"What do we have, Clayton?" he asked the sheriff.

"It's Rupert Townsend. He's either been shot or stabbed. It's hard to tell. I didn't want to move him until you got here."

The doctor stepped up into the carriage and sat opposite the body. Even though Mr. Townsend looked dead as dead could be, the doctor checked his pulse at the neck.

"What a shame." Dr. Tate shook his head. "I'll take the carriage and get him to the infirmary to better examine him."

"I'm going to take Mrs. Pryce back to the hotel," the sheriff said. "I'll send someone to meet you at your infirmary to help you remove the body from the carriage."

The doctor gave a short nod. "Much appreciate it."

Sheriff Marshall looked down at Bijou and me. "Think you can walk to the hotel? If not, you can ride Queenie."

"I'm fine now," I said, standing up. My legs once again felt solid and strong beneath me. "Clarence" —I turned to the boy—"would you run ahead and tell Miss Swind—" I hesitated, reminded that Eliza Swindon was no longer Eliza Swindon. She was Mrs. Rupert Townsend. I cleared my throat to dislodge the lump that had formed there. "Would you ask Mrs. Townsend to meet me in the lobby?"

"Yes, ma'am," he said. He took off at a run, and Bijou scurried after him, barking merrily as if they were playing a game of chase.

The sheriff and I walked toward the hotel in silence, Queenie trailing behind us. I was formulating a script in my mind to impart the unhappy news to Eliza, and the sheriff, never a man of many words, seemed content to let me ruminate.

After he flung Queenie's reins over the hitching post at the back of the hotel, he opened the door for me and I stepped through, my heart heavy and hammering in my chest. I sucked in a deep breath, and calling upon my skills as a thespian, I swept away my own feelings and replaced them with a veneer of collected restraint and stoicism. I would need to be strong for my friend.

When we reached the lobby, Eliza was standing at the reception desk speaking with Mr. Pettyjohn, the hotel clerk, and Jack Duncan, rancher and co-owner of Mr. Townsend's Cougar claim.

Mr. Pettyjohn was a small but slightly paunchy, bespectacled man with a heavy waxed mustache, and equally fat eyebrows. He kept the place running smoothly. Most of the time. He had a tendency toward absentmindedness, which was mildly vexing, but he knew his job well and I really had no room to complain.

Mr. Duncan, on the other hand, was tall and robust in stature, extremely polished, and wore a handsome, well-manicured, dark beard. His eyes, also dark, bore the mark of intelligence. Although his build and demeanor commanded respect, his boyish grin made him instantly likeable.

He stepped forward when he saw us approach. "Mrs. Pryce, is there a problem?"

I went to Eliza and took her hand. It was cold and clammy in mine. She blinked up at me with those soulful brown eyes, and I swallowed hard, fighting the urge to break character. "I'm afraid there is. There has been . . . well . . . an accident of sorts."

"Oh no!" Eliza's hand flew to her mouth. "Rupert?"

I nodded. "He's been—" I couldn't seem to make the words come out of my mouth.

"He's been killed, Mrs. Townsend," Sheriff Marshall finished for me. "I'm so very sorry."

"Killed?" Mr. Duncan shouted.

I raised a hand to quiet him, afraid someone might overhear, although all the guests were in the saloon next door.

"Oh dear. Poor Rupert!" Eliza's knees buckled, and Mr. Duncan quickly came to her aid by wrapping an arm around her waist. He led her over to one of the Queen Anne–styled sofas in the lobby's parlor. Three of the matching, burgundy-tufted divans sat in a *U* shape, surrounding a coffee table. The rest of us followed them but remained standing.

When he got her settled, he handed her a handkerchief and sat down next to her. His care and attentiveness were touching.

The sheriff went on to describe what we'd found, but left out the part about the calling card. I presumed he thought it might be too much for Eliza to hear at the moment.

"Good God," Mr. Duncan said, running a hand over his beard. Eliza pressed the handkerchief to her mouth.

From behind us, at the entrance to the saloon, Kitty and Sally Dean, one of the saloon girls who also moonlighted as one of Kitty's soiled doves, spotted our little group in the parlor and came over.

"What's going on?" Kitty asked, her fists on her ample hips. "What are you all doing in here?"

Sally, a pretty, wisp-thin young woman with large, expressive eyes and a head of luxurious, thick brown hair piled high on her head, stood quietly at Kitty's side, her eyes fixed on the handsome sheriff. As usual. I ignored the pang that stabbed at my stomach, which occurred every time I saw the two together. It was infuriating. Some might call it jealousy, but I refused to give the feeling a name.

Sheriff Marshall again explained what had happened. Sally sat down on the other side of Eliza and placed a comforting arm around her shoulders.

Kitty frowned in confusion. "What could anyone have against Rupert?"

Eliza let out a sob.

"Sally," I said, addressing the barmaid, "would you take Eliza to her rooms and stay with her? Kitty and I will notify the guests that the reception is canceled."

Sally nodded and helped Eliza get to her feet.

"I wouldn't let on that anything is amiss," the sheriff cautioned. "Just say that one of them isn't feeling well or something."

"Right. We don't want to cause alarm," Kitty said.

"No, we don't," the sheriff agreed. "But they're going to find out eventually. Furthermore, the killer might be among them."

I gasped. "You think that whoever did this might be in the saloon?"

Mr. Marshall lifted a shoulder in a half shrug. "Possibly. They could be hiding in plain sight. It's a smart plan."

"But there must be thirty people in there," I said. "And they all trickled in at different times. How will we possibly know?"

"And there have been hotel guests that arrived by train

yesterday and have checked into the hotel," Mr. Pettyjohn added. "Are you going to detain everyone?"

My stomach lurched at the thought. It would take hours, maybe all night or even into tomorrow, to question everyone, and I didn't have the staff or the room to keep them all at the hotel. Half of the rooms were already occupied. A lower percentage than I would have liked, but not in this instance.

"What if the culprit isn't in there?" Mr. Duncan asked. "You'd be spending all your time with the party guests and the murderer could be anywhere."

"He has a good point," I chimed in.

"Parkhurst might be able to help with that. I just saw him at the livery. Guess he didn't want to come to the wedding?"

"I don't think he was on the guest list," I said, recalling what I'd heard coming from Eliza's room. The fact that he'd been in her room at all was still disconcerting, as I hadn't thought they'd been acquainted. Then again, she had claimed he had been there just to procure his fee. That didn't mean they were friends.

"How could he help?" I asked.

"The livery is just at the edge of town. It would be easy for him to see anyone coming or going."

"That could be said about the train depot as well," I added. It was at the opposite end of town.

"No one's getting out of town by train," Kitty said. "About thirty or so minutes ago, I got word from one of the guests that the train's engine broke down. They're sending someone from Denver to work on it."

"Some of the guests who just checked out of the hotel are checking in again." Mr. Pettyjohn tilted his head toward the registration desk where a line of people had formed. "In fact, I should probably get back."

"Please do," I said. "Thank you, Mr. Pettyjohn."

He gave a nod and hurried back to the desk.

"Well, the train delay might make our task easier," I said.

"Our task?" Mr. Marshall regarded me with raised brows.

"Yes. Finding the killer," I said.

"Yes, I know what you meant by *task*. I was referring to the word *our*, Mrs. Pryce. It's best if you leave this to me."

"But how can you possibly do this alone?" I set my hands on my hips. "If you think the killer is among the wedding guests, then you have a lot of people to question. And what if he isn't? How do you know where to begin? You are only one man."

"I'll manage," he said with some finality. Word about town was that the sheriff wanted to hire a deputy, but he and Mr. Archer were at loggerheads over the situation. Mr. Archer, who held the purse strings for town business and was currently acting as mayor, didn't want to spend the money. Thus, Clayton Marshall was on his own.

"I wouldn't sell her short, Sheriff," Kitty said, tilting her head toward me. "Mrs. Pryce here's quite the detective." She gave me a wink. She was, of course, referring to my catching the killer who had tried to pin the former murders on me.

I looked up into the sheriff's indigo eyes with, dare I say, smug satisfaction. At least Kitty appreciated my newfound skills.

"Thank you, Kitty," the sheriff said with some vexation. "But as I said, I'll manage."

I gritted my teeth in annoyance . . . and with a little

indignation at his somewhat cold dismissal of my offer of assistance.

Mr. Duncan stepped forward. "Well, if you don't mind, I'm going to check on Eliza. The poor woman must be completely devastated."

"Not so fast, Jack," Mr. Marshall said. "I need to ask you a few questions."

Mr. Duncan looked affronted. "Me? Whatever for?"

"You and the deceased were business partners. I believe you joined forces recently?"

"Well, yes, but—" Mr. Duncan's face reddened.

"You were partners in the Cougar claim," I put in.

The sheriff turned his hot gaze on me. "Excuse me for a moment, Jack." He took me by the elbow and ushered me some distance away.

"I don't want you involved in this," he said in an irritated whisper.

I pulled my elbow away from his grasp. "Eliza is my friend," I whispered back. "I want to find out who did this. For her."

He took in a deep breath, clearly trying to hold his temper. "That's very good of you, Arabella. But I can't let you do that."

I blinked up at him, my stomach fluttering at his use of my given name. It was only the second time he'd referred to me in such a personal way, and both times it had caused me to feel like a silly schoolgirl. It was most disconcerting.

Suddenly very uncomfortable, and a little warm under the collar, I cleared my throat, shoving my foolishness aside. I raised my chin. "I can be helpful, Sheriff. I'm very resourceful."

Exasperated, he rolled those gorgeous eyes to the ceiling and then set his gaze more firmly on me again.

"Look," he said, this time not bothering to whisper. "I mean it. Don't insert yourself into this investigation."

Quite vexed at being told what to do—or rather, what not to do—I narrowed my eyes at him. I didn't see any gain in arguing with him so I didn't persist.

"What you can do is to tell the guests that the bride and groom will not be at the wedding reception," he added, still obviously feeling he could give me commands.

I gritted my teeth but decided to hold my tongue. For the moment.

I waved Kitty over to me. "Let's give the gentlemen some privacy."

The sheriff walked back over to Mr. Duncan, and they both sat down to talk.

"Kitty, please inform the guests that Mr. Townsend has taken ill and that the couple will not be at the reception, but please have them continue to enjoy the food."

"We're not canceling?" she asked.

"It would be a shame to see it all go to waste," I said.

It was true what the sheriff said: people would find out eventually what happened to Mr. Townsend, but telling them the gritty details at the moment would just cause panic. Besides, what was I going to do with all that ham and roast beef, not to mention the fallen soufflé?

Kitty nodded to me. "Will do."

Just then, Cordelia came through the saloon door into the lobby. "There you are," she said with some exasperation. "The guests are getting restless, not to mention hungry. They are filling their bellies with booze, and things are getting a little, well, chaotic in there."

Kitty and I shared a knowing glance, and she hustled into the saloon.

"Arabella?" Cordelia crossed her arms over her chest. I

could see she'd felt quite abandoned being left to deal with the guests and her patience was nearing its end. "Where are Eliza and Mr. Townsend?"

I tilted my head toward the stairs. "Kitty will have everything under control in the saloon in no time. Let's go upstairs. You aren't going to believe what has happened."

Chapter Six

The next few days were busy with the preparations for Mr. Townsend's burial, and quite unexpectedly, I had to resolve the problem of a leak in one of the gas pipes in the hotel. Luckily, no one was harmed or had become ill, but several of the rooms had gone without light for the last two nights. Mr. Johns had discovered that one of the pipes had come loose from the wall, and in the process, the coupling had come apart, resulting in the leak.

We were all perplexed as to how the riser clamp that fixed the pipe to the wall had detached itself. Thinking on the matter of the stove, the idea did cross my mind that the gas leak could have been due to human intervention, but that might have been a stretch. I suppose things like pipes becoming detached happened for a number of reasons—a swing in temperature, rusted fittings, etc. It was also hard to keep track of all the minutia in a building as large as the Arabella.

The incident had caused a delay in my own investigation into Mr. Townsend's death. After all, I had a responsibility to the hotel and the guests. But now things were going more smoothly, so I could focus on the murder. And it was time for a visit to the good doctor's infirmary.

Stepping through the front door, I noted that the doctor's front room was empty, despite the clanking of bottles coming from the back of the building.

"Hello?" I called out.

The clanking continued, so I followed the sound. I peered through the doorway to see Dr. Tate pulling medicine bottles from a shelf and recording information in a ledger. A quick glance at a table behind him caused my stomach to clench. Under a clean, white sheet, a body rested atop it. No doubt the deceased Mr. Townsend.

"Mrs. Pryce," he looked up with surprise. "I didn't hear you come in."

"I'm sorry if I startled you," I said to him, not quite able to pull my gaze from the table.

"What can I do for you?"

"I was curious to know the manner in which Mr. Townsend was killed. Was he shot or stabbed?"

He glanced over at the body and then returned his gaze to meet mine. "Stabbed. The cause of death was either by suffocation due to a perforated lung, from excessive blood loss, or both."

"Oh." I swallowed. "I see."

"I'd appreciate your discretion for the moment, Mrs. Pryce. The sheriff wants to keep quiet about the cause of death until after the funeral, out of respect for the widow. I thought you should know because you and the boy were the ones to find him."

I nodded. "Yes. Thank you for telling me."

I returned to the hotel in a daze. When I first had seen Mr. Townsend in the carriage, it hadn't seemed important whether he had been shot or stabbed, just that he was dead —obviously killed. But, hearing the official verdict somehow made it seem even more sinister.

The funeral had been a small, quiet affair. I was impressed with how Eliza had borne the events of the last several days with strength and grace. But after the burial, she had retreated to her rooms for some solitude and had not surfaced in three days. I could hardly blame her. I had been sorely tempted to check on her, but respected her wishes to be alone. But now, I was growing concerned that leaving her to linger in her grief much longer might not be beneficial. From my own experience with widowhood, I knew that getting back into the swing of life was the best course of action.

"It's very cryptic that the killer left a calling card," Cordelia mused as she doodled in one of her notebooks, pulling me out of my thoughts.

We were settled in the parlor of the small suite on the fourth floor known as the Owner's Suite. I was seated at the large, walnut desk, and Cordelia had pulled up one of the armchairs to sit in front of the fireplace where the morning fire had reduced itself to glowing orange coals. Bijou had settled herself on the floor in front of it, enjoying the warmth of the wooden floor. The suite was comprised of a parlor, two bedrooms, and a bathing room, replete with bathing tub and water closet—the only two built-in conveniences in the entire hotel—thanks to the foresight and ingenuity of my late husband and, of course, Percival Blank.

There was space here on the fourth floor for expansion,

which I had considered as a project for the future, but funds were a bit tight as there had been a lien placed on the hotel for past debts to the Billings Building and Co., which had been incurred by the former manager. In addition to making repairs and upgrading the hotel, I was diligently endeavoring to pay the debt owed on it with my small stipend. There would be little funds and little time to expand my personal rooms.

And since I planned to leave two months after my year's requirement, it didn't seem necessary. Even though I was used to a stately home on Fifth Avenue in New York—it was nearly as large as the Arabella, annex and all—the cramped quarters on the fourth floor would have to do.

"The image on the calling card was a floral bouquet with a single red rose, a white lily, and a spray of lily of the valley, all wrapped up in a neat little pink bow," I added.

"And that was it?"

I shrugged. "I'd love to show it to you, but the sheriff has it in his possession."

"Oh my!" Cordelia placed a hand on her chest. "I just remembered I've heard of something like this before."

"Sincerely?" I asked, surprised at this declaration, though I wasn't sure why. Due to her vast appetite for reading anything and everything, Cordelia was always "in the know" about things.

"Yes. It was a case somewhere in the Midwest. Chicago, I believe. A man was found murdered in his own home. I don't recall all the particulars of the story or exactly how he died, but the killer left a calling card. I do remember that the murder was of a very personal nature."

"That's what the sheriff said about Mr. Townsend. That the killing was premeditated. How long ago did you read about the murder in Chicago?"

She bit her lip and cast her eyes upward, as if trying to recall. "It was some years ago. I don't remember how many."

"How did the police find the killer?" I asked, hoping for some insight as to how I might proceed. It was true what Kitty said, that I had a knack for investigation, but I had absolutely no formal police training. It's amazing what kind of skills a person discovers they have when trying to save one's own neck.

"I don't think they did. At least that I know of." Cordelia raised her palms in the air and gave another shrug.

"That's ominous. I wonder how many murderers run free in this world," I mused, the thought sending a shiver up my spine.

"The card is definitely a message," Cordelia said. "Goodness, I wish I could remember more about the case in Chicago."

"Do you remember what was on the card in that case?" I asked.

She shook her head. "I'm sorry. No."

"Hmm. That's too bad. It might give us some under-standing into the workings of the criminal mind. The act of leaving something like that at the crime scene almost seems . . . provocative. Like the killer is taunting those left behind. Playing a game, as it were."

"Indeed, it does seem that way. It's very cunning."

"Yes . . ." My voice trailed off. My mind was spinning, trying to determine how to proceed.

"Wait." Cordelia leaned forward. "*Helpful?* What are you aiming to do, Arabella?" she asked with some caution in her voice.

"I'm going to find out who killed Mr. Townsend, of course."

"But isn't that up to Sheriff Marshall?"

"That's what he thinks. But he obviously needs help, and there's no reason I cannot be of assistance."

Cordelia let out a sigh. "This seems dangerous, Arabella. And you have so much to do here at the hotel already. You'd mentioned cleaning up the annex and making repairs to the houses. Some of the porches look as if they're about to collapse."

I sighed in return. Several of the porches and porch overhangs were in pretty bad shape due to the harsh winters here in La Plata Springs. Something I had not yet experienced and was not looking forward to, I might add. The miners and their families had been complaining of the condition of the exteriors of their small dwellings, too, and some of the mothers had also complained about Kitty's girls.

I had to agree that having Kitty's enterprise in such close proximity to children was problematic, but how could I uproot anyone? The brothel was a home to Kitty and her employees. And I needed the income for the hotel. It was a conundrum I didn't want to face at the moment, and finding a killer in our midst seemed to take precedence anyway.

"I will make sure to have the porches fixed before winter," I assured her. Since it was early September, I'd have plenty of time. Wouldn't I? Furthermore, the issue of Kitty's girls would have to wait, as she paid me a handsome sum to run her brothel out of the hotel. That money would definitely help with the repairs.

"How do you intend to find this murderer?" Cordelia asked.

"With your help," I said with a cheery smile. "You have

such an inquisitive mind, and you are so resourceful. Please, Cordelia?"

"Why are you so intent on doing this?" she asked with an air of resignation. She never could refuse me, the dear soul.

"Eliza is the first, well, friend—other than you, of course—that I've had in quite some time and—"

The sound of someone clearing their throat startled me, and I flinched, even though I knew where the sound had come from. Percival had made his presence known, although I couldn't see him anywhere, thank goodness.

"Are you all right?" Cordelia asked. "You aren't coming down with a sore throat, are you?"

I breathed out a sigh of relief that she seemed undisturbed by the noise.

I cleared my throat in earnest. "No . . . No, just a frog in my throat."

"Would you like some tea?" She stood up. "I can go get some. I'll put the kettle on in the kitchen."

Taking the opportunity to avoid what would be a very awkward meeting between Cordelia and Percival, I nodded.

"That would be lovely." I smiled sweetly at her. "Thank you, darling."

The last thing I needed right now was for Percival to reveal himself to Cordelia. I could not risk her going into apoplexy at the sight of a ghost. Or knowing my little secret. I needed her fit and sound if we were going to solve this murder.

I saw Cordelia to the door and then went to the mirror positioned over the desk. In the reflection, Percival was sitting on the love seat, his legs casually crossed at the knees. He lit his pipe with a snap of his fingers, and immediately, the herbaceous aroma of tobacco filled the room.

"That was rude." I crossed my arms over my chest. "I was having a conversation with Cordelia, and you interrupted. And where have you been? I haven't seen you in days."

He removed the stem of the pipe from his mouth and emitted a cloud of thick smoke. "But I have seen you, my dear. You've been quite busy."

"Yes. Do you know what happened to the pipe that caused the gas leak?"

He sighed. "Afraid not." There was definitely a tone of dejection in his voice.

"What's wrong, Percival?" I indulged him.

"You said that Eliza was the first new friend you'd had in quite some time."

"Yes. What of it?"

"I thought we had become friends." He put the stem of the pipe back in his mouth, which was decidedly turned down in a frown. I held back a grin. He was pouting like a child who had been left out of the fun and games in the schoolyard.

"Well, I suppose we have, but . . . it's . . . well, it's different."

He sucked on his pipe and crossed his arms over his chest. "Explain."

"Really, Percival! Jealousy does not suit you." This time I couldn't hold back my smile, amused at his little display of temper. He was often brooding, like a Byronic hero in a romantic play. The melancholic artist who felt things deeply and saw himself as "different" from everyone else.

He let go a sardonic laugh. "I'm not jealous. Just a little wounded."

I recalled he had a similar reaction to some of my encounters with Sheriff Marshall. While I had no intention of allowing a romantic liaison between the sheriff and me, I couldn't deny there was an attraction— perhaps even a connection—between us, and Percival had undoubtedly sensed it, too.

"Oh, come now," I cajoled. "I'm sorry if I hurt your feelings. Of course we are friends. But how could I tell Cordelia about you?"

"I'd like for you to introduce us. Since we are all living here together in these rooms."

"Now hold on." I held up an admonishing finger. "I don't think that would be prudent." A flutter of anxiety rose in my chest, and my fears of being found out suddenly bloomed with a painful memory of the repercussions of my childhood encounter with Oliver Shrewsbury.

While at a picnic with my mother and her friends in the countryside, I had wandered off, bored with the adult conversation. I found myself in a grove of trees, and who should be there but Oliver, sitting on a fallen tree trunk. He had been ill with influenza, and the last we had heard, he'd succumbed to the deathly virus. I was overjoyed to see him.

Upon our return to the city, I had gone to Oliver's parents' home and declared to them that I'd seen Oliver and that I was so happy he was alive and well. My exuberant news had been rewarded with a flurry of tears from Mrs. Shrewsbury and a sound scolding from Mr. Shrewsbury, who had marched me back to my mother.

While my mother was shockingly *not* surprised by the situation, as others in my family had had the same "sensitivity," the ordeal resulted in many long and mentally arduous hours with a spiritualist who taught me to close myself off to this gift. My mother said if I did not learn how to do this, I would be seen as insane, or as a witch, and thrown into an asylum as two other family members had been. If that happened, my career, and her livelihood, would be gone forever. Her words haunted me to this day.

My more recent initial encounters with Percival and previously with Leticia Crookshank had occurred at times when I'd been most vulnerable. They had broken through the walls I had built up. With Leticia, it was at the loss of a treasured gift from my estranged father, and with Percival, it had been when I was facing a possible murder charge. And now it seemed I was quite powerless to shut myself off from him.

Percival pulled me out of my distressing memory. "Not prudent? But why? Cordelia seems like a person who is receptive and open-minded."

"She is, but . . ." Afraid that he would insist, I decided to pour on the charm. "I'd like to keep this friendship . . . well, *you*—" I gave him my most dazzling smile and gazed at him through a flutter of my eyelashes "—all to myself."

A look of satisfaction crossed his face, but he still refrained from giving me any hint of a smile. I decided to offer more. "Please don't be cross with me." I stuck out my bottom lip in a pout. "I need your help."

He uncrossed his arms, took his pipe from his mouth, and tucked it into the top pocket of his velvet smoking jacket. "I suppose you are referring to the murder of Mr. Townsend?"

"You know about it?"

He took in a deep breath and then let it out. "I know everything that goes on in this hotel."

I studied him for a moment, wanting to refute his statement and trying my best to hold my tongue, although my impatience with him was making it difficult. If he knew everything that went on in the hotel, why didn't he know what had happened with the pipe and the more ominous occurrence of the stone in the stove?

While he had been a trusted confidant during the ordeal of the murder accusations, he had not been active in the investigation. He had offered hints and suggestions, but again, for someone who claimed to know everything that went on in the hotel, he had seen relatively little that could have helped my case at that time. Still, he had been some-what of service in a ruse that ended up allowing me to find the culprit.

"Of course you do," I acquiesced. "That is why I need you to be on alert for any sort of suspicious activity at the hotel."

He stood up and then passed through the mirror and into the room, becoming instantly translucent. A wave of icy coldness enveloped me.

"I can also wander the town, if you'd like. It does me good to get out once in a while," he offered with a hint of enthusiasm.

Well, *enthusiasm* might be too strong a word. Perhaps it was more like *interest*.

"That would be wonderful, Percival." I batted my eyelashes at him again. The effect was satisfactory as he broke out into a most captivating smile.

Chapter Seven

Cordelia returned to our rooms carrying a tray. Upon it was a cheery teapot with a floral motif, two teacups and saucers, and two slices of cake.

"Is that the leftover wedding cake?" I asked with a frown.

"Yes. After the guests left, Mrs. Gilroy placed the rest of it in the icebox." She set the tray down upon the coffee table in front of the love seat. We sat on the love seat, and Bijou jumped up between us. She pressed herself to my side, snuggling against me, and rested her head on my lap.

Cordelia poured us each a cup of tea. I couldn't quite bring myself to eat the cake, though. It was a symbol of the couple's future happiness, and now they had no future.

"I still can't imagine why anyone would do this to Mr. Townsend," Cordelia said. "He was such a gentle man."

I nodded, my mouth lingering over the steaming teacup. The warm, toasty vapors of Betty Gilroy's homegrown dandelion tea instilled a quiet in me that I hadn't felt for the last few days. Preparing for the wedding had been quite a lot of work, and then, on the heels of it, we had to bury Mr. Townsend.

"So, if the murder was premeditated and personal," I reiterated, "it would imply that the culprit knew Mr. Townsend, or at least knew of him. But what if it was a random killing?" I finally took a sip of the tea. It had a nutty, spicy flavor, and it had taken me a while to get used to it, but Earl Grey tea, a staple of this Brit's diet, was hard to come by in these parts.

"That is a possibility," Cordelia agreed. "I once read about a series of murders in which the perpetrator killed merely for the thrill of it. He had not known his victims at all. They were just in the right place at the right time."

"Or the wrong place at the wrong time," I said. "That is a chilling thought for several reasons. If the murder was random, that means no one in town is safe, given that the killer is still here in La Plata Springs. It also means they will be harder to catch."

"They could have left on the train already, too. It's up and running again." Cordelia set her teacup down on the saucer with a *click*.

"Yes. But then why leave the calling card? No. The murderer is sending a message. A message they want acknowledged. I don't know why, but I have a feeling they are still here."

"Are you sure you want to do this, Arabella?" Cordelia asked.

I nodded my head firmly. "Yes."

I had spent the last years of my marriage, and my career, solely focused on myself. While I had thousands of fans who'd come to see me perform and I had been invited to dinners and parties by many of New York's elite on a regular basis, there weren't many people I could actually call my friends.

William had provided some companionship, but our lives had been so separate. If it hadn't been for Cordelia and Bijou, my life, though busy, would have been quite empty. Eliza, like Cordelia, had offered friendship, not because of my fame or my money but simply because of who I was as a person, not a performer. We had formed a connection, and I needed more people like that in my life.

"I'm going to start my investigation with Eliza," I declared. "As his wife—well, now his widow—she might know more about Rupert Townsend than anyone."

"She hasn't really known him for very long," Cordelia reminded me.

"True," I concurred. "But they seemed to have grown quite close during their brief courtship." I set my cup and saucer down on the table and stood up, forcing Bijou off my lap. She let out a little yip of disappointment that her pillow had vanished.

"Thank you for the tea, darling." I smoothed my skirt and then picked up Bijou to ask for her forgiveness. She gave it readily with kisses on my chin.

"Well, then I am going with you." Cordelia rose from the love seat. "If you insist on taking on this dangerous investigation, I won't allow you to do it alone."

Touched by her concern, I reached out with my free hand and took hold of one of hers. "Thank you, my dear."

After a quick trip downstairs to fetch more tea and fresh cups, we made our way to Eliza's rooms.

"We've brought you some tea." Cordelia said when

Eliza answered the door. She was wearing an appropriately demure gray dress in velvet brocade.

"May we come in?" I asked.

"That would be nice, thank you," she said.

Cordelia set the tray down on the desk that was positioned against the front wall. Above it was an ornately gilded mirror, similar to the one in my bedroom. It was another one of Percival's favorite haunts. I hoped he would not make an appearance.

After Cordelia poured the tea, we settled ourselves around the coffee table. Cordelia and I on the Louis XVI baroque, gold leaf sofa—my late husband had exquisite taste—and Eliza in the matching armchair. Bijou jumped up and sat on the chair next to her, and with her canine head cocked in sympathy, stared at Eliza. I was about to scold the little imp but stopped myself. Bijou always managed to give comfort, and Eliza was quite taken with her.

"I know this is a difficult time," I started, "but I'd like to ask you some questions, if you don't mind."

"Questions? What about?" She looked at me fondly.

"I'd like to help find out who did this to Mr. Townsend —Rupert."

"That's very kind of you, Arabella," she said, her voice breaking. "I so appreciate it, but the sheriff has questioned me at length. Have you spoken with him?"

I pressed my lips together in a half smile. "Not in the past few days. I've been busy with things here at the hotel." I thought it best to leave out that Sheriff Marshall did not want my help. "Has he made any progress?"

She sighed. "I'm afraid not."

I had suspected as much. Keeping law and order in a town that was growing as fast as La Plata Springs must be a challenge in itself. Add murder to the mix and it was undoubtedly overwhelming.

"Eliza, did Rupert give you any reason to believe he was in danger?"

"No. Not in danger."

"Did he have any enemies that you know of?"

Her eyebrows pressed together, creating a crease of consternation between them. "No. I don't know that many people here, but he knew everyone. They were all here for him. Everyone liked Rupert."

"Yes, they did," I said with some sympathy. It would be natural to feel defensive for a loved one.

"Eliza," I said with some caution, "there was something unusual left at the scene of the crime. Did the sheriff mention that to you?"

"Oh, yes. The calling card. With the flowers on it."

"Does that mean anything to you?"

She shook her head. "No. It is very strange."

"It is," I agreed. "Had he any disagreements with anyone recently?"

I thought of Jack Duncan, his partner in the Cougar claim. Had they had some sort of falling-out? Although, Mr. Duncan's presence at the wedding would indicate that all was well between the two. I wondered what the sheriff had gleaned from him on the day of the murder.

Still clutching the handkerchief, Eliza lowered her hands to her lap and cast her gaze downward. "Well, I . . . I'm not sure it was a disagreement per se, but Rupert and Jack—Mr. Duncan," she quickly corrected herself, "and Boss Archer had a meeting at the General about a week before the wedding. Rupert said that Mr. Archer had come away from the meeting a little . . . well, upset. But the situation seemed to have resolved itself."

"Resolved itself? Do you know what this meeting was about?" Cordelia inquired in her quiet way.

Eliza lifted her shoulder in a half shrug and raised her gaze to meet Cordelia's. "I'm not sure, but it might have had something to do with the mines."

I leaned forward, eager to pelt her with more questions, but I knew I had to pace myself. I didn't want to overwhelm her in her fragile state.

I remained quiet in the hope that she would continue. Bijou reached out her little paw and placed it upon Eliza's leg.

Eliza, absently stroking the dog's head, let out a sigh. "Mr. Archer wanted to buy back Rupert's portion of the Cougar. He offered a handsome price, but Rupert didn't want to sell."

"Buy it back?"

"Yes. Rupert and Mr. Duncan purchased the claim from Mr. Archer some months ago. I guess Mr. Archer figured it wouldn't amount to much, but when they found a lode of silver, he wanted it back."

This news was not surprising. It was pretty well-known that Archibald Archer was trying to buy up all the businesses and mining claims in the area. He owned the majority of them but seemed to want to possess them all. There had been rumors in town that he'd wanted to build a smelter and become the primary smelting site in Colorado.

I harkened back to Mr. Archer's offer of financial help for the Arabella. Did he want to purchase it?

In his last letter to me before he died, William had written a postscript that I was never to sell to Mr. Archer. The reasons why I knew not, but I did know that William had not cared for the man in the least. It was something that I couldn't quite reconcile. Although exceedingly ambitious, Mr. Archer had always presented himself as the perfect gentleman and seemed genuinely concerned about the growth and well-being of La Plata Springs. It had been a mystery to me why William had been so adamant.

"Interesting," I mused.

But the question was, had Mr. Archer stood to gain if Rupert died?

I pulled my top lip between my teeth, trying to determine how I was going to ask my next question.

"Eliza, I know this might be an indelicate question, but what will happen to Mr. Townsend's half of the Cougar now that he's . . . now that he's gone. Does it go to Mr. Duncan?"

Her face flushed pink, and she blinked back tears. Cordelia gave me a look of admonishment. Perhaps I had been too forward.

"I'm sorry. I didn't mean to upset you," I said, taking her hand.

"It's fine." She pressed her fingers to her mouth and shook her head, her eyes doleful. "I'm so embarrassed. I just don't know, Arabella. You'd have to ask Mr. Duncan."

"It's all right, Eliza." I myself wasn't sure how certain assets were handled in these situations.

Eliza's cheeks flushed. "I don't know much about business matters. I've never really had to. When I was in the theater, I had a manager who handled that sort of thing."

"Yes, me too," I smiled at her.

"But, unfortunately, that didn't turn out very well."

"What do you mean?"

The sorrowful, helpless look on her face hardened. "Martin Beale. He turned out to be a scoundrel and a cad." Her eyes filled with tears. "Not only did he break my heart but he took everything I had. He left me destitute."

"Oh, Eliza, I am so sorry."

"That is just unthinkable," Cordelia added. Bijou pressed herself closer to Eliza's hip.

I had to thank my lucky stars—and William—that that particular fate had not befallen me. Even my mother, who was ambitious to the point of nearly working me to death, had not done anything so nefarious. When William and I had decided to find a replacement for her, as my manager, William had scoured the country looking for the best one he could find for my theater and my career. I still had Mr. Thomas Blackthorn in my employ, and I didn't know what I would do without him. Or the lawyer, Mr. Tisdale, who handled the affairs of William's estate. I'd be completely lost without them.

"I continued to work in the theater," Eliza went on. It was clear she wanted to talk, so Cordelia and I sat patiently listening.

"I swore I would never have a manager again. From then on, everything I made I kept in a box under my bed, which provided a living for me. I was also able to save some money, and eventually, it turned into a tidy sum. When I came to La Plata Springs, after answering Rupert's advertisement, he set up a bank account for me, completely in my name. He said he wasn't interested in my money—not that it was very much—only in me."

It was a lovely sentiment and a very kind gesture on Mr. Townsend's part. It seemed he really had wanted to take care of Eliza.

I wondered why she had not told me of her former manager before in some of our intimate conversations. Perhaps she'd been embarrassed or ashamed about that as well.

"And now—" her voice cracked. "And now Rupert's gone. That dear, sweet man."

I reached out for her hand again and gave it a squeeze. I didn't want to press her anymore. She suddenly looked very tired.

But the question remained. What would happen to Mr. Townsend's portion of the claim? Would it go to Eliza? Or perhaps to Mr. Duncan? And then there was Archibald Archer. Just how far would he go to get back Mr. Townsend's portion of the claim? And, furthermore, what significance would the flowers have for him?

Chapter Eight

I wondered how long it would take before everyone knew the truth about Rupert Townsend, that he had been killed in cold blood right in their idyllic little town. And furthermore, that the killer could still be in our midst. Of course, people now knew that Mr. Townsend had died, but most assumed it was due to his sudden "illness." It would only be a matter of time before the truth came out.

My question was answered the following day with a gander at Miss Chatterley's morning missive, which Cordelia must have slipped under my bedroom door. The headline read, Beloved Mercantile Manager Murdered on Wedding Day.

"Oh my," a male voice rang out. "It looks like the cat is out of the bag."

I spun around to see Percival perched on the edge of my bed. Gathering my dressing gown tighter around me, I let out an irritated sigh. "We've discussed this Percival. No appearances in my room until 8:00 a.m. You must give me some privacy, or I'll have to remove your mirror."

I nodded toward the beautiful and ornate gilt mirror that hung above the bureau. It was one of the many lovely furnishings in my bedroom, which was complete with a stately, walnut, four-poster canopy bed, a large bureau, a large desk and chair that I never used (I preferred the one in the parlor) and behind the desk, the absolutely stunning mirror that was framed in gold leaf.

"My apologies." His transparent face took on a doleful look that didn't seem entirely sincere. "I must have lost track of the time. I've been out."

"Really, where have you been?"

"Down at my favorite spot at the river. It's a beautiful morning."

I heaved another sigh. "Well, not for everyone. I hope Eliza was able to rest last night. She was so distraught yesterday."

"I just saw her go out."

"What? You're serious?"

That was odd. Especially given that it was so early in the morning. She usually didn't make an appearance until well after 10:00 a.m.

"Did you see where she was going?" I asked.

He shook his head. "I'm afraid not."

"Why didn't you follow her?" I set my hands on my hips. I needed him to watch out for anything peculiar, and in my mind, Eliza going out so early was indeed peculiar. I hoped she was all right. Shock and grief were nothing to blink at. They could bring out strange things in people, and I was worried about her state of mind.

He gave a shrug. "I didn't feel it was necessary."

"Please, Percival. We must be on our toes," I pleaded.

"Very well. I will pay more attention."

"Thank you."

"Why are you up so early?" he asked.

"I couldn't sleep. I kept thinking about what would happen to Mr. Townsend's portion of the Cougar claim."

"You think it might have something to do with his death?"

"I think money and the potential to make a lot of money is a strong motive for murder."

"Yes . . ." His voice drifted off.

"What is it?"

He crossed his arms over his chest. "Something just popped into my head."

"About Mr. Townsend and the claim?"

"No, about Enrique Valdez."

"Pardon me?"

His transparent eyes took on a vacant stare, as if he was trying to remember something. Mr. Valdez, a gambler and a rake, according to Percival, had been a guest of the hotel some time ago, much before I had arrived, and sadly, he had come to his end here. Apparently, the card player had had more than his fair share of whiskey in the saloon, went up to bed, and then died in his sleep.

"What does that have to do with Mr. Townsend?" I asked, snapping him out of his trance.

"I'm not sure, but— Oh dear, the memory is a bit foggy . . ." His voice trailed off again.

"The memory? I assumed that when a person dies, like yourself, you become all-knowing and memories are clear as a bell."

His gaze shifted to mine. "That is only when a spirit is no longer roaming the earthly realm. While here, we still have our limitations."

"Hmm. That's interesting," I said. "Why are you still

here, then? I would assume that you'd want to rise up to the heavens and be in Paradise."

In my dealings with Oliver and Miss Crookshank, I'd never considered whether or not they were all-knowing. The subject never came up. I did know that Oliver's reason for staying among the living was that he wanted to be near his parents, and Leticia Crookshank was amused and often entertained by the performances in the theater. I figured Percival's reason for sticking around was because he loved the hotel, but he very often seemed at loose ends and, dare I say, even bored.

I had very little religious training, but I did believe in a higher power, and I also believed that when we passed on we did end up in a better place. A perfect place. But it was becoming less clear how or when we got there.

"I certainly would," I added.

He gave a brief nod. "Yes, but I have some unfinished business here on Earth. I am not ready to go."

"What business?"

"As we have discussed, I am uncertain as to how I died, but something keeps poking at me about it. You'll remember that I told you I had been at a party at Boss Archer's place the night of my death."

"Yes, you said you came back—or rather, that Andrew brought you back and poured you into your bed because you had consumed a bit too much liquor."

"Right. I just remembered that Mr. Valdez had been at the party as well. And a woman. A very formidable woman. I believe she was Boss's sister."

"He has a sister?" I don't know why I was surprised by this. Perhaps it was because he had only mentioned a brother to me—Andrew's father, who had died along with his wife, leaving Andrew an orphan. Mr. Archer had taken the boy in and had raised him. A very honorable thing, indeed.

"Yes." He shuddered. "She was a veritable iceberg of a woman. I did not like her."

"And what does this sudden remembrance have to do with your death?"

He tapped his finger against his lower lip but didn't answer. He looked at a loss.

"Well, my dear Percival, you are a mystery to be solved at another time. We need to deal with the one at present."

He sighed. "I suppose you are right. How did Miss Chatterbox find out that Townsend was murdered, I wonder?"

"Are you really that surprised?" I went to the wardrobe to pick out my outfit for the day. "Constance Chatterley has her finger, eyes, and ears on all of the happenings in La Plata Springs. Nothing escapes her notice, which is why I need to speak with her about Mr. Duncan and Mr. Archer. But only after I speak with Mr. Duncan first."

"You suspect them?"

"Perhaps. Mr. Duncan certainly had something to gain from Rupert Townsend's death. And Mr. Archer had wanted to buy the claim back from him. Perhaps the two conspired together? At the very least, Mr. Duncan might know what becomes of the claim now that poor Rupert is dead. Now, if you don't mind?"

I tilted my head toward the wardrobe. I had decided on a dark-gray woolen skirt, a white blouse with lace accents, and a burgundy coat.

"Ah, very well." Percival rose from his seated position on the bed. "I'll pop in later." And in an instant, he was gone.

After I quickly dressed, I plaited my hair. I usually would have had Cordelia arrange it in some sort of upswept creation, but I didn't want to take the time this morning. I was anxious to pay Mr. Duncan a visit.

But first, one of Mr. Gilroy's delectable pastries and a cup of Betty Gilroy's tea was in order. After getting dressed, I went to the parlor. Cordelia was stretched out on the love seat, reading a book, Bijou at her feet. At seeing me, she immediately sat up.

"Oh!" She closed the book. "I didn't realize you were up. You should have called on me to help you get dressed."

"It is of no matter, darling. I'm rather in a hurry."

"A hurry? Where are you going?"

I told her of my plans.

"Oh, well, then I'll go with you."

"If you'd like to join me for a pastry, then yes, but if not, I'd rather you go see what you can find out from some of the miners. See who, exactly, worked for Mr. Townsend and Mr. Duncan. What kind of employers they are . . . or in Mr. Townsend's case, *were*."

"You think one of the miners killed him?"

"I am leaving no stone unturned, dear."

"I'll get right on it," she complied. "I've already had breakfast."

"Really? You've been to the bakery?"

"No. I went downstairs to the kitchen. Kitty was there and fried up some eggs and made some toast for me. It was quite good."

"Wonderful." I frowned with distaste. I found it hard to eat anything but lighter fare for breakfast. And so had Cordelia. That is, until we'd arrived in La Plata Springs. Not only had she become more robust but her appetite had improved as well.

Dear Kitty. Since the fated wedding reception, she had been working double time with the saloon and her brothel, and had also been helping in the kitchen when Mrs. Gilroy was at the bakery. I didn't know how much longer I could impose on the poor woman, or on Mrs. Gilroy. I simply had to find a cook. But I couldn't do so at this very moment, so I stuck to my task at hand.

"Where is Bijou's leash?" I asked Cordelia, but just as the words came out of my mouth, I saw it draped over the parlor door latch. "Never mind. Come, Bijou."

My little canine, a grin on her hairy face, jumped down from the love seat and scampered over to me. She raised herself on her hind legs and pawed at my skirt, eager for me to attach the leash.

I did so and we headed out. We made a quick stop at the reception desk to check in with Mr. Pettyjohn. I found him rummaging through the drawers and key cubbies.

"Mr. Pettyjohn, have you lost something?" I asked with some trepidation. The man, as usual, looked a little scattered.

He whirled around at the sound of my voice, and his expression resembled that of someone staring down the tracks of an oncoming train.

"I, um, well—"

Just then, Maggie Mae Freeman, the head of house-keeping, came around the corner. A pretty, young woman, with strawberry-blond hair and a girlish face, Maggie was a diligent workhorse despite her diminutive stature and fragile features.

"Morning, Mrs. Pryce."

"Hello, Maggie," I said, smiling at her. I had recently promoted her from maid to housekeeping manager. The poor woman had been cleaning all twenty-five rooms of the hotel, and some of the houses in the annex, all by herself since the hotel opened. Why the former manager, Mr. Bledsoe, had not seen to hiring any additional maids was beyond my comprehension. When I had arrived in La Plata Springs, Maggie had been so overworked, she was on the verge of a near breakdown.

Maggie turned toward a tall young woman standing behind her, then urged her forward. I recognized her as one of Kitty's girls.

"This is Lottie," Maggie said.

The woman was all arms and legs. She had a heart-shaped face with wide cheekbones, pink with the blush of youth, and a narrow chin. There was a distinct birdlike quality about her. She reminded me of a graceful flamingo.

I nodded to her in greeting.

"Lottie is . . . Well, she's not really suited to work at Kitty's, and she's looking for a different kind of work. But Kitty is busy in the kitchen and said we should speak with you."

"I see. You'd like to add her to the housekeeping staff?" I had given Maggie carte blanche to hire a few more maids for the hotel. I figured who better to find potential help and then manage that help? She knew every nook and cranny of the hotel and what was entailed in keeping it in tip-top shape.

"Not exactly," she said. "Lottie here is a fine cook, and I know you've been looking for one."

My heart leaped with joy. "Oh! How interesting."

Lottie stepped forward. "I'd love an opportunity to work in your kitchen, ma'am. I've been cooking since I was a child, and those who have tasted my food say it's the best thing they've eaten. I'll work for room and board, ma'am."

This was the most excellent news I'd heard in weeks. "Wonderful. You're hired."

If I was still in New York, I would have vetted the

woman, but I was desperately in need of a cook. If she didn't work out, I would have to make arrangements for another, but for now, I was exceedingly grateful.

Lottie and Maggie exchanged a smile.

"You go on to the kitchen and Kitty will get you sorted," Maggie said.

"Thank you, ma'am." Lottie gave me a pretty little curtsy. "You won't regret this."

I smiled at her. "Welcome aboard." I sighed with satisfaction as she turned and hurried to the kitchen.

I reached out and touched Maggie's arm. "Thank you. I can't tell you what a relief this is to me."

Her face flushed. "You're welcome, Mrs. Pryce."

Bijou tugged on the leash, eager to go outside. I was about to follow her lead when I noticed the expression of sorrow on Maggie's face.

"Are you all right?" I asked her.

"I'm so sorry to hear about Mr. Townsend." Maggie shook her head. "I just can't believe it."

"I know. It's been quite a shock," I concurred.

She tapped her pencil on her clipboard. "I suppose someone is going to have to contact his mother. She lives in Iowa."

"Oh dear. I hadn't thought of that. Is she his only kin?"

Maggie nodded. "They were quite close. He wrote her a letter every week. He once told me he would always take care of her. Said something about his house always being a home for her—should she need it."

"I see." Strange that Eliza had not mentioned Rupert's mother. Then again, the subject of his extended family had never come up. Eliza and I had spoken about all manner of things pertaining to her and Rupert's courtship, though. Given that he and his mother were so bonded, I would think she would have come up *somewhere* in conversation.

"I'll speak with Eliza about it," I said. "Perhaps she should be the one to inform Rupert's mother."

Mr. Pettyjohn let out an exasperated sigh from behind the reception desk. His searching had become a bit more frantic. He had perused the drawers behind the desk multiple times.

"Are you looking for these, Mr. Pettyjohn?" Maggie placed her hand in her dress pocket and held up the master key chain that held keys to every single room in the hotel, with the exception of my rooms on the fourth floor. Only Cordelia, Maggie, and I keys to that.

His face paled, and he cleared his throat. "Ah, yes, thank you," he blustered. "I was just . . . I was just going to retrieve them from the . . . the . . ."

"The office?" she finished for him.

"Right. Yes. I was just on my way, but you've saved me the trip."

Maggie caught my glance and gave a brief roll of her eyes. It wasn't the first time Mr. Pettyjohn had misplaced the keys. I knew something would have to be done about it, but I wasn't prepared to deal with that now.

Chapter Nine

Bijou and I stepped through the bakery door, sending the bells hanging from the doorknob into a tinkling song.

I scanned the covered cake dishes to find an array of raspberry and blueberry tarts, apple pie, and buttermilk biscuits. My mouth watered at the sight of the biscuits. They were the closest thing to an English scone in look and taste, and I found that with a spoonful of jam, it was quite a delectable treat.

As I was perusing the sweets, Betty Gilroy came through a partially opened door that led to the bakery kitchen. Sounds of something thumping against a wooden surface came from behind her at the back of the bakery, and the scrumptious aroma of yeasty bread filled the entire space. Mr. Gilroy, her husband, was preparing his loaves for the day.

"Ah, Mrs. Pryce." Betty wiped her hands on her apron. "You're out and about early. How is Miss Swindon—er, Mrs. Townsend getting on? What a terrible tragedy."

"Yes. I suppose now word will spread quickly about the

murder, considering that Miss Chatterley has written about it," I said with some annoyance. It was true people needed to know about it, but it had all seemed so impersonal.

"Constance delivered the paper herself at dawn." Betty nodded toward the one-page newspaper on the counter. "Said she was waiting until the burial before she followed up on the story with any degree of detail. You've got to give her that."

"Yes. I suppose I do."

"Nevertheless, Constance is Constance. I'm sure she's flitting about town telling everyone. She means well, but that woman loves to be at the center of everything." She rolled her eyes and then sighed. "Poor Rupert. I can't believe he's gone. He's been in this bakery every day since he arrived in town two years ago."

"He'd only been here for two years?" This information took me by surprise. Mr. Townsend had seemed as if he'd been a long-term fixture in La Plata Springs. He had known everyone and seemed privy to every aspect of the residents' lives. I suppose that came from working at the dry goods store, though. There's nothing like working in a place that provides for everyone's needs to get to know them on a deeper level.

"Yes, ma'am."

"I certainly haven't been here very long, but it seemed as though he was on friendly terms with everyone. Do you know if he had any enemies?"

She set her fists on her hips. "Not as I can say. Although —" She hesitated and then shook her head. "No. It's probably nothing."

"What is it?"

She leaned forward conspiratorially and whispered, "I don't think he and Bob Parkhurst got on very well."

"Oh?" This was an intriguing observation on Betty's part. I wondered if that had something to do with his presence in Eliza's room the day of the wedding. He had left looking flustered, or angry, or something. "What makes you say that?"

She lifted a shoulder. "They were civil enough to each other. It was just a feeling I got whenever I saw them together. They are both such happy-go-lucky sorts, but the air grew thick when they were in the same space."

"Interesting," I mused.

"But it could be nothing. My husband says I always read too much into things."

I gave her a smile. "You must be a very observant person."

Bijou, suddenly feeling left out, gave a little yip.

"Well, I can certainly see that someone needs a tasty morsel." Betty leaned over the counter. She gave me a wink and held up a finger, indicating she'd be gone for just a tick. She went to the back of the store.

While Bijou and I were waiting, I casually scanned the little shop, and my gaze was suddenly drawn to the window. A woman passed by carrying a baby on one hip and a colorful carpet bag in her other hand. She must have just arrived on the stagecoach down at the livery.

Betty reemerged holding something in her palm. "Here you go, Bijou." She placed a small piece of butcher paper with a thin slice of ham on top of it down on the floor. Bijou quickly set to gobbling it up.

"And what about you?" She looked up at me, smiling.

"I'll take a biscuit smothered in jam and a cup of tea, please."

"Dandelion or Earl Grey?" she asked with a spark in her eye. "I just got a shipment from my sister."

"Earl Grey, please!" I said with delight. Betty's brother-in-law worked at the Pinehurst Plantation in South Carolina, and he was experimenting with the recipe the British had claimed as their own by adding bergamot oil to strong black tea. The pungent aroma took me back home to London and New York, and often soothed me when I became morose at my fate in living in this tiny, backward mountain town.

Betty bustled about preparing my light breakfast, and she soon laid it on one of the little tables in front of the window. I took a chair and settled myself.

"Does the sheriff have any idea who did this horrible thing?" Betty asked, placing her fists on her stout hips again.

I shook my head. "I don't know. I haven't spoken with him lately."

"Oh, and Miss Eliza? How is she faring?"

I realized I hadn't answered her question when I'd first arrived. "Eliza is . . . Well, she's doing as well as can be, given the circumstances. Apparently, she went out this morning. You haven't seen her by chance, have you?"

"No. You and Constance are the first I've seen this morning. I slept a little longer than usual today. I have been plumb tuckered since the wedding reception, and we've been pretty busy here at the bakery."

"I can only imagine. Thank you for stepping in like that and helping in the kitchen. I have good news: we've hired a cook. Lottie."

"Lottie? Isn't she one of Kitty's sporting girls?"

"Yes. But apparently, it wasn't working out. She said she's a very good cook, and I aim to see for myself."

"Well, I'm glad for you, Mrs. Pryce," she said with a firm nod. "But I'm always ready to help if needed."

"Thank you, Betty. I'll have your payment ready in the next few days."

"You take your time. I know you're good for it. Well, I'd better get back to the kitchen to help my baker man. You just let me know if you need anything else."

"Will do." I savored the fragrant aroma of the tea under my nose as I lifted the cup to my lips. My eye was again drawn to the view out the window. The woman with the baby was now talking with a man in the street, and he pointed her in the direction of the Arabella.

I smiled, glad to know we'd possibly have a new guest. The more guests we had, the closer I would come to finishing the refurbishing of the hotel and paying off the hefty lien against it. All that would lead up to my being able to sell the Arabella at top dollar and get back to my more cultured life in New York.

I quickly finished my biscuit and tea.

"Goodbye, Betty!" I hollered toward the back.

There was no response so I made my way out the door. Betty's observations about Mr. Townsend and Mr. Parkhurst were intriguing. I had set out to speak with Mr. Duncan, but my interest pulled me in another direction for the moment. Now I was intent on speaking with Mr. Parkhurst.

When I arrived at Archer's Livery, the sound of metal upon metal drew my attention to the forge. I walked past the barn where some of the horses for rent were standing in their small, open runs, and others were secluded in the barn's interior in their stalls. I passed the hay shed and then the coach building where coach tickets were purchased, before making my way to the far side of the livery. There, I found

Bob Parkhurst working diligently in the three-sided wooden structure that was the forge, hammering steadily upon his anvil. He was so focused on his work, he did not see me approach.

Behind him, brilliant orange embers cast a menacing glow. The tools of his trade hung from the ceiling, and a large barrel of water was set off to the side of his anvil. He stopped hammering for a moment, and with large metal pincers, he set whatever it was he was working on in the coals. I took the opportunity to get his attention.

"Mr. Parkhurst?"

He turned around. "Oh, Mrs. Pryce. I didn't see you there. Pardon me."

I gave him a smile. "It's no matter."

"What can I do for you?" With the pincers, he pulled out a long, rectangular object—soon to be fashioned into something practical like a gate hinge, or a knife, or even something decorative like a wall sconce—and set it upon the anvil. He then set the pincers on the small table next to him.

"It's this business with Mr. Townsend," I started.

A sheen of perspiration covered his forehead, and his mouth pulled down into a frown. He pushed his shirt sleeves farther up his dark arms, nearly to his shoulders, and then crossed his arms over his chest.

My eyes were drawn to the finely chiseled muscles that rippled under his mocha skin. I was about to force my eyes up to his face when something peeking out from under his sleeve had me riveted. It was a tattoo.

I had not seen many tattoos in my life, but I had heard they were popular among convicts and circus freaks. Also, in England, tattoos had become popular among women of the aristocratic social elite. The placements of the tattoos were always discreet, of course, but they were often bragged about at high tea or gala affairs. It was rumored that even Queen Victoria herself had a tattoo of a Bengal tiger fighting a python, but I found that a bit hard to believe, buttoned-up and proper as she was.

I was not often one to be shocked by such things, but this tattoo made my head spin. It was of a red rose…

"Mrs. Pryce?"

"Yes?" My gaze met his.

"You wanted to talk to me about Rupert?"

"Oh . . . yes. I— Well—" Still distracted by the rose tattoo, I found myself speechless.

His soft brown eyes regarded me curiously, and his full lips turned up in a questioning smile.

I cleared my throat. "The other day, before the wedding, you were leaving Eliza's room."

His smile faded, but he remained silent.

"I noticed you were a bit upset."

His gaze shifted from mine to somewhere over my left shoulder. I got the sense that it was not because something had caught his attention but that he was avoiding eye contact. Still, he said nothing.

"Do you mind telling me why?" I asked.

His jaw tensed. "Why is this important? Why are you asking me this?"

I wasn't sure how wise it was to annoy such a large man who was surrounded by menacing tools, but I persisted. "Eliza said she owed you money, for the use of a horse. I think it odd that you would have gone to her on her wedding day for such a trivial matter. Why could it have not waited?"

He uncrossed his arms and set his fists on his hips. "What are you getting at?"

"Why were you really in her room that day?"

He rolled his eyes to the ceiling. "I was trying to persuade her not to marry Rupert."

"Really? Why? How was her marriage to Rupert any business of yours?" I pressed.

"He . . . he wasn't right for her."

I quirked an eyebrow. This declaration was surprising indeed. "Oh. I didn't realize you knew her that well."

He looked away from me again, and suddenly, I understood. "You had feelings for her."

He nodded. "We met shortly after she arrived in town. We spent some time together before Rupert officially proposed, and well . . . after. It was then that she told me why she'd come to La Plata Springs, to marry Rupert, but she said she wasn't sure she wanted to do it, so we kept seeing each other."

I fought to keep my mouth from falling open. She had been seeing Bob Parkhurst at the same time Rupert had been courting her. And she had shared nothing of this with me.

"Until she finally told me that we couldn't go on," Mr. Parkhurst continued. "She was worried about our . . . differences."

I thought I knew what he was getting at but couldn't be sure. "You mean, your racial difference?"

He nodded. "I told her it didn't matter, but she didn't see it that way."

From the look of anguish on Bob Parkhurst's face, I could tell his feelings for her were deep.

"You love her," I stated.

He took in an audible breath and then let it go. "Yes. And I'm pretty sure she loved me."

"I'm sorry."

He shrugged, trying to convey nonchalance, but I could

see the pain in his eyes. It must have been difficult for him to see Eliza marry Mr. Townsend. I had wondered why he had not turned up at the church like the rest of the townspeople. Now it was quite clear.

Why had Eliza not mentioned this to me? I thought we had shared so much about our lives with each other. That aside, with Rupert out of the way, perhaps Mr. Parkhurst thought he could have Eliza all to himself?

"So . . . you . . . ?"

"I didn't kill him if that's what you're thinking," he finished for me.

"Where were you at the time of the wedding?"

"I was here."

"Did you see Rupert? He came to check on his horse."

The handsome blacksmith crossed his muscular arms over his chest again and fixed me with a curious smile. "Why are you asking me all these questions? I feel like I'm being interrogated."

I straightened my spine. "I want to know what happened to Mr. Townsend. For Eliza's sake. She's my friend. Now, please, did you see Rupert when he came to check on his horse after the ceremony?"

He let out a deep breath. I sensed an air of impatience, but he complied. "I saw him when he brought the horse. He said his horse had thrown a shoe and he had to get to the church. He paid me in advance, and then he left. I put the shoe back on his horse and then hitched him to the carriage again. I tied the horse to the hitching rail, and then I left."

"You left? But he said the horse might be injured."

He shook his head. "Once I got the shoe back on, the horse was fine. I didn't want to be here when he came back. He'd already paid so I didn't see the need to stick around."

"Where'd you go?"

"I went fishing for a bit. It helps me clear my head."

"Did anyone see you fishing?"

He chuckled. "I don't know. I wasn't paying attention. I was pretty preoccupied."

"With the wedding?" I pressed.

He fixed me with a pointed look. "Like I said before, I didn't want Eliza to marry Rupert. I knew she still cared for me, but I told her I would respect her wishes. I wouldn't pursue her anymore. But I still didn't want her to marry him."

"Why, if you respected her wishes?"

He looked away from me and shook his head. I could tell he was tiring of my inquiries. And my questions were obviously painful for him. But I remained steadfast and waited for his response.

He finally met my gaze again. "Because Rupert wasn't an honest man."

"Why do you say that?"

"It was this mine business. He and Duncan . . . they didn't come by that claim honestly."

"What do you mean?"

"They didn't buy the claim from Archer as everyone thinks. They stole it."

"What?"

"They came up with a scheme. They won it in a card game . . . but they cheated."

"I see." I was learning more about Mr. Townsend by the minute, and what I had thought of him before was proving to be somewhat erroneous, if what Mr. Parkhurst said was true. Once kind and friendly, he was now a cheat.

Mr. Parkhurst shook his head. "Problem is, Archer has no way of proving that they cheated."

"Oh. Well, then maybe they didn't," I offered. I didn't

want to believe that Eliza had married such a dubious character. "If it can't be proven, how can you say they cheated?"

He shrugged. "I know a thing or two about Rupert Townsend that might surprise you."

"Like what?"

"It's not really for me to say, Mrs. Pryce."

I could tell from his tone he was tiring of my questions, and the look on his face showed me that he would not reveal more.

Perhaps Mr. Parkhurst was eager to believe this about Rupert because of his hurt feelings over Eliza. This could just be sour grapes on his part. He said he loved Eliza, and Mr. Townsend stood in his way of being with her. It would be easy for him to find fault with him at every turn.

My gaze traveled back to the partially hidden rose tattoo on his arm. What if Mr. Parkhurst's feelings for Eliza had caused him to do something desperate? Yes, finding fault with a romantic rival was one thing, but stooping to murder was another thing all together. Jealousy was a powerful and dangerous emotion. Could it have caused Mr. Parkhurst to take the life of his beloved's husband?

Chapter Ten

When I left the livery, I noticed that the woman I had seen at the bakery earlier was still standing in the street. She had set the baby down, who was now crying, and she was rummaging through her carpet bag.

Bijou and I approached them, and Bijou cautiously went up to the baby and sniffed at its feet. The baby, startled by the dog, immediately stopped crying and emitted what sounded like a giggle. He—or she, I couldn't tell—reached out with a pudgy hand and touched Bijou's head.

"Do you need some assistance?" I asked the woman.

Squatting on the ground, she looked up at me. She was strikingly beautiful, in an ethereal kind of way that was somehow familiar but I couldn't put my finger on how. She had wide, dark eyes and a mane of wavy auburn hair. The baby, still fascinated with Bijou, gurgled and cooed, the previous tears forgotten.

The woman stood up. Her face had a look of heaviness, or distress, about it. "It seems I have misplaced my money pouch," she said, her voice wavering. "I've traveled so far, and now I can't afford lodgings."

"Oh dear," I said with some concern and, I had to admit, a little disappointment. I had hoped for another paying customer. But what could I do? There was a woman and small child in need, and I owned a hotel.

I introduced myself and stuck out my hand.

She took my palm in hers. "Helen Digby." She tilted her head toward the child. "This is Clara."

"Hello, Clara." I bent down and smiled at the baby. She rewarded me with a whimper and a frown. She stuck her thumb in her mouth. I decided not to take it personally, figuring that she was tired, or hungry or— Well, I didn't know. I didn't have much experience with little children. Bijou licked her chin, and Clara broke out into another giggle.

"I can put you up for the night. I own a hotel down the street," I said.

The woman's face finally broke into a smile, and her shoulders sagged with relief. "You are so kind. I will be able to repay you as soon as I find my husband."

"Your husband?"

"Yes. He lives here in La Plata Springs. We've been— Well, we've been apart for some time. But I need to find him."

She picked up the baby and set the child on her hip. The little cherub looked up at me with those large brown eyes and again stuck her thumb in her mouth. Bijou gave a little yelp—sad that her playmate had been taken from her.

"I see," I said. "Maybe I can help. I am a newcomer to La Plata Springs myself, but I've gotten to know some of the townsfolk. Who is your husband?"

She moved the baby to her other hip. "His name is Rupert Townsend."

"Excuse me?" I blinked in astonishment.

"Rupert Townsend," she repeated. "Tallish, thin. His ears stick out." With her free hand, she cupped her ear, pushing it forward. "Do you know him?"

I stared at her like a gaping fish. I didn't know what to say or how to say it. Rupert Townsend had been married already? According to Mr. Parkhurst, he was a cheat, and now he was a bigamist as well. Was this his child? If what this woman said was true—and I had no reason not to believe her—why were they not together? Why did he live in La Plata Springs without her? And what of dear Eliza?

I had thought Mr. Townsend such a kind and upstanding gentleman, but if this was true, on top of what Mr. Parkhurst had said, he was nothing less than a cad!

My stomach folded in on itself, and I felt the blood drain from my face. This could not be happening. Poor Eliza!

"Mrs. Pryce?" Helen Digby's delicate brows turned down in question. "Are you all right? Do you know my husband?"

I swallowed hard and then cleared my throat, still struggling with what to say to her. "Um, yes. Yes, I know Mr. Townsend. Or, well, knew him."

"Knew him?" Struggling with the weight of the baby, she hiked the little girl up higher on her hip.

"There's something I need to tell you, but not here," I said, looking around the street. I didn't want to deliver such shocking news in public. I felt the woman needed some privacy to take in what I was about to reveal.

"What do you mean?" she said, her eyes wide with alarm. "Has something happened?"

"Let's get you to the hotel and I can tell you all—"

"Tell me now!" she pressed, her chin quivering. "Please."

I picked up her carpet bag, which was terribly heavy. I wondered what she had in there. Surely clothing would not weigh so much. Adjusting it more firmly in one hand, I took her by the elbow with the other. I would at least get her out of the middle of the street. I led her over to the boardwalk where we stood between Gilroy's Bakery and Cynthia's dress shop.

"I'm sorry to have to say this, but Mr. Townsend is, well, he passed away." I thought it best not to go into the details at the moment.

"He's dead?!" she said, a little too loudly. Startled at her mother's raised voice, the baby pushed out her lower lip. She emitted a small whimper and then broke out into a full cry. Bijou, in turn, started to bark.

"I'm afraid so," I continued, my hands beginning to tremble. I did not deal with emotional displays very well, and this news, that Rupert Townsend was now married to two women—who were now both widows due to a horrible murder—would cause no end of emotional upset within the town. It was almost too much to take in.

Helen Digby pressed her free hand to her chest. "It can't be true." Her body wavered, and I was afraid she'd collapse. I took the baby from her, which immediately sent the child to crying. Again, I couldn't take it to heart. The poor child must feel her mother's distress.

"But . . . how?"

I really didn't want to elaborate here in the middle of town. "I'll explain everything," I said. "Let me get you to the hotel. You've just received quite a shock."

Her face pinched, she nodded.

Like a robotic automaton, Miss Digby—Mrs.

Townsend? Oh dear, this was all so confusing—picked up the bag and followed me to the Arabella. With the screaming baby on my hip, I hustled her inside and went to the registration desk where Mr. Pettyjohn was sorting through some papers. At the sound of the unhappy child, Mr. Pettyjohn's face soured. He looked equally surprised to see that I was the bearer of the noisy disturbance.

"Mr. Pettyjohn," I said hastily, not wanting to waste any time. "This is Helen . . . Digby." I nodded toward Helen. "She is going to be my guest for the night. Could you please show us to an available room."

"Mrs. Pryce, we have a slight problem."

"Oh? What is it?"

He motioned with his head for me to meet him at the far end of the desk, out of earshot of Helen. I really didn't have time for this. I wanted to get Helen to a room as soon as possible.

With the fussy baby still in my arms, I took his cue. "Yes?" I asked.

"It's the matter of, well . . . squirrels."

"Squirrels?"

"Yes, ma'am. There have been several sightings of them by the guests."

"Ugh! More vermin? I thought we'd gotten rid of them."

A few months ago we'd had an infestation of rats. Percival, taking advantage of the situation, had had his fun with a couple of guests he didn't care for by luring the rats into some of the fireplaces with poisoned food. In a matter of days, some of the rooms—including mine—had reeked with a most unpleasant and malodorous air.

Had Percival been up to his tricks again? Was there a

guest that had gotten under his translucent skin? I would have to have a word.

"Apparently not, madam."

I flinched at the moniker. It was one I despised. I did not care to be addressed as an aging matron, nor as a procurer of ladies of the evening. I had grown to like, and even admire, Kitty Carlisle, but I did not wish to share her title. I had spoken with Mr. Pettyjohn about this several times, but on occasion, he slipped. Given the situation and my desire to get Helen into a room, I decided to let it pass.

"I will deal with the problem later. Now, the room for Miss, er, Mrs. Digby?"

"Well, I must first get her registered, Mrs. Pryce." Always a stickler for details, when he remembered them, Mr. Pettyjohn looked at me quite affronted. He grimaced as Clara's wailing intensified. It was all I could do not to hand the child back to its mother, but I was afraid Helen still had sea legs.

I gave him a pointed look. "We can do that later. This is a matter of some urgency."

"Very well," he said with irritation and pulled his keyring from the drawer. "Follow me."

He led us upstairs to the second floor and proceeded to walk down the hallway toward the back of the hotel. He stopped at room 2B and opened the door.

"Thank you, Mr. Pettyjohn. That will be all," I said, hurrying him away.

We went inside. I had not yet been in this particular room. It was quaint and nicely appointed, but simple. Instinctively, I scanned for mirrors, as Percival liked to pop into the rooms that had them from time to time. There were only fourteen mirrors in the hotel, two of which were in the attic and one of them broken. I figured the last thing Helen needed was an encounter with a ghost. And Percival was quite a discerning ghost. He didn't like everyone, and if one fell into that unfortunate category, they would witness all manner of strange things in their room.

"I'm afraid we don't have a bassinet for the baby," I apologized, making a mental note to buy a couple for occasions such as this. Thankfully, little Clara had quieted for the moment, but the way her face was scrunched up, I feared another outburst was imminent.

"That's all right," Helen murmured. "She slept in the drawer of my bureau at home. She can do the same here." She nodded toward the walnut dresser against the back wall.

"Would you like to sit down?" I asked.

Helen still looked quite distressed and a little unsteady. She went to the tufted, wingback chair next to the small woodstove.

I set the baby on the rug, and Bijou immediately went to her and sat at her feet. The child momentarily broke into a smile and cooed happily. I knew Bijou would keep watch over her.

I took the chair opposite Helen. "Can I get you something? A glass of water? Tea?" I offered.

She shook her head. The color had come back to her face, and she looked a bit stronger. Unfortunately, the baby started to cry again, and poor Bijou did her best to snuggle up and comfort her but to no avail. I looked from the baby to Helen, wondering why she wasn't picking up the child. It must have been the shock. I was about to go to the baby when Bijou licked the child's face and the crying ceased. Sweet Bijou.

"How—" I started. I had so many questions, I didn't

know where to begin. "May I ask—Your name is Helen Digby . . . Why are you not Helen Townsend?"

Blinking up at me, she seemed surprised at my question. Or was she still reeling from the news?

"I—I decided to keep my maiden name. I am the last of the Digbys, and since I do not have a son . . ." She tilted her head toward the baby.

"Yes, I see. How . . . modern of you." Indeed, this was highly unusual, but I had seen it done before, especially in the theater where some of the actresses wanted to keep their stage names different from their married names. I had preferred to take my husband's name because I had liked it better than my maiden name, Janes.

"How long have you and Mr. Townsend been married?" I asked. And if he was already married, why did he marry Eliza? But I kept that part to myself.

"Not long," she said with a small smile. "We met in Addison."

"Oh. When did he live there?" I wondered if that's where he had resided before he came to La Plata Springs two years ago.

"He didn't really. He's from Iowa but had come out West. He was traveling through. We met the day he arrived, and . . . well, it was love at first sight. We were married after three weeks of courtship. Everything was going so well, but then shortly after we were married, we had a falling out, and he left . . ."

She shook her head and pressed her fingers to her lips in dismay. "I was heartbroken."

"Oh my goodness." I reached out and took her hand.

"It wasn't long before I realized I was with child." She looked over at Clara. The baby had quieted and seemed mesmerized by Bijou, who sat staring in her adoring way.

Clara was tugging at the long, silky hair on the poor dog's ears.

"I was very ill when Clara was born. It took me quite some time to recover. Once I was healthy again, I was determined to find Rupert. It just took longer than I expected . . . I thought he'd gone to Denver. I looked and looked for him, but when I didn't find him, I went back to Addison. Then I read about him in the paper, about his Cougar claim, so I came here. And now—" Her voice cracked. She pressed her hand to her throat.

I studied her features. She seemed entirely distraught, but I had not yet seen tears. I don't know why I thought it strange, as I often had difficulty crying, even when I felt like it. After learning how to shut myself off from the callings of spiritual beings, it seemed as if I had cut off a part of myself—or my emotions at least. I still felt them but had become expert at hiding them. Mostly from myself as a form of self-preservation. Perhaps Helen had done the same thing.

"Ah, of course," I said. I supposed a claim that hit would be newsworthy. Miss Chatterley had also told me that Mr. Archer often wanted her to reach out to the other newspapers in Colorado and sometimes farther afield with news of La Plata Springs in order to attract visitors and tourists.

I had to wonder if Helen's reading about Mr. Townsend's success prompted her coming to La Plata Springs or if she was truly heartbroken and had hopes of getting him back for more genuine reasons? Like the welfare of her child, perhaps?

"What happened to Rupert?" she asked, distracting me from my thoughts. "How did he . . . die?"

I sighed, not wanting to impart the horrific news, but she had a right to know. "I'm afraid he was murdered."

Helen's eyes went wide, and her mouth opened into an *O*. "Oh my Lord! Oh my goodness! But—but, when?"

"A few days ago."

She sat gaping at me. I knew this was hard news to take in. And she didn't even know the half of it. I didn't have the heart to tell her about Eliza yet.

"It was quite an unusual scene," I added. "There was a calling card left with the body. On it was a hand-painted image of a bouquet of flowers—a rose, a lily, and lily of the valley. Does that mean anything to you?"

"No . . . no. Not at all. How strange. Why would anyone —" She froze and then blinked rapidly several times.

"Helen?"

She took a deep breath, and then her gaze met mine. "Well, maybe there was something."

"Something? Something what?"

"Did you say a rose?"

"Yes. It was on the calling card."

She went very still and silent, and I could see that her mind was spinning. I waited patiently for her to speak, but it was as if she couldn't. And patience had never been my strong suit.

Eagerly, I leaned forward. "What about it, Helen?"

She snapped out of her trance and shook her head. "No. It's probably nothing. Just a strange coincidence. I'm sure it doesn't mean anything. Sometimes my imagination runs away with me."

"What is it, Helen?" I asked again. "You must tell me if you think it has anything to do with Mr. Townsend's death."

She bit her lip and looked up at me with doubt in her eyes.

"Please," I encouraged.

"Well, Rupert often fancied a card game."

So I'd heard from Bob Parkhurst.

"He would often go to Ginger's Saloon at night after supper. That was a favorite of everyone's in Addison. He was a pretty good card player, as I remember."

Or a cheat, I mused, but nodded, wanting her to get on with it.

"One night, he had a very good night. He won about a hundred fifty dollars."

"My goodness. That's quite a sum."

"Yes. There was a man there at the table. A man named Emory, or Everett, or something like that. Anyway, apparently he lost everything. Lost all his money to Rupert. I told Rupert it wasn't right that the man had lost everything, but Rupert had said a deal was a deal. The man shouldn't have been gambling away his life savings."

Immediately, I thought about Bob Parkhurst's statement about knowing "a thing or two" about Rupert Townsend in regard to him cheating at cards. Could this be what he was talking about?

"What does that have to do with a rose?" I asked.

She sighed. "I told you, I don't think it's significant."

"Please, Helen." Really, this was taking an eternity.

"Well, the next week, that man, Mr. Emor—well, whatever his name was—he came to the house demanding the money back. He said that because of that card game his wife had left him. She'd left town. He blamed Rupert."

She blinked at me as if she'd said something important, but I couldn't make sense of it.

"And?"

"And, well, this might be silly, but her name was Rose."

"I see." This was interesting indeed, and, I'd admit, a strange coincidence. "What did you say the man's name was?"

She pressed her lips together and gave a little shake of her head. "I'm not sure. Like I said it was Emory or Emerson or—"

"Emerson?" I repeated, and then sucked in a breath. "Everett Emerson?"

Her brows pressed together. "Yes. Yes, I believe that was it."

"Oh my." I leaned back against the back of the sofa.

Could it be that the new manager of the dry goods store had followed Rupert Townsend to La Plata Springs to enact his revenge?

Chapter Eleven

Bijou and I left Helen and Clara in their room. Helen had said she was overwhelmed and exhausted and needed to rest. I had managed to avoid telling her that Mr. Everett Emerson was here in town. I didn't want to distress her further.

Finding her in the street had been a distraction to my investigation but helpful nonetheless. So far, I'd learned there were quite a few people who had possible motives for killing Mr. Townsend. There was Mr. Archer, who felt Rupert had cheated him out of the mine. Then there was Mr. Duncan, his business partner. And then there was Bob Parkhurst, who loved Eliza and hadn't wanted her to marry Rupert. Now there was also Mr. Emerson, who had recently come to town and blamed Rupert for his misfortunes. Oddly enough, he and Mr. Parkhurst were the only connections to a rose. If that meant anything at all.

I was just approaching the staircase to go back up to my rooms to tell Cordelia of my recent findings when Bijou startled me with a furious bark. Immediately, a cold draft swept into the hall, and the ghostly form of Percival Blank appeared, perched on the staircase railing.

Surprised to see him there, I gasped. It made me nervous when he appeared in a public place in my presence. Those childhood fears of someone seeing me conversing with thin air and then being thrown into the loony bin surfaced.

"What are you doing here?" I hissed. "Why did you not wait until I was in my rooms?"

Bijou let out another yip. I picked her up to shush her.

Percival shrugged. "Cordelia is there, and I wanted to speak with you. I really think you should introduce us. It's silly that we all can't work together."

"Work together?"

"You know, solving these little mysteries that spring up."

I sighed. "Do you have anything for me, Percival?" I quickly glanced around to make sure no one was there to witness my seemingly deranged behavior.

"Perhaps."

"Really?"

"Yes. I was over at Doc Tate's. Townsend's carriage is still there. It's in the little alleyway between his office and the sheriff's. I wonder if you should peruse it."

"The carriage."

"Yes, I saw something in it that might be a clue."

"You did? What was it?"

"I'm not sure. I didn't stay to look into it further."

"Well, why not?"

Really! Percival gave lip service to wanting to help, but just like in the previous case, he rarely offered any concrete ideas or evidence. He excelled at making suggestions of things for me to do, but he seldom did them himself. Although, I couldn't begrudge him. Oddly enough, he was a great source of comfort for me. Of course, I would never let him know that.

"There were too many people around. The town is all abuzz about the murder, and there were several people wanting to speak with the sheriff about it. You know how I don't like crowds."

"I didn't know that," I said. "And yes, word has spread quickly, thanks to Miss Chatterley."

"Now, back to Cordelia," Percival quickly changed the subject. "I'm sure she would understand your . . . well, your affinity for communicating with spirits, and she wouldn't judge you harshly for befriending me."

I gritted my teeth. "Cordelia is the most rational person I know, and you . . ."

He raised his brows waiting for me to finish.

"You . . . well, you are not a rational thing."

"I think you might be surprised at her ability to accept me, *irrational thing* that I am."

I let out another exasperated sigh. "Nonetheless, I don't want to discuss this now, Percival. I've just discovered some quite disturbing things pertaining to Rupert Townsend, and I simply must tell Cordelia. I'll see you later."

"Can't I tag along?" He gave me that pitiful pout again.

Not willing to spend a second longer on this conversation, I set Bijou down, turned, and went up the stairs.

"Arabella?" The wave of cold air wafted up behind me.

"Oh, all right!" I gave in. "But stay out of sight. I mean it, Percival."

He held his hands up in surrender. "I promise."

Deciding to take him at his word, I proceeded, determined to ignore him, lest my anxieties about him randomly deciding to reveal himself to Cordelia take me over.

"Cordelia!" I burst through the doors of our rooms. She

was sitting on the love seat under the window reading and jumped at my abrupt appearance.

Bijou scooted in after me and went directly to her water dish and then to her bed.

"You will not believe what has just happened!"

"My goodness, Arabella. What has got you so excited? Did you find something pertaining to Mr. Townsend's death?"

Percival's presence was only detectable by the sudden chill that filled the room. I set my handbag on the desk and proceeded to tell her my news.

"His wife? But"—Cordelia's brows knit over her hazel eyes—"that's not possible." She absently crossed her arms over her chest, and she shivered.

"But it is," I continued. "It seems our Mr. Townsend was the duplicitous sort." I then told her about what Mr. Parkhurst had said about cheating at cards. Saying the words brought my ire up. How could Mr. Townsend have been so callous? And then there was Helen Digby. He had grievously wronged her, and now Eliza. I had known all too many men with such selfish natures, and it made my blood boil.

"So, Mr. Parkhurst is in love with Eliza? Goodness," Cordelia said.

"Yes. She had never mentioned Mr. Parkhurst to me, but I saw him leaving her room right before the wedding, and I thought it odd. Now it all makes sense. And there's something even more interesting."

Cordelia motioned with her hand for me to continue.

"He has a rose tattoo on his arm."

"And?"

"The calling card?"

"Ah," she said, tapping her index finger against her lips.

"That is interesting. But perhaps a bit of a stretch, Arabella."

I sighed. "You're probably right, but I think it a strange coincidence."

"And this woman, Helen," Cordelia continued, "Are you sure she was his wife?" Cordelia's voice took on a cautious tone. She rubbed at her arms. "My goodness it's cold in here."

My eyes drifted to the corner of the ceiling where Percival was hovering. Was he making it chillier than usual when he appeared to make Cordelia ask questions? It wouldn't surprise me if he'd tried to force a discussion. He could be very cunning.

He had his arms and legs crossed, sitting in some kind of invisible chair. He pulled his pipe from the pocket of his paisley smoking jacket and was about to flick it to life, but I gave him a quick shake of my head.

He rolled his eyes and placed the pipe back in his pocket.

"Why would she lie, though?" I asked, pretending Cordelia hadn't mentioned the drop in temperature and that Percival was making himself at home above our heads.

"Because Mr. Townsend has become a wealthy man. Perhaps by dishonest means, but wealthy nonetheless." Cordelia stated matter-of-factly. I recalled what Helen had said about how she'd finally found him. I hoped that her reasons for seeking him out were based on love, or even concern for her child, should Clara be his, and not greed.

"Yes. Indeed he had," I mused. "But I don't know, she seemed . . . genuinely distraught. She has a child—"

"Mr. Townsend's child?"

"So she claims."

"Oh dear, this complicates things."

"Indeed. How am I going to tell Eliza?"

"You should definitely tell Sheriff Marshall."

I sighed. "Yes. But he'll just warn me off from further investigating. I'd like to have a bit more information first."

Frustrating as that was, it warmed my heart that he should be so concerned for my safety. But, he really needn't be. I could take care of myself.

Cordelia stood up and began to pace the floor in front of the love seat. "I don't think you should tell Eliza. Not yet."

"I'm not sure I can keep it from her. I did not tell Helen about Eliza. What if Helen starts enquiring about Rupert to the townspeople? She would surely mention that she is his wife."

"If only we could find proof of their marriage . . . " Cordelia said, "But how?"

"Helen said she and Rupert were married in Addison. It's simple enough. We find a record—either a church record or a legal record."

"Of course." Cordelia smiled. "I can make a trip to Addison if you'd like. I've been wanting to go there. I've heard they have an extensive library. It's only thirty miles from here. I can take the stage and be there and back in a day."

"Yes. Wonderful, Cordelia. Meanwhile, I'm going to have to inform Eliza of this new . . . development with Helen Digby. I don't want her finding out on the street."

My stomach turned at the thought. Not only was her husband dead but she now had to find out that he might have been a cad to boot. But she had to know. I decided I would keep Mr. Parkhurst's suspicions about Mr. Townsend's cheating to myself for the moment, though. It would be hard enough for Eliza to hear about Helen, and that situation seemed more pertinent.

"I'll take the first coach out tomorrow morning," Cordelia said.

"All right," I agreed. "Helen also mentioned something else of interest."

"Yes?"

I told her about Everett Emerson and his wife, Rose.

"Mr. Emerson who works at Archer's Dry Goods Store?"

"How many Everett Emerson's from Addison could there be?" I asked.

"Goodness. Another rose connection. How strange. Well, I suppose he could be a suspect." Cordelia tapped her index finger against her lips again.

"That's right," I said. "Well, I'd better tell Eliza the news of Helen Digby. I'll see if she is back in her room. She went out this morning. Have you seen her or heard from her?"

Cordelia shook her head. "No. Should I have one of the maids build a fire? It's so drafty in here all of a sudden."

"Perhaps later." I hadn't noticed it before, but Percival had disappeared. But it could have only been seconds ago as there was still a chill in the air. "I have an errand for you to run, if you don't mind."

"Certainly. What can I do for you?"

"I'd like for you to find Miss Chatterley. I intended to seek her out after my breakfast at the bakery, but then other things came up that I had to look into, particularly Helen."

"What do you want with Miss Chatterley?" she asked.

"To see if she has found out anything of interest about the murder or the calling card. If there has been talk about it in town, she would surely know."

"I'm on it," Cordelia said, reaching for her coat and hat. "Are you sure you don't want me to ask Maggie to tell one of the maids to build you a fire?"

I shook my head. "I'll be out myself. But thank you."

She shivered again, put on her coat and hat, and left.

Immediately, Percival appeared in the mirror, and Bijou barked.

"My goodness. You'd think your dog would be used to me by now," he said with an air of distaste.

"She doesn't like to be surprised. And neither do I," I said with some irritation.

"So, Mr. Townsend had two wives," Percival reiterated. "I wonder if there are more lurking about somewhere."

"That's doubtful. But it's something that needs to be explored. It seems that our Mr. Townsend was a man of mystery."

Chapter Twelve

I went to Eliza's room and knocked. There was no answer. She was obviously still out, but where could she have gone?

Perhaps if I walked through town I would run into her, and since Cordelia had been happy to oblige me in going to see Miss Chatterley, I decided to heed Percival's advice and examine the coach. He did have a point. I wondered if the sheriff had had the forethought, or the time, to thoroughly examine it yet. And while he was known as a good lawman, he was not a trained detective like a city policeman, so I still maintained that he needed all the help he could get.

Bijou and I made our way downstairs, where Mr. Pettyjohn was busy checking in some new guests. I strode across the lobby and decided to go outside via the Bella, just to check that things were going smoothly in there. I still had much to do with the business of the hotel. I really didn't need the distraction of trying to find a murderer. But I wanted to help my friend. And the townspeople were at risk if the killer was still among us. Furthermore, as far as I could tell, the sheriff had found nothing conclusive. I would have to inform him of my findings, but I knew it would just cause him to try to shut me down again, and I had just gathered some momentum.

I entered the saloon to find it quiet, which was a bit surprising. Although the miners were not present in the middle of the day, as they were slaving away in the mines, the townsfolk liked to gather here for lunch, beer, and gossip.

Bijou, spotting Kitty standing near the bar, leaped from the steps that led down to the saloon in one single bound and ran to her.

"There she is!" Kitty leaned down and picked up my little imp, hugging her to her chest. Bijou panted happily.

"Hello, Kitty."

"Mrs. Pryce. What can I do for you?"

"Please call me Arabella, dear. I think we are good enough friends for that, don't you?"

"All right. Arabella. What can I do for you?" She gave Bijou a nice scratch behind her ears.

"Nothing really. Though, I'd like to thank you."

"Thank me? For what?" she asked with a chuckle.

"For Lottie. It greatly eases my mind knowing we have a cook."

"It's you I should thank," she said with a tilt of her head. "Lottie hasn't been with me for very long, but I could tell from the start she wasn't cut out for the sporting business. A girl's gotta have a toughness about her to work for me, and Lottie's a tender soul. She has no family and nowhere else to go, and I couldn't see turning her out into the world. I appreciate you giving her a chance."

"I am grateful to have her," I assured her.

"The guests seem to like her food so far."

I heaved a sigh of relief. "Then all is well, for Lottie, for you, and for me."

"That it is."

I smiled, thankful to have such an industrious and generous person helping me to better the hotel. "I was just on my way out and wanted to check in. Everything all right? It's pretty quiet in here."

She let out a sigh. "Yep. I think everyone is still in a bit of shock over Rupert. He was a big part of the community. He will be missed."

"Yes, I suppose so," I agreed, biting back my chagrin at his alleged dishonesty. "Kitty, do you know Mr. Emerson very well?"

"He's stopped in at the saloon a few times, and he's also . . . well, you know, visited the annex." By which she meant visited one of her girls.

"What is your impression of him?"

She turned her mouth downward and gave a little shrug. "Seems a nice sort. Quiet. Doesn't say much. Why?"

I couldn't really go into the details of why I was asking because then I would have to mention Helen, and I didn't want to do that until I spoke with Eliza first. "Oh, it's nothing," I said. "Just curious. He's new in town, is he not?"

"Yes. Been here about three weeks, I'd guess."

"Did he know Mr. Townsend? Did they get on?"

She set Bijou down, who, wanting more attention, danced at her feet. Kitty set her hands on her hips and gave me a dubious look from beneath her heavy brow. "What are you getting at, Arabella?"

"Well, I know he replaced Rupert as manager of the dry goods store. And since he is new here—"

"That doesn't mean he killed him," she said.

"True." I had to agree his being new wasn't sufficient reason. Goodness knows I was all too familiar with that kind of prejudice. The first day I had arrived in town, I myself had been accused of murder, but I wasn't ready to tell her why Mr. Emerson *might* want to move to La Plata Springs, that is to do Mr. Townsend in.

"You're right," I said, looking at the ceiling and then back at her. "I wish I hadn't brought it up."

She gave me a wry grin. "Is this you investigating the murder?"

I remembered her words to the sheriff about my being a good detective.

I lifted my shoulder in a nonchalance. "Maybe."

"All right," she said. "You've proven you've got instincts, I'll give you that. Want me to nose around a bit about him? I could talk to the girls. It's amazing what their customers talk to them about."

I gave her a smile. "That would be helpful, Kitty. Thank you."

"I doubt there's anything in it, but it's worth a try," she said. "And there's one more thing."

"Yes?"

She took in a breath and let it out slowly. "It's your friend Eliza."

"What about her?"

She shook her head. "I can't quite put my finger on it, but there's something familiar about her. Like I've met her before or heard about her somewhere. *Before* she came to town. It's been nagging at me ever since she arrived."

"Perhaps you had heard of her. She was an actress some years back. It's one of the many things we have in common. I don't think she was very well-known, but maybe you saw one of her performances in Denver?"

She pressed her lips together. "I haven't been to Denver in quite some time. . . No, that's not it."

"Well, what is it?" I asked. I wasn't sure what she was getting at, and I was starting to feel at little defensive for my friend.

"It's nothing." She batted a hand in the air. "Maybe she just reminds me of someone. I'll see what I can find out about Mr. Emerson."

"Thank you, Kitty." I gave her a warm smile. "Come, Bijou."

I quickly made my way out of the saloon and crossed the main street. I headed toward Dr. Tate's office, which was next to the sheriff's office at the end of the road. Sure enough, even from a distance I could see the front of Mr. Townsend's carriage peeking out of the little alleyway between the two buildings, just where Percival had said it would be.

The day was brilliant with sunshine, and the early fall atmosphere was crisp and smelled of pine. I picked up my pace, happy for the exercise. I hadn't had much time lately to take in the air.

When I finally approached the two offices, Cynthia Mayes, the owner of the dress shop, was coming out of the sheriff's office. She was a woman of mature years, tall and slender with an angular yet attractive face, and deep-set dark eyes. She had a wonderful sense of style and was the perfect model for her beautiful clothes, which she made in the latest fashions. It always surprised me that she was able to keep up with the trends living in this back-water burg.

"Hello, Mrs. Pryce," she greeted me warmly, but her brow was knit with concern.

"Miss Mayes." I gave her a friendly nod. I wondered what business she had with the sheriff. Her face looked so grave. "Everything all right?"

She sighed. "It's just this business with poor Rupert. He was such a wonderful man."

"He was," I said in my best consoling tone. She obviously had not known of any ill behavior on Rupert's part.

She raised her chin with a defiant air. "That woman didn't deserve him."

"Who? Eliza?" Her statement took me by surprise.

"After his money, she was."

Those defensive feelings for my friend reappeared. That thought had never crossed my mind. Eliza had been quite well off on her own. She'd worked hard and saved her earnings.

"Why would you say that?"

She huffed. "Do you know how many dresses she's asked me to make for her since she's arrived? Six! What woman needs six dresses? And all of them on Rupert's account. I can scarcely keep up. I have other orders to fill as well, yours included. I'm going to have to hire help."

I failed to see why Eliza's penchant for lovely dresses was cause for such hard feelings. And what business of Miss Mayes's was it whether or not Eliza's beloved fiancé wanted to shower her with gifts? Furthermore, I'm sure those six dresses cost a mighty sum. I would think Miss Mayes would have appreciated the business.

Not wanting to give voice to my increasingly irritated feelings, I merely said, "Oh, I see. My dress can wait, Miss Mayes." I waved a hand, assuring her that I was in no hurry.

She paid my statement no mind and continued. "I came to tell the sheriff what I've just told you. That she was only after Rupert's money. And, now with him gone . . . "

Now I could not hold back my ire. "You think that Eliza was responsible for Rupert's death?"

She sniffed, and then turned up her nose.

"That's ridiculous!" I said. "Not only that but it's impossible. I was with her the whole time Rupert was gone."

Bijou, sensing my irritation, gave a little yip.

Miss Mayes's mouth turned down, giving her the look of a child who'd been called out in a tall tale but didn't want to admit their mistake.

"Well, I just thought the sheriff should know my thoughts on the matter."

I gave her a tight-lipped smile, not wanting to debate with her. "Good day, Miss Mayes."

"Good day," she said and walked on.

I put her negative thoughts about Eliza out of my mind and focused on my task ahead. "Let's go, Bijou."

I approached the carriage. Still a bit flummoxed as to how it got down to the river in the first place, I looked for any kind of scuff marks. Perhaps whomever had killed Rupert had driven it down to the water's edge? Or the horse had been frightened and had taken off only to end up there? I recalled the awkward angle of Rupert's body. There was always the possibility that someone had set Rupert's body in the carriage after killing him and then ushered the horse away from the scene.

Nevertheless, the vehicle looked pristine from the outside. Except for the wheels. They were a little muddy, but that had probably come from being so close to the river.

I opened the door and peered inside. Bijou, probably

thinking I was going for a ride, let go a rapid chorus of barking.

"Bijou! Quiet. Give me just a minute."

She whined but obediently lay down and set her chin on her front paws. My stomach curdled at the sight of the gory bloodstain on the back of the seat. The blot was large and flowed down onto the floor. I stepped up inside and closed the door behind me, settling myself in the opposite seat.

It was a fine carriage, its walls overlayed with ivory silk and the cushions upholstered in gold velvet. Silk window curtains were tied back with entwined silk tassels decorated with tiny floral bouquets tied with string. The flowers looked like sweet little white wedding bells surrounded with oval-shaped leaves. I reached out to touch one of the bouquets and—

I sucked in a breath.

The flowers were lily of the valley! Just like on the calling card. It seemed I was seeing flowers everywhere. But I supposed that wasn't unusual. It was like when you learned a new word or heard about an unusual color, and all of a sudden, it popped up everywhere. But, still. It was something. And the flowers did pertain to the case, if only minutely.

But these lily of the valley weren't fresh flowers. They were made of silk.

I wondered if this was what Percival had alluded to earlier. Had the sheriff seen this and made the connection with the flowers as well?

Something on the floor, wedged between it and the base of the seat, caught my attention. Whatever the thing was, it was made of some kind of metal. I leaned over and tried to pull it out, but it was stuck underneath pretty tightly. On closer inspection, the item seemed to have tines. Quickly taking a hairpin out of my hair, I placed the end of it between the tines, and after a few attempts, I was able to drag it out.

It was a silver haircomb. It was simple in design and had a floral motif. Flowers again. But I had seen many hair-combs with floral designs. Yet, could this, too, mean some-thing integral to the murder? Its tines were grievously bent, some of them probably due to my prodding and poking, but the other tines looked like they had been smashed together from being forced between the wood of the floor and the wood at the base of the seat, perhaps by someone's heel?

Was this Eliza's haircomb? How long had it been here? It might not be hers at all. Maybe it belonged to someone else? A friend of Rupert's? Someone he might have courted before he'd met Eliza? Perhaps Helen?

Either way, it might be evidence. I would have to share it, and the strange coincidence with the flowers, both the lily of the valley that were tied to the curtain tassels of the carriage and the roses, as well as everything else I'd learned, with the sheriff. He would not be pleased with me for inves-tigating. Yet, it would be remiss, and grossly negligent, to keep these things from him as they could possibly help find the killer. I would just have to remain strong and steadfast in my determination to continue my search, despite his protests.

I shoved the comb in my reticule and then went to open the latch of the coach door, but it wouldn't turn. I tried again, but it was stuck. I jiggled the latch, pushed, pulled, and jiggled again, but nothing. I was locked in the coach.

"Everything all right?" a voice came over my left shoul-der. The smell of pipe tobacco overtook me. I turned to see Percival sitting on the seat next to me.

"What are you doing here?" I said in exasperation. I

really wished he wouldn't appear when I was in public. It sent all kinds of anxieties, rational or not, straight to my belly. What if he chose to show himself to someone who didn't understand the phenomenon of the spiritual realm? And what if they saw me conversing with him like we were old friends—well, we were friends, new friends—but still, they might think me a witch. Or worse, insane. That threat of the asylum always lurked in the back of my mind.

He himself admitted that he'd caused trouble for people at the hotel that he didn't care for, and it was already rumored that he roamed the hallways. It would be terribly difficult to sell the place after my tenure here if too many people knew of Percival, the Arabella's resident ghost. And I had every intention of selling and getting back to my life in New York. I wanted nothing to hinder that further.

"Did you find it?" he asked, seemingly unperturbed at my annoyance at his being there.

"What do you mean by 'it' exactly?" Really, I needed to get out of this coach and Percival needed to pop out of sight.

"The thing I saw wedged under the seat." He looked down at the haircomb in my hand. "Was that it?" He puffed on his pipe, sending a plume of ghostly smoke around his transparent head.

"Yes." I fiddled with the handle again. It was positively stuck, and I was trapped.

Hearing my voice, Bijou barked from outside the coach. I hoped she wouldn't draw attention to it. Aside from Percival and any explanation I might have to give about talking to— what would appear to be—myself (like a madwoman), it would be difficult to explain what I was doing in this empty carriage.

A little discomfited that he'd followed me here and frustrated with the blasted handle, I left it alone for a moment and whirled around on the seat to face him. "But what does it mean? To whom does it belong? Does it have any relevance to Mr. Townsend's murder?"

With his palm turned toward his face, he curled his fingers and examined his nails. "I don't know. I just thought it might be useful," he said, quietly. From the tone of his voice, I realized I had been impatient with him.

"I'm sorry, Percival. I know you are trying to help." I tried the handle again to no avail. "I really must get out of this carriage!"

Bijou barked in agreement.

I surveyed the open window. I would have to climb out. But how to manage it? Headfirst or feetfirst? How I wished I hadn't picked the larger bustle this morning, nor my favorite lavender satin skirt and white lace blouse. Surely it would not emerge from this unscathed, but I simply had to get out. And I refused to call for help like a damsel in distress.

I decided I would depart feetfirst, as if climbing over a fence. I just needed to get my bottom on the lower ledge of the window.

Since the carriage cab was not tall enough for me to stand up, I was in a crouched position. Carefully, I lifted my skirts and put one leg outside the window and rested my backside on the ledge. At that moment I was grateful that Mr. Townsend's carriage was not parked in the center of town. Still, I hoped that no one cared to make a visit to either the doctor or the sheriff at the moment. I would hate for someone to see my stockinged leg hanging from the coach.

Grabbing on to the top of the window, I swung my other leg around and dangled it outside, too. I'm sure my limbs hanging out the window looked like the disjointed legs of a broken doll. Fearing someone might see the spectacle I had created of myself, I needed to get down from my perch, but now that I was here, I couldn't fathom how.

Perhaps if I turned on my belly and then slid down the side?

It took a little bit of doing with the volume of my skirts twisting around my body and my corset allowing me no mercy or room for breath, but once my stomach was resting on the edge of the window, I could push myself off and land on my feet, god willing.

A jolt of embarrassment stabbed at me as I felt the cool mountain air wafting over my drawers. Because of the tangled mess of my skirts, my bum was exposed for the world to see. Luckily, we were in an alleyway, and I might be able to get down with no one the wiser.

I looked up to see Percival, still lounging on the seat in his casual way, grinning from ear to ear.

"Oh, do stop it!" I said. Really, the man—ghost—was so vexing!

I pushed myself from the window, preparing to land on my feet, when my skirt caught on something. I heard a terrible rip and then tumbled to the ground, landing on my backside, my skirts well above my knees.

Chapter Thirteen

Bijou yelped as I almost landed on her. Pain shot through my tailbone and up into my lower back. I groaned in agony.

"Need a hand?"

I looked over my shoulder to see Sheriff Marshall, his arms crossed over his broad chest and his cobalt eyes scrutinizing me as I lay in the dirt. My stomach folded in on itself in my humiliation. How long had he been standing there? Had he seen my bum hanging out the window in all its glory? I gave an audible groan of mortification. The man always seemed to find me in the most undignified situations and had even accused me of being accident-prone, which wasn't true in the least.

"You really should be more careful, Arabella." Those heart-melting eyes twinkled with mirth, and I cringed as heat blazed up into my cheeks.

"What are you doing here?" I asked.

Bijou stood on her hind legs and rested her paws on his shins. He bent down and ruffled her ears, and she panted happily, grinning up at him.

"I work next door?" He offered his hand to help me up with a smile. Embarrassed enough, I did not want to appear helpless so did not take his hand.

Gathering myself together as best I could, I struggled to get up, though I'm sure I looked like a clumsy dolt wrestling with my bustle and the fabric of my skirts and petticoats, which were woefully askew.

Once on my feet, I smoothed everything down, and another glance at the sheriff found him silently chuckling, those broad, square shoulders bouncing up and down with delight. Completely chagrined, I put on my best acting face and chose to ignore him.

"I've found something I think might be of interest to the case." I straightened my hat on my head and ran my hand up the back of my hair, ensuring that it had not escaped the pins holding it in place. At least all seemed in order there.

"In the carriage?" he asked, his tone suddenly serious, trying his best, I gathered, to hold back another chuckle.

"Yes, in the carriage!" I snapped. Really, this awkward situation was beyond the pale. Bijou let out a bark of agreement.

"I thought I told you I didn't want you involved." He gave me a stern look. "I mean it, Arabella. Stay out of it."

I set my hands on my hips. "But I've just now found two things of interest in the coach, one of which I'm pretty certain you might have overlooked."

Any hint of amusement left on his face vanished in the blink of an eye.

He started toward the door of the coach to look inside.

"Don't!" I reached out and touched his arm, afraid Percival was still lurking inside with that smug smile on his face.

He glanced down at my hand and then raised his gaze

to meet mine, his brows lifted in question. I quickly pulled it back.

"I mean, you can't. The latch is stuck."

Ignoring me, he reached out and flipped a small toggle on the handle—obviously a lock I hadn't known about—and then pushed the handle downward. An audible click made my embarrassment complete. He opened the door.

"Seems fine to me," he said, that trace of amusement in his expression returning.

Oh drat! This was the absolute end of my dignity. My face burned with heat. I gritted my teeth and closed my eyes momentarily to collect myself. He looked inside. Thank goodness Percival had decided to vacate the premises.

The sheriff perused the interior for some moments and then turned back to me, a look of annoyance on his face. "All right," he said in submission, "so what did you find?"

I pulled the comb from the reticule and held it up for him to see.

"What is it?" he asked, screwing up his face at its mangled condition.

"It's a haircomb. A woman's haircomb," I said.

"And?" He raised his arm and leaned it against the carriage.

"Well, this could be evidence."

With his other hand, he rubbed his chin with his index finger and thumb. "Probably belongs to his fiancée. Perhaps they were out—alone—and well, you know . . ."

"Know what?" I blinked up at him.

"Um. You know, maybe they got a little . . . amorous."

I wasn't entirely sure, but I thought I detected a faint pinkness to his cheeks. So it was his turn to be embarrassed. I smiled in delight.

"Perhaps." I widened my grin, and he quickly looked

away, occupying himself with another sweep of the carriage.

"Do you notice anything else?" I asked, feeling a bit smug.

He gave a half-hearted shrug of a shoulder. "No."

"The flowers?"

He turned to look at me. "What about them?"

"Lily of the valley. The same flowers that were on the calling card."

He stepped up into the carriage and sat opposite the bloodstained seat. He pulled the calling card from his front pocket. "You're right." He glanced over at me.

"Yes, I know." I gave him a prim smile. "And they're silk. Not real. Lily of the valley blooms in early to mid-spring."

"You know your flowers," he said with a downturn of his mouth.

"I know a lot of things that might surprise, you, Sheriff."

I didn't really know much about flowers, but I recalled that particular flower showing up in the bouquets I often received from fans after a performance, but only in the spring.

He turned back to the bouquet and loosened it from the curtain swag. He turned it in his fingers. "Could be a coincidence." He examined them closer.

"It could, but I discovered two other things this morning pertaining to the flowers."

"My, you have been busy, Arabella." His usually merry eyes clouded over with annoyance. "Well, let's hear it."

I told him about Mr. Emerson and his wife, Rose.

The sheriff's brows shot up, and he scoffed. "Now, that really sounds like a coincidence."

"But don't you see? Mr. Emerson blames Rupert for his wife leaving him. He has motive."

"I think you're jumping to conclusions. The fact that Mr. Emerson's wife's name was Rose is probably just a fluke."

I then told him about Mr. Parkhurst, the tattoo, and his unrequited love for Eliza.

The sheriff pulled his chin back in surprise. "You think Bob's a suspect?"

"I think jealousy is a strong motive for murder. And roses obviously mean something to him. Why else would he have one permanently drawn on his arm?"

"You saw the entire tattoo?"

"Well, no, his sleeve was covering the upper half, but I know it was a rose, and . . . he could have been the last person to see Mr. Townsend alive," I added.

"What do you mean?"

I told him what Mr. Parkhurst had said about going fishing after conversing with Mr. Townsend and then fixing the horse's shoe. "I don't believe he has anyone to corroborate his whereabouts at the time of Mr. Townsend's death."

The sheriff didn't have anything to offer on that account. Instead, he cleared his throat and changed the subject. "Bob's tattoo and the rose on the calling card are purely happenstance."

"But a strange coincidence, wouldn't you agree? Just like the lily of the valley in the carriage?" I still was not entirely willing to let the rose-tattoo theory go.

He rubbed his chin. "I don't know, Arabella. It seems unlikely. A lot of people like roses. You see them in bouquets and artwork all the time."

"Artwork?" I repeated. "You don't strike me as an admirer of art."

He raised his brows. "There are a lot of things about me that might surprise you, Arabella."

Touché. Sometimes I wished the things in my head would not come out of my mouth.

"Very true. Forgive me," I conceded. "But why are you always so skeptical, Sheriff Marshall?"

He gave me a pointed look. "It's my job. I have to look at things in a practical way, Arabella. I can't afford to go chasing every whim, as you seem to be doing."

I sucked in a breath, offended. "I beg your pardon?"

He lifted a placating hand in the air. "That said, I will take into consideration what you have told me."

Somewhat satisfied that he was not completely discounting my findings, I rewarded him with a half-hearted smile.

"Do you know who decorated the carriage?" he asked.

I shook my head. "I have no idea. I had some of Kitty's girls decorate the hotel's carriage for Eliza to arrive in at the church, but I don't know about this one. Perhaps Mr. Townsend arranged to have it decorated?"

"Think it could have been Eliza?"

"I doubt it. I was with her for much of the week. She and Mr. Townsend had decided to stay apart for the week leading up to their wedding. She wouldn't have had access to his carriage as he would need it."

"Well, it might be helpful if we could find out who put these flowers in here," he said.

I brightened at the fact that he seemed to find some value in my observances. "I'll see what I can do."

"I'll handle this, Arabella," he said, the steeliness returning to his features.

"But what about finding out if Mr. Parkhurst was truly fishing at the time of the wedding?"

"I said I'll take care of it."

"Oh, really, Sheriff! Don't you see that I can help? Haven't I just proved it?"

"You've learned about Mr. Emerson and his wife, Rose, but we don't really have all the facts: you found a woman's hair comb, probably Eliza's, and you've noticed the lily of the valley flowers, which is most likely another coincidence. Those flowers look very wedding-y."

"Wedding-y?" It was my turn to laugh.

He shrugged. "They look like wedding bells."

"How very perceptive of you, Sheriff."

I wanted to ask why he hadn't made the connection between the flowers and the calling card before but held my tongue. "And what about Mr. Parkhurst?" I asked instead.

He pulled his lower lip between his teeth, hesitating to answer. "I've known Bob a long time. He's not the jealous type. But like I've said before, I'd rather you not insert yourself in the investigation," he said with some impatience. "I'm sure you could be of better use to Eliza in a different way."

"Well, then I suppose you don't want to hear what else I've learned?" I set my hands on my hips.

"Oh lord." He rolled his eyes. "There's more?"

I smiled. "It may have no bearing on the case, but it certainly brings to light Mr. Townsend's character."

"Go on," he prompted.

"A woman has arrived in town claiming she is Rupert's wife."

At that little bit of news the stern set of the sheriff's mouth softened. "You're serious?"

"Dead serious, pardon the pun. But please keep quiet about it. I haven't told Eliza yet."

"Did this woman have any kind of proof?"

I swallowed. "I— Well . . . I didn't ask her for proof. That would have been awkward and, quite frankly, rude."

Perhaps I shouldn't have taken the woman at her word. She just had seemed so frazzled at the news of Rupert's death, so genuinely upset. Though, now I wished I had thought to inquire about some kind of proof, but Cordelia would be taking care of that tomorrow.

"Who is she?" he asked.

"She said her name was Helen Digby. She claims she kept her maiden name instead of taking Mr. Townsend's. She's staying at the Arabella."

"I'll have to speak with her. This is a serious matter."

"Do you think it pertains to the case?"

"When did she arrive in town?"

"This morning."

"So she wasn't here the day he was murdered?"

"Right." I nodded. "She has a baby with her and . . . she seemed devastated at the news that Rupert had passed, and in such a violent manner."

"Wait . . . a baby?"

"Yes, that's why she came to town. Rupert didn't know about the child, and she wanted to tell him. They'd had a falling out, and Rupert had left. She said it had taken her some time to find him. I think she wanted to reconcile."

"You'll have to tell Eliza."

"I will."

"All right. But leave the rest of this to me."

I narrowed my eyes at his condescending statement. "You're welcome," I said flatly. I did not fancy his dismissive tone but didn't see much point in arguing with him any further.

"Thank you," he said, but I could hear the reluctance in his voice. "But please stay out of this."

I straightened my spine at his apparent need to repeat the command. "I don't see why—" I attempted again.

He gently took hold of my arm and pulled me a fraction closer to him. Those dreamy blue eyes gazed at me intently, causing that most disconcerting flutter in my chest. "I care for you, Arabella. I don't want anything to happen to you."

I blinked up at him, and my throat suddenly went dry. Heat crawled up my neck and into my face. He had succeeded in rendering me speechless with his candor, and I wasn't quite sure how to take it in.

"Shall I walk you back to the hotel?" he asked, startling me out of my stupefaction.

"I'm not going to the hotel," I managed to say. "And I am quite able to get around town on my own."

His face fell slightly. He nodded and then tipped his hat to me. "Well, then good day, Arabella."

I took a deep breath and mustered a smile, trying to wrangle in my infuriating emotions. "Good day, Sheriff."

He gave me that disarming smile again. "Let me know when you're ready for that riding lesson."

"I certainly will," I said, knowing full well that day would never come. I much preferred a bicycle. I had spent many a wonderful hour riding my bicycle through Central Park and missed it dearly. I would have to send for it, or perhaps order a new one from Columbia Bicycle Company —one with a basket on the front for Bijou, of course.

"Come, Bijou!" I said, clapping my hands, and then we continued on our way.

Chapter Fourteen

The sheriff didn't put much stock in it, but I had a strong feeling about the flowers in the coach. Yes, they weren't unusual as a wedding flower, but the fact that they were also one of the flowers on the calling card gave me pause. But what significance did they have? I believed that in knowing this, it would lead me to the murderer.

And who had put the flowers in the carriage? The sheriff had been right to question that. Perhaps Mr. Townsend had availed himself of one of Kitty's girls as I had for that purpose? Which led me to wonder if he had ever availed himself of one of them for other purposes. He didn't seem the sort, but he also didn't seem the sort who would have two wives, either, or cheat at a card game.

I had to admit, I had trouble understanding men and the workings of their minds, or their hearts, or, well—quite frankly, anything else about them.

I slowly made my way down the street, musing on my lack of comprehension of the male sex when I noticed Mr. Duncan, Mr. Archer, and Eliza all standing in front of the

General hotel. I was a little taken aback when I noticed that Eliza had her hand tucked under Mr. Duncan's arm in a most intimate way. He was dressed impeccably, as usual, and wore green-tinted spectacles. He held her hand firmly to his side and had placed his other hand over hers.

Perhaps I was reading into things. It would make sense that Eliza would lean on such a close and personal friend of her late husband's. I myself had leaned greatly on Mr. Tisdale, my husband's lawyer, and also Mr. Blackthorn, my manager, when William had died. Having to oversee one's deceased husband's affairs was an overwhelming task, and in working with William's closest business and personal allies, I had formed a unique bond with each man. And romance had been the furthest from my thoughts at such a time. Or ever, quite frankly.

Mr. Archer's face was an unpleasant shade of red, bordering on purple, which made the whiteness of his beard all the brighter. His body was stiff, his movements jerky, and he held a menacing finger up toward Mr. Duncan's face.

Mr. Duncan, on the other hand, seemed quite calm. Eliza held her free hand up to her mouth. It was clear that whatever was happening, it was causing her some distress. Poor dear. She'd been through so much already.

I could not hear what Mr. Duncan was saying, but he spoke to Mr. Archer in an even tone. In fact, the tone completely lacked any kind of emotion.

Suddenly, Mr. Archer's face paled, and he stepped backward, faltering a little, as if what he'd just been told had been a blow. What on earth were they talking about?

As I approached the small trio, Mr. Archer, rubbing his forehead in what looked like a great deal of consternation, turned on his heel and went back into the General without so much as a by-your-leave.

"Eliza, there you are," I said, pretending I had not seen the confrontation, though I was bursting with curiosity at what had gone on between the three of them. "I was worried about you. You left the hotel so early."

The previous apprehension on her face dissipated, and she greeted me with a warm smile. "Oh, I'm sorry to have worried you, Arabella. Mr. Duncan sent me a note early this morning requesting a meeting. He had some news for me."

"Oh?"

Her hand still clutched his arm, and she looked up into his face, He gave her a nod of what looked like approval or permission. She then turned her attention back to me.

"Rupert was such a dear man." Her voice cracked, and she held her gloved fingers to her throat, as if unable to continue.

Mr. Duncan patted her hand. "It's all right, Eliza." He then turned to me. "Rupert had a very special gift for Eliza. He was going to tell her about it on their wedding night, but . . ."

Eliza closed her eyes and shook her head in anguish.

"Yes." I reached out and placed a hand on Eliza's shoulder.

"He has gifted Eliza with his half of the Cougar claim."

"Goodness!" I exclaimed. "That's . . . wonderful, Eliza." Did she know that her late husband and Mr. Duncan had possibly obtained the claim through dubious means?

She nodded in agreement.

"It looks like Eliza and I are business partners now. I just have to get some paperwork completed."

"I see." I wondered what kind of stake Helen might have in Rupert's estate. I figured that, legally, his gifting Eliza with the claim would have nothing to do with what

Helen might have inherited, if anything. Did Mr. Townsend have a will? Surely, he must have.

"Jack has been so wonderful through all this." Eliza beamed up at him. "I don't know much about such things, but he's going to oversee the management of the mine for me. I'm sure Rupert would approve."

He looked down at her adoringly, which made my stomach lurch. Her husband was not yet cold in the ground, and the familiarity with which the two carried on gave me pause.

William and I had not had a passionate marriage. We had come together because he needed an heir he could trust with all his investments and holdings, and I needed to get away from my overbearing mother. We had grown to love each other, each in our own way, but romance never had been a part of our relationship.

Yes, William had been ever so thoughtful and bought me trinkets, sent me flowers, and the like, but we had been more akin to friends. Even still, at his death I had been quite devastated, and I don't recall looking at a man the way Eliza was looking at Mr. Duncan then or since. Or perhaps ever. Although, Sheriff Marshall did at times leave me quite tongue-tied. But I put that down to his good looks and nothing more.

I hoped Eliza was not jumping into anything too soon. How could she really know her feelings when she was clearly still grieving? Yet, grief did strange things to people. Perhaps I was reading too much into this. I decided to turn back to my investigation.

"Was everything all right with Mr. Archer?" I asked.

The two of them exchanged a glance. Then Mr. Duncan turned to me. "I'm afraid Archibald was a bit taken by surprise by news of our . . . partnership."

"Why would he care?" I looked from Mr. Duncan to Eliza and then back to Mr. Duncan again.

"When Archer sold the claim to Rupert and me—" he started, but I cut in.

"Excuse me, Mr. Duncan, but isn't it true that you and Mr. Townsend 'won' the claim in a card game?"

He shook his head and let out a little laugh. "That's what Archer is telling everyone, that Rupert and I cheated him out of the Cougar. It was an attempt to save face. We did play cards with him, and he did lose to each one of us, but it was money, not the claim."

"What do you mean by Mr. Archer trying to 'save face'?"

"Boss fancies himself quite the astute businessman, and he is, I'll give him that. But even those with such business acumen make mistakes sometimes. Boss never thought the Cougar would amount to much so he offered it to us for a song. Even at that, Rupert was a little short of the funds. Archer sold Rupert's half to him at an even lower price, but there was a condition."

"Oh? What was the condition?" I asked.

Eliza spoke up. "The condition was that if Rupert wanted to sell, or be rid of the claim for any reason, or that if—" she blinked rapidly, as if holding back tears "—something should happen to him . . ."

"Then Archer would have first right of refusal on Rupert's half of the claim," Mr. Duncan finished for her. "But the agreement became null and void when Rupert gifted his half to Eliza."

"I see. And today was the first Mr. Archer knew of this? That Rupert had gifted his portion to Eliza?"

"Yes." Eliza nodded. "Like Jack said, Mr. Archer never expected the claim to be so lucrative. He tried to buy the entire claim back from Jack and Rupert a few times, but they had no intention of selling."

Now that Mr. Townsend was dead, Mr. Archer had assumed he'd get at least his half of the claim back. Was he so angered at not being able to buy back the claim that he would stoop to murder in order to get Mr. Townsend's half? It was an interesting prospect and one that I wanted to explore.

"All this excitement has quite worn me out," Eliza said, smoothing her hair. "I think I'd like to go back to the hotel."

The thought that she might run into Helen at the hotel crossed my mind. What if Helen had been talking to others at the hotel about her claims of being married to Mr. Townsend? I knew all too well how quickly word spread in this little hamlet.

I hadn't had the chance to tell Eliza about her yet, and I dreaded breaking the news. Cordelia was traveling to Addison tomorrow to verify Helen's claim of marriage to Mr. Townsend. Would it be too late at that point? I wanted to protect Eliza from hearing about this from anyone but me, but I needed to know for sure. I'd have to speak with Helen again as soon as possible. Speaking with Mr. Archer would have to wait for the moment.

"I was just heading back there," I said to Eliza. "Shall we go together?"

"Oh, well—" She looked up at Mr. Duncan.

He gave her an assuring nod. "You go on. I'll call on you later."

"Come on, Eliza. I'm sure you'd like to rest." I hooked my arm through hers and led her away from Mr. Duncan. She turned back and bade farewell to him with a wave of her hand.

Chapter Fifteen

We engaged in chitchat on the way back to the hotel. Eliza was a little subdued, but I couldn't help noticing that there was a glow to her cheeks and, dare I say, a faint smile on her lips. It struck me as unusual for a woman who had just lost her husband. But then again, Eliza had flawless skin and her cheeks had a natural rosiness to them—something that many women might envy. As far as the smile, perhaps she was still remembering her late husband's kindness in giving his half of the Cougar claim to her. It was indeed a generous gift.

When we arrived at the third-floor landing near her rooms, I took hold of her elbow. "Eliza, may I come in with you? I have something to tell you."

Her face lost its rosy appearance, and a look of concern flashed in her eyes. "My goodness, Arabella. You sound so serious."

I nodded. "It's a serious matter."

She took her key out and opened her door. I followed

her inside. She removed her hat and set it and her reticule on the bureau next to the door. "What is it, Arabella?"

I gestured toward the sofa. "Shall we sit?"

Once we were settled on the sofa, I began. "I went to the bakery this morning—to get my tea—and, well, I—" I hesitated, deciding in the moment not to tell her just yet about my visit to the livery and my previous conversation with Mr. Parkhurst. I was also finding it hard to come up with the words to tell her about Helen.

"Yes?" Eliza encouraged.

I cleared my throat. "On my way back, I . . . I ran into a woman. She'd just arrived in town and was coming from the stage stop at the livery . . . and—"

"Arabella, what is it?"

"She . . . she said she was looking for her husband."

"And? What does this have to do with me?"

I detected a hint of impatience in her voice, but I was finding this terribly hard to tell her. I took in a deep breath to gird myself and then let it out in a rush. "And she said her husband was Rupert Townsend."

Eliza sat very still, looking at me blankly, then blinking slowly. It was as if she were a statue frozen in time. The only part of her that was moving were her long, sable lashes. Then she let out a quick laugh. "Why, that's preposterous." Her face took on a look of disbelief. "I'm his wife."

"I don't have any kind of proof," I continued, my heart wrenching for her. "But I just wanted you to know about this woman . . . before you . . . well, in case you happened to run into her."

She stood up and, turning to face me, set her hands on her hips. "Well, whoever she is, she's lying."

"Perhaps," I said, glancing up at her. "But, we need to look into this."

Eliza's face hardened. "I want to meet her."

I got to my feet. "There's more."

"More?"

"There's a child."

"What?"

"A little girl. She claims the child is Rupert's."

Eliza pressed her palm to her forehead. "This is unbelievable."

"Like I said, we don't really have any proof. Cordelia is going to go to Addison tomorrow to—"

"Where is she?" Eliza interrupted. "I want to meet her."

"I'm not sure that's such a good idea."

"Arabella, please. I want to meet this woman and . . . her child."

I sighed. I supposed I couldn't blame her. I would want to do exactly the same if I were in her position. I almost regretted telling her. This news, coming on the heels of her husband's death, had to be a blow.

"Where is she?" she demanded.

"Here. In the hotel."

"Take me to her."

I sighed, feeling like I'd opened up a whole new can of worms.

———

We made our way to Helen's room and knocked.

She opened the door. She had changed her clothes and looked refreshed. The sound of the baby whimpering came from behind her. "Yes?" she inquired, an expectant look on her face.

"Hello, Helen. This is my friend Eliza. May we come in?"

Helen looked from me to Eliza and then back to me again. "What's this about? I'm trying to get the baby to take a nap."

"Please, it's important," I said gently.

She sighed and then ushered us into the room. The baby, sitting in one of the bureau drawers, her face red and wet, suddenly went quiet in our presence. She looked up at us with big, teary brown eyes.

Eliza glanced over at the child, and her shoulders visibly stiffened.

"It seems we have a bit of a problem," I started. "You see, Eliza here . . . well . . . she—"

"I married Rupert Townsend four days ago," Eliza cut in.

"You what?" Helen's brows rose nearly up to her hairline.

"You heard me. I married Rupert Townsend. I'm his wife."

Helen's mouth dropped open, the reality of Eliza's words sinking in. "But . . . but I'm his wife," she said, her voice a fraction louder than a whisper. "And, Clara, my baby—" she pointed at the child who had shoved her entire fist in her mouth and had resumed whimpering "—is Rupert's child."

"Ladies," I said, wanting desperately to defuse the situation, "perhaps we should sit down and—"

"Do you have proof of this?" Eliza asked, ignoring me.

Helen straightened her shoulders. "As a matter of fact, I do. I have our marriage certificate." She went over to her carpetbag and rummaged through it. Finally, she procured a very thick, stiff envelope and pulled out a piece of paper. She handed it to me.

My stomach sank. It was indeed a Colorado marriage

certificate signed by Rupert Townsend and Helen Digby, dated 1883—roughly two years ago. It was also signed by an officiant named David Houston. So much for Cordelia going to Addison tomorrow. Here was our proof.

"Oh my," I said on a sigh. I handed the paper back to Helen and turned to Eliza. Her face had gone stony.

"But why are you carrying that around?" Eliza asked, her tone sharp.

"Because I've left everything in Addison behind. I was hoping for a new start with Rupert. I brought everything I had."

Eliza faltered a bit, and I took hold of her elbow.

"How could he have done this to me?" She turned her gaze to me. "He lied. He was living a lie."

"With both of us apparently," Helen added in that whispery quiet voice.

"I'm so sorry, for both of you," I said, still in a state of shock myself.

"And now he's dead," Helen said with a touch of sorrow in her voice. "He never got to meet his daughter."

I looked over at Eliza, who was now gazing out the window, her thoughts seemingly a mile away. After a few awkward moments of silence, she turned her attention to Helen. "What do you intend to do now?" she asked.

Helen shook her head. "I don't know. I had planned to see if Rupert would take me back now that we have Clara. I thought it unfair for her to be raised without a father."

"If you don't mind me asking," I cut in, "what happened between you and Rupert? Why did he leave?"

Helen glanced at Eliza. "Like I said, we had a falling out. He didn't want to stay in Addison, and I didn't want to leave. We were both so stubborn about it. So we parted ways. That was before I knew I was pregnant."

"Why didn't you seek him out when you realized you were with child?" I asked.

She sighed. "I should have, but I wasn't sure where he'd gone. And I knew he wouldn't change his mind, and I wasn't going to change mine until—" she looked over at the baby who had gone quiet, still gnawing on her fist "—I thought of Clara. It wasn't fair to her, so when I'd read about him in the paper, I decided to come here to be with him."

I wondered what these two women were going to do now that Rupert was dead. Who had a claim to his belongings? His home? His assets? Eliza had his share of the claim, so she would be in good stead financially—if the mine continued to produce. But what about Helen? And what about Rupert's house always being a home for his mother?

"You'll stay here at the hotel," I offered. "Until we can get things sorted."

"This is absurd!" Eliza burst out. "You aren't really going to let her stay here, are you? It would be so . . . uncomfortable."

Helen held up a placating hand. "It's not necessary, Mrs. Pryce. I suppose I'll move into Rupert's house. He told me he had one here. Even though he's gone, it gives me great comfort that he saw to it that I'd be taken care of."

"Pardon me?" Eliza said, her voice shrill.

"He's left everything to me. Unless he changed his will."

"Um, well, moving into the house might be a problem," I said.

Both women swiveled their heads in my direction, confusion written in their faces.

"I— Well, I heard from Maggie that Rupert had

intended his house for his mother." I glanced at Eliza. "Did Rupert mention anything about that?"

"How would *the maid* know about that?" Eliza snapped. I was a little taken aback at her tone, but this was indeed an upsetting situation.

I shrugged a shoulder. "They were friends? But we don't know anything for sure. Eliza, did Mr. Townsend say anything to you about a will?"

She shook her head. "No. I knew nothing of a will."

"Well," I said, "if what you say is true, Helen, that a will exists—"

"One does," Helen said resolutely.

I gave a firm nod. "Then Rupert probably had a copy, and we need to find it."

Chapter Sixteen

I suggested we delay our search for the will, or a clue as to what law office he might have employed to procure such a document, until morning, when everyone was fresh and a little more clearheaded.

It had grown dark and both Eliza and Helen were exhausted, not to mention a little emotional, and the baby, tired and hungry, was beside herself. Eliza and I left Helen and Clara, and then I accompanied Eliza upstairs to her rooms.

"Are you all right, dear?" I asked when we got to the door of Eliza's rooms.

"I honestly don't know," she said. "When I answered Rupert's advertisement for a wife, I never would have imagined that he was already married."

"Yes. The audacity of the man," I said in sympathy. I could barely hold back my ire at poor Eliza's misfortune.

She sniffed, shaking her head, and then she caught my gaze. "Do you trust her? This Helen Digby?"

I shrugged. "I don't know her well enough to say if I do

or do not trust her. If she hadn't shown proof of her marriage to Mr. Townsend, I might not be so ready to believe her, but—"

"I suppose you are right. But what about this will? What if I am left with nothing?"

"You have partial ownership of the Cougar claim," I reminded her. "Which has proven lucrative so far."

"Yes. Yes, it's true. But I was so hoping to be settled by now. With Rupert, in his home—" Her voice broke, and I reached out and pulled her into an embrace.

"We'll see what tomorrow brings. Hopefully, we can get to the bottom of this sooner rather than later."

Leaving her, I felt as if I had a lead stone in my chest.

I spent the rest of the evening with Cordelia and Bijou. We had gone to the Bella for a dinner of smoked pork, potatoes, and carrots. Lottie truly was quite handy in the kitchen, and she was doing a good job of keeping our patrons fed.

After dinner we stepped outside for Bijou's sake and took a quick walk up and down the main street. A warm glow of gas light loomed up from Second Street, the residential street that was parallel to and directly to the west of Main.

Since many of the La Plata Springs residents had adequate to more-than-adequate means, due to the success of the mines, many of the houses, large and small, were quite beautiful, built in the Queen Anne Victorian, Colonial Revival, Edwardian, and Gothic Revival styles.

"Cordelia, I meant to ask," I said, "Did Miss Chatterley have any new information on Rupert's murder?"

"No. I'm afraid not. She had lots of gossip about other things, though."

"Oh? What other things?"

She shook her head. "I'm afraid I don't remember. Once she said she didn't have anything new on Mr. Townsend, I stopped listening. I find conversation with her a bit taxing."

I smiled. "I know what you mean."

"What are your thoughts on this Helen Digby?" Cordelia asked as we stopped to let Bijou do her business. I sensed a note of skepticism in her voice.

"She seems a nice sort," I said absently. "She was genuinely upset when I told her of Mr. Townsend's murder. Why do you ask?"

We walked on, and she shook her head. "Oh, nothing. It's just not every day you hear of a man having two wives."

"I can't argue with that."

"Do you think she aims to stay in La Plata Springs?" Cordelia asked.

"I suppose that depends on if she stands to inherit Mr. Townsend's house and any of his other assets."

"I see," she mused. I sensed she had something more to say.

"Cordelia, is there something on your mind?"

"What?" She batted a hand in the air. "Not really. There is just something about Miss Digby that unsettles me."

"Like what?"

"I can't explain it."

Although I didn't want to admit it, I had the same reservations about the woman, but like Cordelia, I could not say why exactly. Perhaps it was because she dropped in on us at such a difficult time. Everything seemed upside-down.

"Back to Mr. Townsend's assets. I suppose the Cougar is out of the question for Miss Digby, as it will belong to Eliza," she added.

"Yes. That is true. We are going to Mr. Townsend's home tomorrow to see if we can find a copy of his will. Or to find out if he has acquired the services of a lawyer. I wonder if there is a lawyer here in La Plata Springs. I've not seen a law office per se."

"No," she said. "But there are a few in Addison. Hopefully, as La Plata Springs grows, the town will attract more professional people."

We made our way back to the hotel. After a quick stop at the reception desk to check on things with Mr. Pettyjohn, we climbed the stairs to our rooms. I stopped on the second-floor landing. "I'd like to check on Helen before we retire."

"Very well," Cordelia agreed. "I'll come with you."

As we neared her room, I could hear the baby crying.

"Poor Clara," Cordelia said. "I'm sure the child is exhausted from traveling today. Babies don't like their routines disrupted."

We stopped at the door, and I knocked. The crying stopped for a moment but then quickly resumed, even louder. I knocked again.

"Do you think Helen's asleep?" Cordelia asked.

"With all that crying? I don't see how. I hope she's all right."

"Helen," I said through the door. "Helen, is everything all right?"

Clara's wailing reached a crescendo, and I began to worry she would disturb the other guests.

I reached into my reticule for the ring of room keys I kept on my person at all times when in the hotel. I had forgotten to remove them before our walk. I knocked one more time, just to be sure. Bijou, sensing my apprehension, barked.

"Shhh, girl," Cordelia admonished her.

I turned the key in the lock and opened the door. Little Clara was sitting in her drawer, her face red as an apple and shiny with tears. Her blanket was on the floor.

"She's not here," Cordelia said.

I went to Clara and lifted the unhappy child into my arms and immediately grimaced. Her little bottom was wet.

"Oh dear." I held her at arm's length, which only sent her crying into a fever pitch. "She's wet."

Bijou jumped up onto my skirts, whining. She was obviously distressed at the child's upset.

"Do you know how to—" I looked at Cordelia, who vehemently shook her head, her eyes wide with that look she often had when in the presence of violent emotion, as if being faced with an oncoming train. I quickly looked around for a nappy. I noticed the bed was still made, neat as a pin, and it looked as if nothing in the room had been touched, aside from the open drawer.

"Cordelia, look in Helen's carpetbag. Maybe there are some nappies in there."

She walked the small area of the room. She looked in the wardrobe, which was empty, and then behind the chair positioned near the fireplace. "It's not here."

A sinking feeling hit my stomach. Had she left town? And without the baby? If so, what were we to do with her? Panic stabbed at my chest. I knew nothing about caring for a child, and obviously, neither did Cordelia.

"Where do you think she's gone?" Cordelia asked.

Fear closed my throat. I looked into Clara's screaming face and was suddenly engulfed with pity for the poor child. She must be hungry, and frightened, and uncomfortable with her cold, wet nappy. Something in me snapped me out of my paralysis. I set the child in the drawer and laid her down. I quickly removed the wet nappy and wrapped her in the sheet that lined the drawer. I picked her up again and held her tight to my chest. Bijou stopped whining and had settled herself on the floor at my feet.

I was about to suggest we take the baby to our rooms when Helen appeared at the door, carpetbag in hand.

"What are you doing here?" she asked. Her eyes were disturbingly cold and accusatory.

"We heard the baby crying," Cordelia said flatly, clearly annoyed.

"Where were you?" I couldn't deny the relief I felt at her presence, even though she seemed perturbed at us for coming into her room.

"I . . . I, uh, went to fetch some milk for the baby."

"In the kitchen?" I asked, wondering why she would need her carpetbag for such an errand.

"No. At the bakery. But it was closed."

"I'm sure there is milk in the kitchen," Cordelia said. "Why didn't you go there?"

"I . . . well, I didn't want to impose any further." She looked over at me. "With you being so kind to let me stay here and all."

"Don't be silly!" I said. "You need to feed your baby. And I'm sure we can spare some milk. Cordelia, go fetch some for her, would you please?"

Cordelia had fixed a narrow-eyed gaze on Helen and didn't respond.

"Cordelia?" I repeated.

"Of course," she said dryly. "I'll be back in a moment."

Awkwardly, I held the baby out to her mother. Helen set down the carpetbag and took the baby into her arms, but there was no warmth or tenderness in it, which gave me pause.

"Why didn't you take Clara with you?" While I knew nothing about children and child-rearing, common sense dictated that you did not leave such a small child alone for any length of time, or at all for that matter.

She adjusted the child on her hip, and Clara began to whimper. "She was sleeping."

"Oh, I see. Her nappy was wet. I took it off and—" I pointed to the soiled garment that I had hung on the corner of the drawer.

She took the baby to the drawer and laid her down in it. She then went to the carpetbag and pulled out a number of square pieces of cloth. Silently, she set to putting one of them on the baby. I stood there awkwardly, not sure what to do or say. Bijou jumped up on my skirt, and I lifted her into my arms. Panting, she watched Helen and the baby intently.

"Here we are," Cordelia said from the doorway. She handed a jar of milk to Helen, who took it and set it on top of the dresser.

"Well," I said cheerily, trying to break the tension in the room, "it looks like you have everything in hand here."

Helen gave me a curt nod and continued wrapping the nappy around the baby. From her dress pocket, she produced a large pin.

"We will leave you to it, then," I finished. "See you tomorrow?"

"Yes, fine," Helen said.

I caught Cordelia's gaze. She seemed as confused as I was about the coolness with which Helen had responded to our presence. I would have thought she'd be grateful that we'd tended to and offered comfort to her unhappy child, but perhaps she'd just had enough for the day. She was probably worried about the will and what, if anything, she stood to gain. It would be frightening to have to raise a child with little or no means. It was unfair to judge her too harshly, I reasoned.

We left her finishing up with the baby, who had thankfully quieted now that her mother was back and tending to her needs.

"Was that strange?" Cordelia asked as we climbed the stairs.

"Oh, I don't know," I said with nonchalance, wanting to give Helen the benefit of the doubt.

"But she left her baby."

"Only for a few minutes. She said the child had been sleeping."

"But why take the carpetbag?"

"To carry the milk?"

Cordelia put a hand out to stop my ascension. "Did she aim to buy a dozen bottles? Come now, you have to admit . . ."

"Yes, yes," I said on a sigh, not wanting to give in to the notion that Helen's behavior had been a bit questionable but finding it hard not to do so.

Yes, in the words of Hamlet, something was rotten in the state of La Plata Springs.

Chapter Seventeen

The following day around midmorning, the four of us—Eliza, Helen, myself, and Bijou—were setting out for Mr. Townsend's home. As we were standing in the lobby waiting for the hotel carriage, Sally Dean approached us. I'd hardly recognized her as she was not wearing her customary barmaid's ensemble of bright-green bustier and knee-length skirt. Instead, she wore a simple, two-piece cotton dress in a charming and understated brown-on-ochre-leaf print.

"Hello, Sally," I greeted her. "Don't you look nice."

She gave me a charming smile. "Thank you, Mrs. Pryce. Kitty is allowing me the day off."

I was glad to hear it. Sally spent long hours on her feet during the day at the Bella and then more long hours on her back in the evening and throughout the night. I wished I could afford to pay Kitty's girls more to get them out of that life, but I was no match for what Kitty could give them and all the benefits she offered. They were like a little family—tightly bonded and loyal to one another. Although I didn't approve of them "sporting" at the

Arabella, I was grateful for the work they did in the saloon. They kept the place running, and the revenue generated from the Bella was more than helpful for the running of the hotel.

"Where are you ladies off to?" she asked.

Helen, holding the baby, shifted Clara to her other hip, jostling her quite roughly. The baby whimpered, threatening to cry.

"We have . . . well, we have an errand to attend to." I didn't feel it was appropriate to offer any of the details of our mission.

Clara's fretting gave way to wailing. Helen let out an irritated sigh and rolled her eyes. "For Heaven's sake, Clara," she said. "I just fed you."

"Oh, the poor thing." Sally laid her hand on Clara's back. Her large dark eyes were filled with compassion. "May I hold her?"

Without answering, Helen held the baby out to her. Sally took the child and hugged her close. Immediately, Clara's crying ceased. She laid her little head on Sally's shoulder, sniffling and snuffling into it.

"You have quite the touch," I said, impressed with the tenderness she showed the child.

"I love babies. I have lots of little brothers and sisters. Before I came to La Plata Springs, I used to help my mother care for them." She turned to Helen. "If you'd like, I could watch her while you go on your errand."

"That's a grand idea," Eliza said with some disdain.

"Thank you," Helen said. "She'll need feeding at noon." From her oversized handbag, she pulled out a feeding bottle full of milk and handed it to her. "I've left more milk in the kitchen icebox."

"Wonderful." Sally smiled brightly, her eyes lit with

enthusiasm. "Come on, Clara. Let's find you a toy to play with."

Mr. Ellis, the hotel's carriage driver, pulled the carriage up to the front of the hotel and we bade Sally and Clara goodbye. After Helen and Eliza got in, I noticed a commotion down the street, next to the livery.

The sheriff was standing nearby, and Dr. Tate's carriage pulled up.

"Something's happened," I said. "Mr. Ellis, take us over there."

When we arrived, several men were loading an unconscious Mr. Parkhurst into Dr. Tate's carriage.

Mr. Ellis pulled the coach up alongside the sheriff.

"What's happened?" I asked him.

"Looks like Bob was attacked from behind. Someone took an iron fence post to the back of his head. He's alive, thank goodness, but he's pretty badly injured."

"Oh my goodness. When did this happen?" Eliza asked, her voice unsteady.

"From what I can tell, about fifteen minutes ago. I saw him getting his tools set up for the day when I rode into town. I came back to ask him to fix a hinge that had sprung loose at the jail and found him on the ground."

"Did anyone here see anything?" I asked.

"No," he said, shaking his head. "But one of the horses is missing."

"How awful," Helen said.

I looked over at Eliza, who seemed quite stricken. "Are you all right?" I asked her. I considered asking her about what Mr. Parkhurst had told me about their relationship—which she had neglected to tell me—but now was not the time.

"Yes . . . Yes, it's just— The poor man."

"It seems there is nothing we can do," Helen said matter-of-factly. "We really must get on. I don't like to be away from Clara for very long. May we proceed?"

"Of course," I said, a little taken aback by her abruptness. But I supposed the fate of Mr. Parkhurst did not concern her, especially when hers was held in the balance.

The carriage ride was tense and silent. There was a frosty chill between Helen and Eliza, and my mind was awhirl with what we had just witnessed at the livery. Why an attack on Bob Parkhurst? To steal a horse? Or was it for another reason?

Thankfully, it was not a long ride, as Mr. Townsend's home was nestled in the foothills about a mile to the east.

We pulled up to the house, a lovely, two-storied Victorian home painted bright blue with white trim. It was of modest size with a peaked roof, wraparound porch, and a corner entrance.

I told Mr. Ellis to wait for us, and we entered through the front door. Many of the dwellings here did not have locks on their doors, as there really had been no reason. However, with the town slowly growing, I knew this would not last.

The interior of the house was plain and the furnishings sparse. There were no window coverings, aside from a bedsheet hanging from the window that faced the street. Indeed, Mr. Townsend had needed a woman's touch to make this place feel like a home.

A parlor was situated to the right of the staircase that led up to the second floor. To the left, I found a small room furnished with a desk, which was set in front of another window facing the street. Next to it was a standing lamp. Adjacent to the fireplace stood a bookcase full to bursting.

A chair at the desk, with its back facing the window, was

tucked neatly under it. I pulled out the chair and began looking through the drawers. I found a number of papers in a file drawer but nothing that resembled a will. On top of the desk sat a writing set, complete with two pens, an ink bottle, ink well, and letter opener. Next to the letter opener was a small key with a neat little tassel hanging from it. I wondered what it might open, but none of the drawers had a keyhole.

The sound of heels on wood echoed from the staircase. One of the women was headed to the second floor.

I left the little room and decided to go toward the back of the house. There I found a small kitchen, containing an icebox, a cast-iron stove that looked to be of the new gas-heated type, a wooden larder, and a small table with two chairs nestled in a nook surrounded by three windows. It was a charming room.

I took a gander throughout the space. I opened the doors of the larder to find nothing but some garden vegetables, a tin of flour, and a small tin of sugar. I suppose looking here was probably futile, for who would leave their will in the kitchen? But I wanted to leave no stone unturned.

As I was about to move away from the kitchen, Helen came in, holding a metal strongbox.

"I found this in the wardrobe of one of the bedrooms upstairs." With both hands, she held it out toward me. "But it's locked."

"Ah. Yes," I said, motioning her over to the table. She set the box down. "This is exactly where someone would keep important documents."

"I couldn't find a key, though."

I inhaled sharply, remembering the small key in the little room at the front of the house. "But I found one."

I hurried out of the kitchen, Helen on my heels. Eliza was coming down the staircase as we passed it.

"I think we've found something," I said to her. Both women waited at the stairs while I swiped the key off the writing set on the desk. I held it up to them. "This looks to be the right size."

Sure enough, the key opened the box. Inside, we found a string of pearls, some cash, a signet ring, and two rolled documents, each tied with string.

"Oh my goodness." I picked up one of the documents and slid the string off. Opening it revealed that it was a deed to some property.

"Look." I held it out for Eliza and Helen to see.

"It's a copy of the Cougar claim," Eliza said. "See there." She pointed to Rupert Townsend's name, which had been crossed off and replaced with another. Eliza Townsend's. The initials *RT* and *JD* were printed next to her name.

"What's the other document?" Helen asked.

I took off the string and unrolled it. My heart jumped as I read the flourished scrawl aloud. "Last Will and Testament of Rupert Townsend." It was dated 1883. Two years ago. Helen and Eliza crowded closer to me, and we read.

Helen stood back, crossing her arms over her chest. "See, I told you," she said smugly. "He left everything to me."

Sure enough, Rupert had written that his lawful wife, Helen Digby, a.k.a. Helen Townsend, had full rights to his house and anything in it. He'd also left a sum of money in Archer's Savings & Loan in her name. He'd signed the bottom of the document with his full name, Rupert Arthur Townsend.

"I can't believe this," Eliza said, a waver in her voice.

"I'm so sorry." I took hold of her hand. "Mr. Townsend was not honest with either one of you, and it's shameful what he did in marrying you both."

An uncomfortable silence ensued. I cleared my throat. "Even though his actions were dubious, to say the least, Mr. Townsend has taken care of both of you," I added. I hoped my statement of positivity would give the two women some comfort. At least both of them would be financially secure.

Helen nodded in agreement. "I'm sorry, too, Eliza. It's not fair what Rupert did to us. But you have your claim, and I have his house and some money. Surely, that accounts for something."

Eliza sniffed and ran a finger under her eye and wiped away a tear. "Yes. I suppose you are right."

I reached out, and with my other hand took Helen's as well, impressed that both women were acting so graciously. "This has been a trying situation for both of you, but now you can move forward in your lives and put all this behind you." I squeezed both their hands. "Now, there is just one thing left to do."

"Which is?" Helen asked.

"Find Rupert's killer. Then you will both have closure to this awful situation and justice will be served."

Chapter Eighteen

Once we got back to the hotel, I left each one of them to their own devices, and with that sorted for the time being, I could focus on finding Rupert's killer.

I had thought Bob Parkhurst might have been a strong suspect, but someone had set out to kill him, too. Yet, there had been no calling card left at the scene. At least not that the sheriff had mentioned. But if Mr. Parkhurst *was* Rupert's killer, maybe someone had attacked him in revenge for Rupert?

I pulled my bottom lip between my teeth. The latter scenario was possible but didn't feel quite right. Bob Parkhurst might have been hopelessly smitten with Eliza and terribly upset at her rejection of him, but would his feelings prompt him to kill?

After tending to some paperwork in the manager's office in the annex, which was actually my office, I had come away with an overwhelming desire to flee the premises. The mountain of bills that seemed to be accumulating by the minute left me feeling closed in and desperate. How was I ever going to catch up on the meager stipend William had left for the operation of the hotel?

Thank goodness Lottie had agreed to work for room and board. Thinking about her and the kitchen, I was reminded of the stone that had been placed in the stove on the day of the wedding. I hadn't had time to think about it with everything that had transpired lately, but the question remained: Had someone put it there to sabotage Eliza and Rupert Townsend's big day or mine? And did it have something to do with the murder? Unfortunately, there had been no clue left behind as to who the mischievous culprit was.

At moments like this, when overwhelmed with my responsibilities at the hotel, Mr. Archer's offer to buy the Arabella was all too tempting, but should I do so, it would leave me and my future in a very precarious situation.

Thinking of him, I wondered if he had felt desperate to get back the Cougar claim. How it must have stung to lose it and then to find out there was no way of getting it back now that Eliza was the owner of Rupert's half. According to Eliza, he had learned of it after Rupert had been killed. If Mr. Archer had killed Rupert, he would have done so in vain. I recalled the look of horror on his face when I came upon him, Eliza, and Mr. Duncan. Had he realized his grave mistake? There was only one way to find out.

I quickly jotted off a note requesting he meet me at my office later this afternoon on the pretense of hotel business. A niggle of guilt tapped at my gut at my dishonesty, but I wanted to ensure he'd come.

And now I needed to speak with the next suspect on my list, Mr. Emerson. I stowed the account books and the remaining bills in the desk.

"All right, Bijou," I said, looking down at the beloved hairy little creature at my feet. "Let's get back to the investigation!" I took up her leash, attached it to her collar, and we set off for the dry goods store.

From the side entrance that led to the annex, Bijou and I made our way across the street. Archer's Dry Goods was located next to the post office, and both businesses were where the townspeople gathered.

I entered the store to find it bustling. Not the best circumstance to question Mr. Emerson about his possibly killing someone, but I made my way to the counter where he was helping a customer check out. After a friendly ding of the cash register drawer, the customer left, and I stood facing Mr. Emerson.

"Good day, Mrs. Pryce," he said with a nod. He was a beefy man, with a tree trunk of a neck, thick arms and legs, and a perpetually serious expression on his face. During my time in La Plata Springs, I had yet to see the man smile. However, if what Helen had said was true about his wife leaving him on account of Mr. Townsend, I suppose he did not have much to smile about, given he was still pining for her.

"Hello, Mr. Emerson." I tried to give him a disarming smile but had trouble making my mouth work with what I was about to use it for.

"What can I do for you?" he asked in his gruff way.

Suddenly paralyzed with not knowing how to begin, the lie slipped from my lips. "Lottie has sent me to request a delivery of flour and pinto beans."

"I hear she's taken on the job of cook for you over there," he said, setting his sturdy hands on the counter.

"Yes. I am so grateful."

He nodded. "She's a good girl, Lottie. How much do you need?"

"A forty-pound bag of flour and ten pounds of pinto beans." I really had no idea whether we needed them or not, but no hotel kitchen in the Southwest could ever have too much of those staples, that much I had learned.

He took a clipboard from behind the counter and studied a sheet of paper attached to it. "I can have the delivery brought round to the hotel late this afternoon."

"Excellent."

"Put it on your tab?" he asked.

"Please."

He wrote something on his clipboard as I floundered for a way to keep the conversation going. My mind had gone completely blank.

Someone came up from behind me. "Mr. Emerson, do you have any cinnamon?" It was Cynthia Mayes. Bijou let out a cheerful bark at seeing her, but Miss Mayes ignored her.

"Oh, hello, Mrs. Pryce." She nodded a greeting to me.

"I have some on order," Mr. Emerson answered. "It should be here by the week's end."

"Oh my." She sighed. "Well, I guess making my favorite pumpkin spice cake will have to wait another week."

"Yoo-hoo!" Constance Chatterley came up behind us. Today she was wearing a rich-gold ensemble with dark-chocolate lace. The color was all wrong for her and gave her complexion a rather washed-out look. Her hat, which was enormous, spouted feathers from the top of it, making her look like a chocolate fountain.

"Mrs. Pryce," she said, "I am so glad I ran into you. I was just about to go over to the hotel when I realized I

needed more ink for my printing press. Mr. Emerson, I'll need three canisters please."

"Coming right up," he said and left the counter. He disappeared into a back room. I held back a sigh. It had not been a good idea to come to the store to speak with him. I should have figured a way to have more privacy.

Miss Chatterley set her hands on her hips and looked at us intently. "Did you hear about poor Mr. Parkhurst? Someone tried to kill him! Hit him in the back of the head with a metal fence post! I say, someone is wreaking havoc in this town. First, Mr. Townsend, and then this!"

"I had not heard," Miss Mayes said, concern in her voice. "Will he be all right?"

"He's with the doctor," I said. "I suppose only time will tell."

"Yes, poor man," Constance concurred. "You will never guess what *else* I heard." Her eyes shone bright with excitement. "I heard that a woman came to town claiming to be Rupert's wife. And him having just married Eliza Swindon!"

"No!" Cynthia said. "That can't be true!" Her cheeks drained of color.

Constance turned to me. "Isn't that so, Mrs. Pryce? I understand she is staying at the Arabella, as your guest?"

Both women looked at me expectantly. I had hoped word of this would not get out. It just complicated matters, and I knew that it would humiliate Eliza.

But how could I evade the truth? The proverbial cat was already out of the bag.

"Yes, it's true."

"Oh my land!" Miss Mayes said, clutching her chest with one hand. She faltered and caught herself with her other hand on the counter. Bijou whined at the woman's distress.

I reached out to offer assistance. "Are you all right, Miss Mayes?"

She collected herself and left the store without another word, Bijou padding after her. My little urchin was left standing in the doorway watching the woman walk away. I looked over at Constance who, with lips pressed together, shook her head in dismay.

"Poor Cynthia," she said in a loud whisper. "She'd been carrying a torch for Rupert for quite some time. Ever since he took her for a carriage ride well over a year ago. He just didn't show the same interest."

A carriage ride? My thoughts immediately went to the haircomb. Could it have been hers? Had it been left there a year ago, or had it been more recent? Had Cynthia Mayes misconstrued Rupert's intentions? Has she been so distraught and angered over Rupert's marrying Eliza that she did away with him?

Her reaction to Rupert's having another wife indicated that her feelings for him had not waned. She'd been just as shocked as Eliza.

"Miss Chatterley, have you any new news on Mr. Townsend's murder?" I asked, hoping to glean any more information that might give me more insight.

She clicked her tongue and shook her head. "I'm afraid not. Only that there was a calling card left on his body. Quite chilling, if you ask me."

So, word *had* gotten out.

Just then Mr. Emerson emerged from the room with a wooden box. "Here you go, Miss Chatterley. Three canisters of ink."

"Oh, thank you, Mr. Emerson. Please put it on my tab."

"Will do." He held out the box for her.

"It looks rather heavy," she said, giving him a brilliant smile. "I wonder if you could bring it round . . . later?"

"Well, Miss Chatterley, I have a delivery to the hotel and some others to make. It might be quite late."

"Oh, I don't mind. Late is fine." She beamed at him again.

"All right." He turned and went back to the counter, setting the box on top of it. "I'll bring it by this evening."

Miss Chatterley gave him a finger wave and then glanced at me. "He's such a nice man," she whispered, her eyes twinkling, and I wondered if she had feelings for Mr. Emerson.

Another customer walked into the store, and Mr. Emerson was again diverted.

"Yes, he is" I agreed.

"So, what are your impressions of this woman who's recently come to town? Rupert's *other* wife?" she asked.

"To tell you the truth, I'm not quite sure." I didn't know how much information I should give her, lest it end up in her paper. "I was very surprised at it all. You say that Miss Mayes had inclinations toward Mr. Townsend? Do you know if he had any other romantic interests here in town, or elsewhere, before Eliza answered his advertisement?"

"Can't say I do. I was just as surprised as you to find this out."

"I see. Could I ask you a favor, Miss Chatterley?"

She laid a hand on my arm. "Constance, please. And yes."

"I'm not sure this information should end up in the paper for now. It would be painful for both women involved, and it might hamper my—I mean, the sheriff's investigation."

"Yes. I quite agree," she said. "The sheriff said as much.

I do think the people of La Plata Springs need to be informed of things that affect the community, but I'm not sure this particular bit of information should be imparted in such a public way. For now."

My previous, less than positive impressions of her shifted in that moment. It was true she was inclined to gossip, but from what she'd just said, it seemed she indeed was concerned about the townsfolk and the welfare of La Plata Springs.

"Thank you, Miss—Constance," I said with a smile.

"You're quite welcome, Mrs. Pryce."

"Arabella."

Her eyes lit up with delight. "Arabella, then."

She walked out of the store with a definite spring in her step. Bijou padded back over to me and lay at my feet with a sigh.

"Is that all, Mrs. Pryce?" Mr. Emerson said from behind the counter.

I cleared my throat. "Actually, no. I have a few questions for you, if you don't mind?"

"I'm rather busy. Can it wait?"

"It will only take a moment," I said, mustering my courage. "I've taken an interest in the death of Mr. Townsend."

He crossed his burly arms over his chest. "What does this have to do with me?" The tone of his voice took on a gravelly quality that reminded me of the roar of a bear.

I swallowed the intimidation I was feeling. "I understand you knew him when he was staying in Addison for a time."

His brows pressed down into a *v* over the bridge of his nose, and his eyes darkened. "I did. What of it?"

"Did you ever play cards with him?"

He shifted his weight, set his hands on the counter, and leaned into them, broadening his bearing. "Maybe."

I swallowed again, not sure how to go about asking if he'd lost his life savings to the man and, thus, his wife. "Did you like Mr. Townsend?" I asked instead.

Mr. Emerson emitted a slight growl, which only added to his bearlike demeanor. My heart quickened. "Not particularly," he said with a note of caution in his voice.

I braced myself to ask the question I needed to ask him. "Was that because you lost a good deal of money to him in one of those card games?"

His face clouded over, and his eyes narrowed. "Who told you that? And why are you asking me about it? It's none of your business."

I straightened my spine and pressed on. "I heard it from a reliable source."

"Who?"

"His wife."

"Miss Swindon or his other wife?" He shook his head and began to laugh—a great big guffaw. I wasn't quite sure what to make of it, but then the laughter stopped and the cloud that had previously darkened his features returned to his face.

"How do you know that?" I asked. "Did Miss Chatterley tell you?" She had said she would keep it out of the paper, but had she refrained from telling individuals?

"No. But it's still a small town, Mrs. Pryce. Word travels."

The bells on the door jingled, and two women came through and began perusing the shelves. Mr. Emerson's eyes followed them. "Look, like I said, I'm rather busy at the moment."

Ignoring him, I soldiered on. "Are you married, Mr.

Emerson?" I knew I was treading into dangerous waters but wanted to push the boundaries a bit, to see what he might reveal, either in expression or words.

"Why do you want to know?" He growled but didn't answer the question.

Interesting. The trembling returned to my arms and legs at the menacing look on his face. "I, um, well, I was wondering if you and your wife would like to come to—"

"Afternoon." A deep, male voice sounded from behind me. My heart sank as I recognized it as the very voice of Sheriff Marshall.

"Sheriff," Mr. Emerson said with a nod of his head. "What can I do for you?"

"Nothing, Everett. It's Mrs. Pryce I'm after." He gently took hold of my elbow. "I'd like a word. Outside, if you don't mind."

"But I was—"

"Now, Arabella." He took a firmer hold on my arm and marched me out of the mercantile.

Once outside, I jerked my arm out of his grip, annoyed at his presumptuousness. "I beg your pardon!"

"You need to leave this alone, Arabella. I'm tired of warning you. If you don't stop, I may have to—"

"Lock me in my tower again?" I glared up at him.

"Maybe."

"On what grounds?" I demanded.

"You're interfering with an investigation. And for your own safety. Now, with what's happened to Bob . . ."

"Do you think the attack is related to Mr. Townsend's murder?" I asked.

He shrugged a shoulder. "I don't know, but I aim to find out."

"Was there a calling card left at the livery?"

"No, but look, the last thing I need is for you to—" He paused. There was something in his voice I hadn't heard before. Fear.

"I can take care of myself, Sheriff." I insisted. "You needn't worry about me. I am no concern of yours."

"But you are." His tone softened, and those damnably gorgeous indigo eyes scanned my face. The trembling I had experienced before with Mr. Emerson returned, but this time it was different. It was accompanied by a pounding in my chest and a shortness of breath that was most disturbing.

He cleared his throat. "Everyone in this town is my concern. But it seems you are at the top of the list right now. I went to the hotel looking for you—"

"You did?" I asked, ignoring the flutter in my stomach.

"Yes. I had heard that you were going about town asking questions. Even after I asked you not to."

I needed to tamp down this unbearable discomfort I felt in his presence, lest I become a simpering fool.

"So you think you have the authority to tell me with whom I can speak now?" It came out sharper than I had planned, but I needed to regain my composure.

He pulled something from his vest pocket and handed it to me. It was the calling card with the bouquet of flowers on it.

"Why are you giving this to me?" I asked, confused.

"I'm not giving it to you. I'm showing it to you."

"But I've seen it before." I crossed my arms over my chest. "I was the one who found it."

"This is another one."

Fearing the worst, my heart beat a staccato. "But you said there was no card left at the livery."

"There wasn't."

"Well, then where did you find it? Was someone else—"

He put it back into his pocket, and he regarded me with concern. "I found it under the door to your room. Like I said, I went to see you but no one answered the door. As I was about to leave, I noticed a corner of this sticking out from under the door."

I sucked in a breath, and my pulse picked up speed like a train racing down the tracks, out of control. "The killer came to my rooms—"

He took me gently by the arms. "They know what you are doing. Stop this, and let me do my job."

Looking up into his eyes, I found myself mute with fear and further silenced by the worry I saw in them. He genuinely cared about me, and the thought of that struck a bit of terror into my heart. I didn't know how to respond to it so I diverted from it. I had another concern that was more pressing.

"What if Cordelia had been in? What if she had stumbled upon the killer as they were leaving the card? They could have . . ."

"Yes," he agreed. "Don't put her in further danger."

She had gone to Addison to see the new library today. I wondered if she had returned yet. I needed to go to her and warn her.

"I won't," I complied.

The sheriff let out a breath and gave me a fraction of a smile. "Good."

"But—"

"But? I don't like the sound of that." He crossed his arms again.

"Did you ask Mr. Emerson about his wife, Rose? I didn't get the chance."

A stern expression replaced the previous tenderness in

his face. I may have been pushing the new boundary, but I couldn't seem to help myself.

"Yes, I did."

"Does he blame Mr. Townsend for her leaving him?"

"He does."

"Did you ascertain his whereabouts around the time of the wedding?"

"He claims he was at work, at the dry goods store."

"Can anyone corroborate this claim?"

The sheriff let out another breath. "Everyone was at the wedding."

"So he could be lying."

"Maybe. But I don't think he is. I believe him."

"How can you be so sure?"

He shrugged. "I can't, but I don't think he killed Rupert."

"Well, how do you know that?" I asked in exasperation.

"I'm a pretty good judge of character, Arabella, and I've had a lot of experience with the killing sort, and Everett Emerson doesn't strike me as that kind of man. Underneath all that muscle is a kind soul. He was deeply wounded when his wife left him, but he's not the type to seek revenge. He knows deep down the fault lies with him for his money problems, and—"

I blinked up at him. "And?"

"I think I've said enough—too much, really. You don't need to know any of this because you should not be investigating this crime, Arabella. And, now, because of what you've done thus far, the killer has you in his sights. You need to be careful."

"*His* sights? What makes you think the killer is a man? It could be a woman, you know. In fact, that would make the most sense. Why would a man leave a calling card with a bouquet of flowers on it? Did you know that Cynthia Mayes was in love with Mr. Townsend?"

He pulled back his chin in surprise. "No. No, I did not know that."

"Constance Chatterley said she'd been carrying a torch for him since last year. He took her for a ride in his carriage and she took it to mean something, but he didn't return her feelings. What if she was angered that he sent away for a wife? She's made it clear she doesn't care for Eliza. And you should have seen her face when I told her that Rupert already had a wife when he married Eliza. Perhaps the hair-comb is hers? She might have lost it back then, a year ago, but what if she lost it when she killed Rupert? Surely, there might have been a struggle . . ."

He held up his hand to silence me. "I will look into this, Arabella. You need to get back to running your hotel."

"You see, I can be helpful," I argued.

He set his hand on my shoulder. It was warm, and it sent a tingling down my arm. "Yes, you have been helpful, but you need to stop. Please. I have half a mind to put a guard at your door."

"Oh!" I gently slapped him on the arm. "Not that again! I won't stand for it." When he had me under suspicion regarding the last two murders in La Plata Springs, he had set Mr. Johns—one of my employees, no less—at my door to keep me jailed in. It was better than the jail at his office, mind you, but it was humiliating nonetheless.

"Don't test me, Arabella. You must be careful." He handed me the calling card. "On second thought, you keep this to remind you of what is at stake."

Looking up into his knee-melting eyes I knew in my heart that Sheriff Marshall truly was concerned for my welfare. Possibly deeply concerned, which both thrilled and terrified me.

"Go back to the hotel. Mind your business. Please. For me."

I blinked up at him, and then a slow smile crept across his handsome face. "Once this is all over, we can start on those riding lessons," he said.

I returned the smile. "We'll see, Sheriff. We'll see."

Chapter Nineteen

I had hoped to speak with Mr. Archer that afternoon, but when I returned to the hotel, Mr. Pettyjohn presented me with a note from "Boss" stating that he was unavailable due to some business at the mines but that he hoped we could get together soon. I'll admit, I was somewhat relieved, as should he be the killer, it was best I was not with him alone.

That evening, Cordelia and I chose to dine at the Bella instead of having our meal brought upstairs to the parlor. Truth be told, I was a little skittish after hearing about a visitation to my rooms from the killer.

I hadn't told Cordelia yet but thought I should. I was vacillating between not wanting to worry her and wanting her to be on alert. I was also afraid she would insist I stop my investigations, as the sheriff had, but I wasn't sure I wanted to let it go. I was pretty deep into it, and that calling card being delivered to my door as a threat made me angry. So, suffice it to say, I hadn't entirely made up my mind as to whether I'd stop or not.

For now, I wanted for Cordelia and me to be in the

company of others. Well, not entirely. We took the booth at the back of the saloon, the one that the former manager had claimed for his own. I had also claimed it as a favorite. It was easy to see what was going on in the saloon but afforded a good deal of privacy as well.

Once we were seated, Sally Dean came over to us. Bijou, nestled next to me, raised herself on her hind legs and rested her paws on the table, happy to see Sally and no doubt hoping for a pat on the head.

"Evening, Mrs. Pryce, Miss Danson . . . and Bijou." She offered a broad smile and round blinking eyes. She was again attired in her alluring costume. It gave her a hardened appearance, so different from how she had looked in that simple day dress. I found the latter suited her much better.

To Bijou's delight, Sally gave her a friendly scratch behind the ears.

"Hello, Sally," Cordelia and I said in unison and then chuckled at our folly.

"I'm sure you've heard about Bob Parkhurst," she said.

I nodded. "Yes. Do you know how he is faring?"

"He's still unconscious."

"It's so awful," Cordelia added.

"It is," Sally agreed. "He's such a good man. I can't imagine why someone would attack him. Anyway, what can I get you?" Sally asked.

"I'd like some champagne," I said.

Champagne was not easily found in these parts, but I'd had Kitty special order it from Denver. It was the one extravagance I allowed myself to help me endure my tenure here in the ruggedness of the Colorado Rockies.

"Sarsaparilla for me," Cordelia added.

Sally was about to leave us to fulfill our order, but I stopped her. "My dear, did Kitty speak with you about Mr.

Emerson? She said she was going to ask you girls what you knew of him. I take it he is a customer?"

"Yes, she did mention something. He hasn't spent time with any of the other girls, just me."

"Ah. Of course." It was well-known throughout the town that Sally Dean was a favorite among Kitty's customers. She was also a favorite of many others in the town because of her cherubic looks and her sweet nature. Even the Sheriff was partial to her, but I couldn't figure out in what capacity. I could not determine whether or not he had been a customer, was still a customer, or just liked the girl in a platonic way. And if I'm honest, the first two of the three scenarios brought up feelings in me that I did not care for. I had never considered myself someone who succumbed to romantic jealousy, for I had always been the one on the other side of it. Many of my fans had been male admirers, much to their wives' chagrin. I did nothing to encourage the admirers, of course, and didn't quite understand the animosity of their wives toward me, but now that I myself had been visited by the green-eyed ogre, I had a bit more compassion for them.

"Well, what is your impression?" I asked, getting back to the matter at hand. "Do you think he could have killed Mr. Townsend?"

"No, ma'am."

"Really? Why? Even Sheriff Marshall said that Mr. Emerson blamed Rupert for his wife's leaving him." I left out the part where the sheriff had said he didn't believe Mr. Emerson to be the sort to kill. He could be wrong after all.

Her gaze dropped to the table, and her generous smile faded. She didn't offer more, and Cordelia and I shared a glance.

"Sally?" Cordelia said, encouraging her to continue.

"Well, Kitty doesn't like us to talk about our customers, but she said I could tell you on account that he really isn't a customer . . . anymore. Emerson and I are sweethearts."

"Oh, I see." A little surge of happiness lifted my heart. Did this mean that she was no longer availing herself to the men of the town? More importantly, it most definitely meant that there was nothing between her and the sheriff at present. Not that I cared, of course.

"At the time of the wedding, and before the reception, we were together," she continued. "We've both been working so much—me here at the saloon and not, well, you know. Kitty has been so gracious about the whole thing. To make up for my lost wages in the annex, she's given me more time at the Bella."

"Yes," I said with a smile. "That is gracious of her."

"And Everett's been so busy at Archer's Dry Goods that we take whatever time we can to be together. Even if it's just for a quick cuddle or to exchange a few words."

"Thank you, Sally. You've been most helpful."

"I'll get your drinks now." With a bow of her head, she left us.

"Well, that puts Mr. Emerson in the clear. He has an alibi." Cordelia pulled something from her satchel. It was a notebook turned to a page with a list of names. She put a line through Everett Emerson's name.

"You've compiled a list of suspects?"

"Yes," she said. "I had Mr. Emerson on it and Bob Parkhurst, but I don't know if I think him a suspect anymore."

I had to concur. The calling card that was left under our door was left after Mr. Parkhurst had been attacked.

Cordelia continued. "And then there are Archibald Archer and Jack Duncan."

"Don't forget Cynthia Mayes," I cut in. I nodded toward the front of the Bella, where Miss Mayes was sitting at a table eating dinner with a woman I did not recognize.

Cordelia's chin dropped. "The dressmaker?"

"Apparently, she was in love with Mr. Townsend. It was unrequited love, mind you, but she had taken at least one carriage ride with him. I wish I knew if it was her haircomb I'd found in his carriage."

"Could be Eliza's," she said. "Have you asked her?"

"Not yet."

"Well, best ask her. Perhaps you can ask Miss Mayes about it as well. Now."

I thought about the calling card and the sheriff's warning to stay out of the investigation. "Yes. But I don't want to put her on the spot in front of her guest. I'll find the right moment."

My attention was diverted by a fluttering near the ceiling over the bar. I stifled a gasp as my gaze found Percival hovering there. Luckily, the ceilings were quite high, and he didn't seem to garner any attention from any of the patrons. He wafted over toward us and settled himself on the back of the booth bench on Cordelia's side of the table. Panic seized my chest, and I fought to breathe. What in the devil was he doing here? He never visited the saloon.

Cordelia pulled her elbows to her sides and shivered. "Goodness, but there's a draft in here."

"Yes," I choked out. I folded my arms across my chest, feigning cold. "I'll have to see to that."

"Just one more thing to add to the list of repairs," she agreed, giving me a sympathetic smile.

Percival pulled his pipe from the pocket of his smoking jacket, and before I could shoot him a warning glare, he flicked it aflame. The spicy odor tickled my nostrils.

Just then, Sally returned with our drinks on a tray.

"Thank you, Sally. That will be all." Nervous that Percival might choose to reveal himself, I dismissed her with a wave of my hand.

With a confused and affronted look on her face, she gave me a nod and left. I'd have to find her later to apologize.

"What's that wonderful, familiar smell?" Cordelia asked.

"Someone must be smoking a pipe," I answered all too quickly and sipped at my champagne. "But back to your list."

"That's it, really. But . . ." She set her pencil down.

"But?"

"There's something I have to tell you," she said with some caution in her voice.

"What is it?"

"It's Helen Digby."

"What about her?"

"Well, yesterday I went to Addison."

"Yes, to the library. How was it?"

"It was wonderful. But I made another stop."

"Oh?"

"I went to St. Alban's Church to speak with Pastor David Houston. I know that Helen had shown us her marriage certificate, but there was just something about her that I found—" she cocked her head as if searching for the right word "—questionable."

"I agree. I've had those thoughts myself. And did you speak with Pastor David Houston?"

"No. But I did speak with a Pastor Charles Green. He was Pastor Houston's replacement."

"Oh?"

"Yes. Apparently, Pastor Houston recently retired and moved back to the South where he was from."

"And what did Pastor Green say?"

"Not much. He was quite preoccupied. He'd just learned that a man in the community, a member of his parish, was dying and he needed to go to him. I was lucky to catch him at all."

"Oh dear. How terrible."

"Yes, he was in quite a rush as you can imagine. Anyway, I asked him about Helen Digby and Rupert Townsend. Of course, he knew nothing of them. I asked if I could see the church's marriage records, but he said the church secretary was out sick and he needed to get on. We agreed that I could come back later. Like I said, he was in quite a hurry and a bit flustered." She took a sip of her sarsaparilla and then set down her glass. "I want to go back first thing tomorrow," she said. "I want to check those marriage records."

My gaze drifted toward Percival, who regarded me with raised eyebrows. I did my best to ignore him, my shock at his being there having turned to a slow burn of anger. His persistence in presenting himself while Cordelia was in my company rankled. At least he'd positioned himself behind her instead of in front of her. It seemed he was honoring my wishes to remain unseen, and I appreciated that.

I carried on. "Cordelia, why do you doubt the validity of the marriage?"

She shook her head. "I'm not sure. It just didn't seem in character with Mr. Townsend to be so insincere."

"But he might have been courting Cynthia Mayes while he was advertising for a wife. They had been in his carriage together. Constance thought that Miss Mayes had miscon-strued Rupert's intentions, but you never know . . . "

I darted my gaze over to Miss Mayes's table.

"Do you still have the haircomb?" Cordelia asked.

"Yes. I have it in my reticule." I held it up.

"We need to find out if it is hers. And, if there was any sort of romance going on. You should ask her." She cocked her head and blinked at me expectantly. "It looks like you'll have your opportunity soon. It seems they are close to finishing their meal."

I took in a deep breath and raised my chin. "It does," I said, all the while thinking about the calling card left under the door and that I had agreed to the sheriff's request that I stop my inquiries.

"But I'll wait until they get up to leave. No need for her friend to hear this," I said by way of excuse once again.

Something caught my eye at the corner of the ceiling. Percival was floating over toward Miss Meyer's table. From my vantage point, I could see in the reflection of the mirror, his form descending from the ceiling. He hovered above the table. To my relief, no one seemed to notice him, but I feared what he might do. I sucked in a breath and squeezed my eyes shut.

A yelp emitted from that direction. I opened my eyes to see Miss Mayes's companion jump up from the table. A large, wet stain covered the front of her dress.

Miss Mayes rose from the table and, using a handkerchief, tried to help the woman blot up the mess, but the wet stain was far too large. She and the woman exchanged a few words and then the woman picked up her handbag from the table and left the Bella.

"Looks like you don't have to worry about embarrassing Miss Mayes now," Cordelia said. Percival came back to us and resumed his position behind Cordelia, a devilish grin on his face. I did my best not to acknowledge him.

She was right, of course. But if Miss Mayes was the killer, might I be putting myself in more danger by further provoking her? Whomever left the calling card under my door meant to scare me—or worse. The sheriff had made that clear.

"Right," I said, "but there's something that *I* need to tell *you.*"

She leaned forward eagerly, all ears, her hands wrapped around her glass.

"The sheriff has warned me, yet again, about my efforts at finding Mr. Townsend's killer."

She gave a chuckle. "That's never stopped you before."

"I know. But this might be different."

"How so?"

I told her about the calling card left under our door.

"Oh my." She sat back against the booth, unwittingly resting on Percival's lower leg. She shivered again, and her face had gone quite pale. I glared at my ghostly friend, and he scooted over closer to the wall. I tossed back the rest of the champagne in my glass, hoping it would help relieve my anxiety at his presence here in front of God and everybody. I would have to have a word with Percival about his surprise visits once again.

"It's from the killer. Whoever it is knows what we're doing," she said.

"Yes. I don't want you to come to any harm, Cordelia."

She opened her eyes wide. "Me? What about you, Arabella?"

I sighed. "This new development has given me pause. Perhaps we should leave it alone, Cordelia. What if she—" I tilted my head in Miss Mayes direction "—is the killer? I might be putting us at even more risk if I pelt her with questions. We may be out of our depth here, not to mention in grave danger."

Saying the words made my blood boil. I detested the fact that someone had thought they could control me with fear. How dare they?

"That's true." Cordelia worried her lower lip. "But the killer doesn't know how much we know. If he, or she, thinks we know a good deal and are close to finding the truth, aren't we in danger anyway? It might be best if we help the sheriff get to the truth as fast as possible. To prevent the death of anyone else."

I nodded, considering. The sheriff would not be happy with me for continuing, but Cordelia was right. We were already knee-deep in this, and time was of the essence.

"Besides, it's not like you to back down," she said with a wry grin.

"No. It is not." I narrowed my eyes. Her words bolstered me. I would not be intimidated or cowed into submission, and I didn't take kindly to threats. "I'll be right back."

When I reached her table, Miss Mayes had settled herself in her chair once again and had recommenced eating her bowl of stew.

"Is everything all right here?" I inquired. "I saw your friend left quite in a hurry."

Miss Mayes dabbed at the corners of her mouth with a napkin. "Oh, hello, Mrs. Pryce. She spilled her drink down the front of her dress, and she had to go change her clothes."

"Oh dear. I hope it isn't ruined."

"Some sodium bicarbonate and water should do the trick," she said. "It's rather strange, really. I've never known Olivia to be quite so clumsy."

"We all have our days." I gave her a tense smile. "May I sit?"

She inclined her head toward Olivia's abandoned chair, and I sat down.

"Miss Mayes, I've found something that I think might belong to you."

She blinked at me in surprise. "Oh? What is it?"

I set my reticule on the table and pried open the strings holding it shut. I pulled the bent haircomb from it and held it out to her.

After a cursory glance at it, she raised her gaze to meet mine. "No. That is not mine."

"I found it in Mr. Townsend's coach."

Her jaw tightened. "And why would you think it belongs to me?"

"Well, I understand that Mr. Townsend had given you a ride in his carriage."

She glanced away. "That was a long time ago."

"Oh, I see. Were you courting?"

Her eyes met mine again. "We— Well, no, not exactly. I had thought that maybe . . ."

"You liked him."

"Yes. But he—" she cleared her throat "—did not return my sentiments. Not in that way. Like I said, that was a long time ago."

"You must have been quite disappointed. Mr. Townsend was a lovely man." Based on what I knew so far, that was definitely in question, but the statement served my purpose for the moment.

"I don't see how this is any of your business," she said through straightened, thin lips.

Perhaps I had gone too far. I held up a placating hand. "I'm sorry. I didn't mean to pry. I just know what it is like to have been given the wrong impression by a man."

"Ah, yes, like you and the sheriff?" Her hardened expression softened, and she smiled sweetly at me, revealing a somewhat snaggled eyetooth that I had not seen before. I got the sense that there was no sweetness behind the gesture.

"I beg your pardon?"

"I've seen how you look at him."

I fought to keep my mouth from dropping open. This was the most absurd thing I'd ever heard. She was way off the mark. "Well, I'm afraid your eyes have deceived you. I have no designs on any man in La Plata Springs. My life is elsewhere. I am only here . . ."

Her forehead raised in question.

"What I mean to say is, I am a widow and I have no interest in another romantic relationship—certainly no interest in another husband."

"Of course," she said with a look of smug satisfaction on her face. She had successfully and completely turned this conversation around on me, and I had to gain purchase again.

"So, this is not your comb?" I held it up again.

"I told you it is not. It's probably that woman's."

"Eliza?"

"Yes. She wasted no time getting her hooks into Rupert. She's a fortune hunter, that one. You know, she came into my shop yesterday and purchased a very expensive new frock that I had ordered from New York for display. I often do that so the women of La Plata Springs have an example of the latest trends. You know, to spark ideas for what they might want me to make for them. Anyway, the dress was a gorgeous ebony silk with a lovely pattern of emerald dragonflies and Our Lady's Tears flowers. She insisted on purchasing it and offered more than I paid for it. Why she needs more dresses, I have no idea, but—"

"Our Lady's Tears flowers?" I cut in.

"Yes. Lily of the valley."

My heart skipped a beat. "Did you say lily of the valley?"

She nodded. "Beautiful. Like little bells. We Catholics believe that when Mary was at the cross, crying as she watched her son die, her tears, when they fell to the ground, turned into the little flowers."

"I see."

"They are also called May Bells."

How odd that Eliza chose that particular dress. Given the lily of the valley on the calling card left on her dead husband's body, I would think it would be the last thing she'd want. And furthermore, was it a coincidence that Miss Mayes had ordered the dress with that particular fabric?

"Does that mean anything to you personally? Lily of the valley—or, er, Our Lady's Tears, Miss Mayes?"

She shrugged. "No. Not particularly. Why do you ask?" She picked up her glass of beer and took a sip, her gaze fixed on mine. Something in her eyes made me shiver. I reached into my reticule and pulled out the calling card the sheriff had given to me. I presented it to her.

She set down her beer glass and took the card, looking it over. "What's this?" she asked.

"It was left under my door. There was also one left on Mr. Townsend's body. Have you not heard of this before?"

She raised her gaze to meet mine. "No. Why are you showing this to me?"

"Lily of the valley?"

She peered closer at the card. "Oh. Yes."

"Why did you choose to purchase a dress with a lily of the valley–patterned fabric? Was it merely a coincidence that the pattern coincided with one of the flowers on the calling card?" Or perhaps, if she was the murderer, she'd ordered it to taunt the grieving Eliza and Eliza had purchased it to get it out of the window display?

Her face paled. "I—I told you. It is of the latest fashion."

"And are you certain you'd not heard of or seen the calling card before?"

She regarded me for a few seconds, and I could see the wheels in her head spinning. "You say the calling card was left on Rupert's body. Do you think I left it there? That I killed Rupert?"

I maintained direct eye contact with her but didn't answer.

She leaned forward in her chair and whispered, "You think I am the poor desperate spinster who was jealous of his new wife."

"I'm not sure what I think, Miss Mayes. I just find it curious that you ordered that particular dress."

She pulled down the front of her coat firmly with both hands. "I will not sit here in your tawdry establishment one second longer and be interrogated like this. Good day, Mrs. Pryce."

She stormed out of the Bella.

Ignoring all the eyes upon me, I returned to Cordelia at our booth.

"Oh dear," she said. "That did not go well. Do you think she's our culprit?"

I sat down and leaning my elbows on the table I rested

my head between my fingers. "I'm not sure," I said. "But if what she told me is really the truth, I may be barking up the wrong tree entirely."

Chapter Twenty

The next morning, I woke with my eyes burning. They also felt like they had piles of sand in them. I'd had a restless night, my thoughts churning at what Miss Mayes had told me about the dress with the pattern of dragonflies and lily of the valley. Would Eliza really have chosen such a reminder of her husband's death?

I sucked in a breath. Or perhaps it was something else. Not a reminder of his death but of him himself? If she, as Miss Mayes had said, insisted on purchasing the display dress, maybe she did so as a reminder of him and their love? I remembered the lily of the valley secured in the curtain ties of his coach. Perhaps the flowers had meaning for the two of them. The thought gave me some succor, but all the same, I needed to speak with Eliza about it.

It was still a bit early for calling, so with Cordelia off to Addison to query St. Alban's church records again, I spent a good couple of hours working. The first thing I did was make a list of things I needed to take care of at the hotel. I would have to launch an entirely new investigation to find out who had sabotaged the hotel's oven, too. While it might have been the very person who'd killed Mr. Townsend, there was also a possibility that it was someone who did not care for me and wanted to ruin the party. I wrinkled my nose at the notion.

In addition to the problem with the oven, I still had to contend with the squirrels. Mr. Johns and Clarence, the hotel bellmen, had set several traps and had been successful in capturing some of the scoundrel vermin but not all. I feared there might be a nest, or several, hidden in the walls where baby squirrels were being raised for the sole purpose of making things difficult for me at the Arabella. And while I had seen to most of the leaks in the roof already, there was still water damage on several of the room's ceilings that needed mending.

And then there was the less palatable task of finding someone to repair the outhouse wall on the second floor, where someone had punched a hole in it.

Mr. Blank and my husband had come up with an ingenious design for a three-story outhouse, which connected to the building by a narrow walkway on each floor. The fourth four, where Cordelia and I lived, had more modern plumbing that carried the waste underground and out to the river.

The way the outhouses worked was thusly: Each floor had two stools, and the refuse was collected into one tower per floor, each tower butting up against the other. At the end of the line, everything fell into an enormously large pipe in the ground, and the waste was carried to the river. I aimed to change this, as having taken an accidental tumble into the river on my way to La Plata Springs, the thought of refuse in it was beyond the pale. I would bring modern plumbing to the Arabella in time, but for now, I had to contend with the hole in the second-floor outhouse wall.

I heaved a great sigh. My next task was to write a letter pleading for more money from Mr. Tisdale, my late husband's lawyer and the keeper of my freedom. I had already gone to him on a few occasions and he'd complied, but I could tell from his hasty scrawl that this was not at all what my late husband had in mind. I wondered how much William had really known about what it took to actually run the hotel. He had always had a manager do it, and now that manager was me.

"Everything all right, my dear?"

I looked up from my papers to find myself staring into the face of Percival Blank in the mirror. Given the mounting list of tasks I needed to accomplish, it was indeed pleasant to see him. When he wasn't surprising me in the company of others, I found his presence to be quite calming.

"I don't know, to be honest," I said. "It seems that once I get one thing repaired in the hotel, another springs up. I can't get ahead."

"Ah. The privies."

"Yes! Who would slam their fist through the wall in such a place?"

"Perhaps whoever did it, did not enjoy the company of the person sharing . . . the experience . . . and there was an altercation."

"Ugh! Don't be disgusting, Percival. Why anyone would choose to bring a friend along for that kind of business is beyond me. Sometimes, I really wonder about people."

"Well, there are two seats . . ."

"Is there something you needed?" I asked, wishing to discuss almost anything else.

"Not particularly. I was curious about your conversation with Miss Mayes. Did it render anything useful?"

I pulled my lips between my teeth, took in a deep breath, and then let it out. "Maybe. I fear I have offended the good dressmaker."

I proceeded to tell him about the dress and my quandary as to who really chose it and my reasoning for why each woman may have done so.

"The lily of the valley. This seems like more than a coincidence." He brought his fist to his chin and tapped his curled index finger against it.

"Yes. If Miss Mayes is Rupert's killer, and the one who left the calling card at my door, I have just put myself and Cordelia at great risk."

"And what of your friend Eliza?" he asked.

"At risk? From Miss Mayes? Well, I suppose she might be."

"I saw something that might be of interest to you."

"Yes?"

"It concerns Eliza."

"Oh? What is it?"

He pulled his hand from his chin and curled his fingers toward his palm, examining his fingernails as was his habit when he was being cagey. "I think you need to see for yourself. And you might want to hurry."

"Why don't you just tell me?"

"If I merely tell you, then you may not get all the information you need. She is at the church."

"The church? But it's not Sunday."

Without so much as a by-your-leave, he popped out of sight.

"All right, then," I said to my own reflection in the mirror and then flinched. Was that vertical crease between my eyes a new development? Could it be a permanent wrinkle? Or did it just appear when I was vexed? I heaved another sigh. I was wasting the best years of what was left of my fleeting youth in this town worrying about the hotel's outhouses and invading squirrels, and murder, of all things! What had my life come to?

"Come, Bijou." I rose from the desk and reached for her leash. "There is something Percival wishes us to see. Never mind that it is a most inconvenient time," I said with a roll of my eyes.

Bijou jumped up from her bed and scurried over to me. She obediently sat while I attached the leash to her collar.

At least someone was looking forward to this outing.

I walked at a fast clip, partially because Percival had told me to make haste but also because I was a bit unsettled. Was the person who had left the calling card under my door watching me? I scanned the area for Miss Mayes but did not see her. I glanced down the street toward her shop where two women were looking at the window display with some interest. It was half past ten, and I believed she opened her store at ten. My thoughts were confirmed when the two women opened the door and stepped inside.

Across the street from the dress shop, Mr. Parkhurst was lying unconscious at the doctor's infirmary, and at the opposite end of the street, Mr. Archer was standing in front of the General talking with someone who looked like a laborer. He was pointing to the upper portion of the building and paid me absolutely no mind.

It was beginning to feel like I was further and further

away from the truth, and the disconcerting feeling of being watched was growing.

Was I to live in perpetual fear of coming to the same fate as Mr. Townsend? The idea rankled. I had never really been afraid of anything in my life, save for disappointing my public or my reputation coming to ruin, but that was different. I was never in fear of someone physically harming me before. Well, I take that back. When I had discovered the perpetrator of the two previous murders in La Plata Springs, I had been in physical danger, but that was in the moment. It hadn't been hanging over my head like it was in this case, and I didn't like it. I determined right then and there that I would not be cowed by such trepidation. I would not show weakness.

My curiosity at Percival's cryptic suggestion returned. What in the world had he wanted me to see? Why couldn't he have just told me? I didn't have time for this. However, I had wanted to speak with Eliza about the dress, so this would be my opportunity. At least the errand would be of some use.

I continued toward the church, my pace even faster, slowing only to let little Bijou catch up.

Finally, a bit out of breath, I entered the church, and what I saw sucked the air out of my lungs. Eliza and Mr. Duncan were standing at the altar in front of the priest, exchanging a kiss.

"What is going on here?" I burst out loudly.

The two of them turned to face me. Eliza held a beautiful bouquet of fall wildflowers in her hands. She reached out and touched Mr. Duncan on the arm.

"Give me a minute please, Jack."

She walked down the aisle toward me. Despite my shock at the situation, I couldn't help but notice her beautiful dress. It was emerald green in satin brocade with red and green velvet trim. The overskirt was opened in the front, revealing a crepe underskirt embossed with silk flowers, and it was draped high at the sides and bouffant at the back. It was stunning. Another new purchase, no doubt.

Quickly, I was snapped out of my admiration of the dress as she approached me with open arms. "Arabella, I—I can explain."

I stepped back, not feeling keen for an embrace at the moment.

"Eliza, what are you doing? Are you marrying Mr. Duncan? You've only just buried Rupert."

Eliza lowered her arms and clasped her hands in front of her. "It's complicated, Arabella."

"Well, I can see that. What are you thinking?"

"Look, I know this seems rash, but Jack and I—"

"You weren't seeing him behind Rupert's back like you were with Bob Parkhurst, were you?" I whispered.

Her eyes widened in surprise. "How did you know about that?" she whispered back. She took me by the elbow and ushered me out the door to the front steps of the church. Bijou, panting furiously, plunked herself down at my feet.

"I spoke with Bob Parkhurst," I continued. "I wanted to know why he was in your hotel room on the day of your wedding and why he was so upset. You lied to me, Eliza."

I realized I had been putting off bringing this up before, and then when we'd seen that Mr. Parkhurst had been injured, Helen had been with us. I suppose I didn't want to believe that Eliza had lied, only that she had been embarrassed and didn't want to speak of it. But it suddenly seemed like a betrayal of sorts.

She bit her lower lip and scrunched up her face, closing her eyes tight as if to block out my accusation. "I'm sorry,

Arabella. It's just that Mr. Parkhurst and I— Well, it was just a passing fancy."

"Not to him it wasn't. He loves you. He thinks you love him back."

"I never loved him. I loved Rupert. When I first arrived in town, Bob happened to be at the train station. I was having trouble with my bags, and he helped me. A couple of days later, I was taking a walk down by the river. I was having second thoughts about answering Rupert's ad, and I got cold feet. It seemed absurd to agree to marry someone I had never met before. Anyway, Bob was passing by, and he ended up walking with me. He was so kind. We saw each other every day for a few weeks. I thought about breaking things off with Rupert, but I just didn't have the heart to do so. So, yes, I was seeing them both. But in the process, I fell for Rupert, and Bob just wouldn't accept it."

"But why didn't you tell me about this?"

"I was afraid of what you would think of me. I didn't want to lose your respect. Or your friendship. It's meant so much to me, Arabella. Really, it has."

My anger was slowly giving way. Her friendship had meant a lot to me as well. I felt I had found a kindred spirit with our love of the theater and tea, and our messy upbringings. But I couldn't shake the feeling that she was not entirely what she seemed. The dress came to mind.

"I had a visit with Cynthia Mayes today."

A look of confusion crossed her face. "How . . . nice?"

"She said you bought yet another new dress, the one in the window display. You are keeping the woman in high cotton."

Her cheeks turned a pleasing shade of pink. "Oh. That. Yes, I can't help myself. Jack said to buy something for our honeymoon. We aren't . . . taking it right away. It's some weeks off."

I would not be deterred. "She said it was made of a patterned black silk of emerald dragonflies and lily of the valley."

She smiled. "Yes. It's quite beautiful, but Arabella—" she pointed to the church doors "—I really must get back—"

"Why lily of the valley? Like the design on the calling card left on Rupert's body . . . and more recently under my door?"

"Pardon? Under you door?"

I took in a deep breath. "Yes. It seems the killer is trying to frighten me off the investigation."

"Oh, my dear." She reached out and touched my arm.

"Why the dress, Eliza?"

"Lily of the valley was my mother's favorite flower. Like I told you, I lost her when I was very young." Her eyes softened with sincerity, and she gave me an indulgent smile. "That's why I chose it as my wedding flower. I even had Rupert's coach decorated with them. They were silk, of course. And rather hard to come by, I might add. I would have liked to have had them at the reception, but . . ."

"Didn't it give you pause when a calling card with that very flower on it was left on Rupert's body?"

She gave a shrug. "I guess I didn't think about it. Weren't there two other flowers on the calling card? I suppose I just associated them all together, without singling out the lily of the valley."

Her explanation did make sense, but I couldn't let it go. I supposed I was still stinging from the lie she had told me. "But it seems so . . . insensitive to have purchased a dress made with a fabric that has that particular flower pattern after the killer used it on the card."

She pulled her hand away and looked up at me with those impossibly large, luminous eyes. "I don't mean for it to be insensitive. Quite the opposite. It's a remembrance. Of them both." She dropped her gaze. "I'm still quite devastated about Rupert. "

"So then why are you marrying Jack Duncan?"

She sighed. "Like I said, it's a bit complicated."

I folded my arms at the waist, taking hold of both my elbows. Bijou let out an audible sigh. "I'm listening."

"Archibald Archer claims that Rupert and Jack somehow cheated him out of the Cougar claim, which isn't true."

"Yes, Mr. Archer had sold the claim to them for a song."

"Well . . . yes and no."

"Excuse me?"

"He did lose the claim to Rupert and Jack in the card game. But they won it fair and square."

I shook my head. "I'm sorry, Eliza, I'm confused. First, Mr. Parkhurst said that they cheated Mr. Archer out of the claim. Then Mr. Duncan said that Archer sold it to them. And now we are back to Mr. Archer losing it in the card game again. What's the truth? Do you even know the truth?"

My words came out harsher than I'd intended, but my head was spinning. Who was lying and who was telling the truth?

Eliza's mouth turned down in a frown, and her eyes lost their soft glow. I had offended her, but none of this was making sense.

After a few moments, she explained. "Mr. Archer had had a bit to drink that night. He had been losing all night.

His nephew, Andrew, tried to get him to leave the game, and he refused. They argued, and then Andrew finally left. Mr. Archer insisted on continuing the game. He said he was putting half ownership of the claim into the pot on one condition: should he lose it, he would have first right of refusal should the winner decide to sell it, or if . . . well, if something happened to them. He first lost to Jack and then to Rupert. They were both happy they'd won, but they did feel bad for Mr. Archer. He really was in no state to keep gambling, so Rupert and Jack agreed they would tell everyone that they had purchased the claim from Mr. Archer."

"But to get out of the condition, Rupert gifted his half of the claim to you."

"Yes. Like I said, he won it fair and square. He didn't want Archer pressuring him to sell. It had become so lucrative."

"So then why are you marrying Mr. Duncan? Were you seeing him behind Rupert's back as well?"

"No. It's not like that. I don't love Jack."

I released my elbows and pressed my fingers to my forehead, trying to understand this very odd situation. "I am not following, Eliza."

"It's a business arrangement."

"Excuse me?"

"We are pooling our resources. We thought we would be stronger together. Combine our wealth."

"You're marrying him for the money?"

She looked at me blankly. I couldn't believe what I was hearing . . . or that she'd so frankly admitted it.

"But you have your own money. Your savings. And now half the claim," I said.

"My savings have dwindled to practically nothing,

Arabella. This is a way for me to secure my future. I can't go back to poverty. Surely, you understand that."

Her words struck a chord. It was true. I would do almost anything to avoid impoverishment again. As I was demonstrating by living in La Plata Springs.

"But marrying just for the money? Is that really going to make you happy?"

"You married for reasons other than love, to get away from your mother. And you married a very wealthy man, am I right? I don't see how you are any different from me, Arabella. It's called survival."

As much as I wanted to argue my case, I found that I couldn't. "Is that why you married Rupert and broke Mr. Parkhurst's heart? For the money?"

Her face hardened again. "No. I told you. I fell for Rupert. I loved him. I still love him. Not Bob."

She let out a breath, and her face morphed again to its usual gentle expression. "Arabella." She reached out and took hold of my hand. "Please don't think poorly of me. When I learned that I did not inherit Rupert's house and his assets, I panicked. Yes, I have the claim, but I'm a terrible manager of money. I know this about myself. What if I squander the money my half of the claim provides? I'll have to go back to acting, and I can't live the theater life anymore. It's too difficult living hand to mouth. I don't have your kind of acclaim to make the sort of money I need to sustain me. This way, I'll be taken care of. The money will be safe. It's what Rupert would have wanted for me. Jack is a kind man, and I trust him. And I have come to love La Plata Springs. I'll be happy here. Can't you be happy for me?" She regarded me with pleading eyes, and her delicate brows turned up like a cute puppy dog's.

I sighed. "Of course I'm happy for you. It's just so . . . soon."

"I know. But Mr. Archer will not be swayed. This way, Jack and I can stand firm together," she reiterated.

"What will people think?" I couldn't help myself. Try as I might to rid myself of the fear of others' opinions of me, I worried about what others might think of Eliza.

"We'd like to keep this secret . . . for a while. Out of respect for Rupert. That's why we are postponing a honeymoon."

I pulled my chin back a little affronted. "You had planned to keep this secret from me?"

She gave me that pixie-faced smile. "Of course not, darling. I had planned to tell you soon after. You are my dearest friend, after all. I can't keep anything from you."

I regarded her countenance for a moment. She simply looked up at me with a serene expression on her face. It seemed that I had wanted to ask her about something else. Suddenly, I remembered. I reached into my handbag and pulled out the haircomb.

"I almost forgot. Is this yours by chance?"

Her smile faded. "No. No, it isn't. Where did you find it?"

"It was in Rupert's carriage."

She shrugged a shoulder. "It looks like it was once beautiful. What a shame it's all bent up like that."

"Yes," I said, placing it back into my bag, her stilted reaction to the comb giving me pause but I wasn't sure why. Had she just lied to me again?

She indicated with her hand toward the church doors. "I really should—"

Some people passed us by on the street, looking in our direction.

"You'd best get back inside," I said. "People might be wondering why we are standing on the front steps of the church with you dressed so exquisitely. You know how La Plata Springs is. Tongues will wag."

Her smile returned, and Eliza wrapped her arms around me, pulling me into an embrace. Her petite frame felt delicate and fragile against me. It was as if I were being hugged by a tiny bird.

"Thank you, Arabella."

She let me go and then slipped back inside the church. I let out another sigh, shaking my head.

I hoped she knew what she was doing.

Chapter Twenty-One

I left the church still somewhat bewildered. I worried that Eliza was making a mistake, but what could I do? I had voiced my concerns, and she seemed undeterred.

From across the street, I spotted Mr. Archer leaving the General. Based on what Eliza had just told me about how he'd lost the claim, once again, the thought that he could be Rupert's killer took precedence in my mind. At the time of Rupert's death, Mr. Archer had not known that Rupert had gifted his half of the claim to Eliza. And from what I'd learned thus far, Mr. Archer was not a gracious loser.

"Mr. Archer!" I called, trotting toward him. "Could I have a word?"

I caught up to him, somewhat winded, and he looked genuinely pleased to see me. He took off his hat and ran a hand over his bushy silver hair and then held it between his fingers. His pale-blue eyes crinkled in the corners, giving him the look of an indulgent and kindly grandpapa. Based on his appearance alone, I couldn't imagine this man having such ruthless tenacity as everyone seemed to think. Then again, I had known many men whose effusive charms could be quite disarming, thus providing them with a clear advantage to get what they wanted—no matter what it took. Maybe even murder.

"What can I do for you?" he asked. "I'm sorry I couldn't meet with you yesterday. Have you changed your mind about selling the Arabella? If not, I'm prepared to raise my offer."

His comment took me off guard. *Raise the offer?*

My thoughts immediately went to the squirrels and the outhouses and the long list of repairs still to tackle. I could be rid of them forever. But was he prepared to offer me a price that would rival my inheritance?

Hardly. My heart sunk.

"Mr. Archer, with all due respect, I've told you I cannot sell. My husband wanted me to retain ownership. It was important to him, and I want to respect his wishes."

"But, my dear Mrs. Pryce, your husband is gone, God rest his soul. You have done him proud by coming here and seeing to the business of the hotel, but as it is losing money—"

A zing of adrenaline spiked through my heart. "How do you know that?"

He gave me a slippery smile. "My dear, I own the bank. I can see money coming in and money going out—the latter of which, in your case, often exceeds the former. You have been in arrears since you arrived."

I pulled in a fortifying breath. "That is largely on account of the prior management's poor work and neglect of the hotel. You know this. I am doing my best to bring it back."

"Why be saddled with all that bother? I can make every one of those problems go away. For a very nice price."

I have to admit, again, that his offer was quite tempting. I could leave this town where I felt I didn't belong and go back to my beloved theater and my adoring fans. But even when my year was up, there was the matter of William's request that I not sell to Mr. Archer under any circumstances. I still did not quite understand why. Perhaps he'd felt that Mr. Archer had a nefarious nature? A nature that was inclined to murder? In fact, if he was the killer—or even if he was not—was he the one trying to frighten me off by leaving the calling card in an attempt to get the hotel?

I desired to leave the present conversation and confront my questions head-on.

"Mr. Archer, what do you know of Mr. Townsend's murder?"

"Beg pardon?" Confusion flooded his features at my abrupt change of subject.

"Do you have any insight into who might have killed him?"

He ran the brim of his hat between his fingers and pressed his lips together. "I'm afraid I haven't a clue. Such a shame. He will be missed in this town."

"Did you and he get along?"

He shrugged. "He was my employee. He was a good worker."

"He worked for you until the Cougar claim became lucrative, you mean."

His brows pressed together. "Yes. What are you getting at, Mrs. Pryce?"

"Where were you after the wedding and before the reception?"

"Excuse me?"

"The day of Rupert Townsend's death. Where were you after the wedding and before the reception?" I repeated.

He shook his head and chuckled. "My dear, I thought we were discussing the prospect of me buying your hotel."

"It's not for sale," I reminded him. "Please answer my question."

His face clouded over. "I get the sense that you are insinuating something, Mrs. Pryce."

"It's my understanding that you lost a great deal to Mr. Townsend and Mr. Duncan in a card game—the Cougar claim, in fact. Am I right? "

"I—I sold it to them," he said, suddenly avoiding eye contact with me.

"And you had first right of refusal to get it back should something unfortunate befall Mr. Townsend. And then something did . . . befall him."

Any trace of the kindly grandpapa vanished, and his eyes hardened to the likeness of ice. "I don't know what business this is of yours, Mrs. Pryce. I have already been interrogated by the sheriff. But to answer your question, after the wedding, I went to the General. I had a gift for the couple and I went to retrieve it."

I held his cool gaze, and something in his eyes told me he was telling the truth. But how to be sure?

"Do the rose, the lily, and lily of the valley hold any significance for you?"

His white, caterpillar brows came down low over the bridge of his nose. "The what?"

"The flowers. Do they mean anything to you?"

He pulled back his chin and blinked at me with concern. "Mrs. Pryce, what are you talking about? Are you unwell?"

"The flowers were printed on a calling card left on the

body. There was also one left under the door of my rooms. I won't be intimidated," I added.

He scoffed. "You've certainly got that right. You are rather a hard woman."

My jaw tightened. *A hard woman? I should think not!* I was anything but *hard.* Strong, maybe—though sometimes I wondered—but hard? Was that how people saw me? The familiar feelings of insecurity and anxiety swirled in my belly.

He crammed his hat back on his head. "My offer for the hotel still stands. Perhaps you'll see sense and change your mind."

"Not for the time being." I gave him my well-rehearsed stage smile. "I won't keep you then," I said with some terseness.

The muscles in his jaw twitched under his great white beard, and he nodded. "Good day, Mrs. Pryce.

Chapter Twenty-Two

Over the next few days, as much as I had wanted to pursue my investigation, my time had been taken up by the squirrels and the other problems at the hotel. It was slow going, as the little devils seemed to multiply by the day, and I had trouble locating a handyman to address some of the needed repairs.

It seemed that Mr. Archer had absconded them all for odd jobs at the General, his mansion, and his other businesses around town. Was this a deliberate move on his part? Was he trying to make things difficult for me in order to persuade me to sell? Or was he trying to distract me from my investigation of the murder?

Nevertheless, I would not be deterred from my mission. After all, to my knowledge, the sheriff still had not made much progress in finding any sort of solid evidence in the case. Or at least none that he had shared with me. Aside from the calling card that had been placed under my door, which only served to muddy the waters.

Thinking of Mr. Townsend, I wondered how Eliza was

doing in her new life as Mrs. Duncan. I had not seen her since that day at the church, and I sorely missed her. Had she moved out of the hotel and taken up house with Mr. Duncan? If she had wanted to keep their marriage a secret for the time being, setting up house together would not be wise, and someone would undoubtably find out. And surely, Eliza would not leave the hotel without saying something to me.

Yet, I had to admit I found her behavior of late quite perplexing. Was she no longer concerned with the fact that someone had brutally killed her late husband? A man she'd claimed to love?

Remembering the calling card left under my door, I certainly had a care. Someone had threatened me, and I did not take kindly to threats. Yet, as much as I wanted to spend my time finding the culprit, I had to deal with the squirrels who had managed to find their way into some of the rooms. And, the lovely gaping maw in the second-floor privy.

Mr. Pettyjohn had come up with a temporary plan and had employed Clarence and Mr. Johns to patch the holes with two-by-fours, but the result was far from aesthetically pleasing. It would not do for long. And they still had not ascertained the vermin's entry point. The task seemed to grow more impossible by the day.

Thank goodness for Cordelia. In addition to my duties at the hotel, I still had to manage business at the theater and my Park Avenue mansion through correspondence and the occasional visit to the post office, where I often availed myself of the telephone exchange. She assisted with these tasks, and I don't know what I would've done without her steady devotion to me and my enterprises. She really kept things going. And she was of great help with Bijou, who truly wasn't a burden but who did need frequent visits outdoors, where they were now.

But back to the damnable squirrels. I could not afford to have guests fleeing the Arabella in disgust and going over to the General. It just would not do to have that hanging over my head. Furthermore, it would bolster Mr. Archer's argument that I should sell to him. Tempting as it was, if I agreed to sell, not only would I be going against William's wishes and in doing so lose my inheritance but it would prove I had failed. And failing was out of the question. For if I failed, the hotel's reputation would be tarnished and, in turn, so would mine.

While the repute of the hotel could someday be repaired, my own would have a permanent mark against it. Being a person of celebrity, my successes *and* my failures would become known through the news. Word traveled fast around here, too, and thanks to Miss Chatterley, who was fascinated by my theater and my extraordinary life in New York, word of my hotel and my doings in La Plata Springs would naturally find its way to the larger cities' newspapers.

But, I digress . . . There could be another reason for the squirrels' presence, I realized. Looking into the mirror positioned above the desk, I summoned Percival.

He appeared immediately, and I inquired about the recent infestation. "Why do you assume that it was I?" he asked, looking quite insulted.

"Come now, Percival. You've done this kind of thing before." I reminded him of the rats he had lured in a few months ago in order to play tricks on the guests.

"Yes, I have admitted my guilt with the rats, but I swear on my life—er—my death, I have nothing to do with this particular outbreak of rodents."

"But how are they getting into the hotel? I thought I had all the holes where the rats had entered sealed up."

He came out of the mirror, his form instantly turning translucent. He stood next to the desk, and the familiar chill filled the room, making me shiver.

He lit his pipe with a flick of his fingers, and the pleasant aroma of spicy tobacco surrounded me. "Squirrels are industrious," he commented. "Especially this time of year when they are 'squirrelling away—'" amused with himself, he gave a chortle "—their stores for the winter."

I sighed, ignoring the pun.

"How did things go at the church? Did you find your friend?" he asked.

"Yes, thank you for suggesting I go there. Did you know the nature of her business at the church?" I asked.

"Not exactly, but I thought it terribly odd that she and Mr. Duncan went there together."

"Why didn't you go yourself?"

"Oh, I never go inside churches. I'm not welcome, for obvious reasons. So why were they at the church? Together. During the middle of the week."

I considered whether or not I should tell him of Eliza's news. But then I realized, who would Percival tell? He wasn't in the habit of speaking to the guests, even if he delighted in sometimes scaring them by moving things about. And besides, he'd seemed to have already guessed.

"I don't know if I should say. I promised to keep it a secret."

"Come now, my dear. Do you not trust me?" he asked, raising his hands, reaffirming my thoughts in regard to his discretion.

I told him of Eliza's latest nuptials.

He puffed on his pipe and then let the smoke gently

swirl from his mouth. "As I had thought. So she was not a beneficiary of Mr. Townsend?"

"Aside from the claim, no. Miss Digby is his heir."

"And what about his mother?"

"It seems she was excluded from the will, as far as I could tell. The will stated that everything go to Helen."

"Interesting," he mused. "If he and his mother were so close, I wonder why the change."

I gave a shrug. "Perhaps his mother is already financially secure. Maybe when he met and married Miss Digby, he wanted to provide for her."

"Hmm." He took another puff from his pipe and then blew a series of smoke rings in the air. "I saw them talking," he said as he watched the rings float toward the ceiling.

"Who?"

"Helen and Eliza."

"Really? When was this?"

"Yesterday. In the second-floor hallway."

"How peculiar." Eliza had made it clear she didn't want Helen at the hotel. "What were they talking about?"

"I'm not exactly sure. I kept my distance. I didn't want to startle them."

"Thank you for that," I said. "Could you glean anything from watching the conversation?"

"It seemed a little contentious."

"They were arguing?"

He shrugged. "It seemed so from their body language. I couldn't hear much. I did hear Helen mention the will."

"I see. Anything else?" I sat forward, eager for more.

"No."

I sighed. "You know, sometimes you could be of more help, my friend. You always seem to get just part of the story."

His brows lowered. "Really, my dear Arabella, you wound me. You must not want to hear what I saw over at the General."

"Actually, I do."

His face broke into a satisfied smile. "Old Archibald and Jack Duncan almost came to fisticuffs."

"What?"

"Indeed. As a matter of fact, I heard Archibald threaten the man."

"Threaten how?"

"As in, 'You will pay for this!'"

"Oh my goodness." I remembered the dark look on Mr. Archer's countenance when I mentioned his losing the card game.

"The good sheriff just happened to be there and broke up the fight."

"Well, I hope no one was hurt."

"Didn't seem to be. Do you reckon Boss killed Mr. Townsend? He sure seems anxious to get that claim back." Percival blew another series of smoke rings in the air.

"It's possible. Mr. Townsend was killed before Mr. Archer learned that he had gifted his portion of the claim to Eliza. He could've been counting on their agreement, of getting the claim back if something happened to Rupert."

"If he did kill him for the claim, he'd done so to no end, it seems."

"Yes. I initially thought it might have been Mr. Parkhurst." I continued to tell him about Mr. Parkhurst's feelings for Eliza and how he'd felt slighted when she'd agreed to marry Rupert. And the rose tattoo on his arm. "But now it seems unlikely."

"Who attacked him, I wonder?"

I shrugged. "I have no idea. I suppose the attack might

not have been related to Mr. Townsend's murder. As far as I know, there was no calling card left at the livery, and a horse was stolen as well. Perhaps the attacker bludgeoned Mr. Parkhurst in order to take the animal."

He frowned. "I see. What about Mr. Emerson?"

"He had an alibi." I told him about Mr. Emerson and Sally.

Just then the door opened and Cordelia popped in, followed, to my surprise, by Eliza. Percival quickly vanished.

"Hello, you two," I said, glad to see them both.

Cordelia held up a teapot wrapped in a festive teapot cozy to keep it warm. Bijou scampered into the room, jumped onto the love seat, and curled up into a ball.

"I've brought Eliza and tea," Cordelia said.

"Wonderful," I said. "I'm parched."

Cordelia always seemed to know what I needed before I knew it myself. I turned to Eliza. "How are you doing, Eliza?"

She plopped down on the love seat. "I'm exhausted. But I think that with Helen's help, we have dealt with all Rupert's affairs."

I remembered what Percival had said about seeing Helen and Eliza speaking in the hallway. "How are things between you and Helen?"

Cordelia poured us each a cup of tea, and I joined Eliza on the love seat. Bijou crawled over and set her head on my lap. Cordelia then took the Queen Anne chair situated perpendicular to the love seat.

"A little awkward, I must admit." Eliza furrowed her brow. "I am still quite hurt that Rupert had been so duplicitous, but that is not Helen's fault. She, too, was treated unfairly. I suppose that gives us something in common."

I pressed a hand to my chest, impressed with her

generosity of spirit. Not many women in her position, having found out that she'd married a man who was already married to someone else and that someone else having shown up on her doorstep, would be so magnanimous.

There was a knock on the door. Cordelia set her teacup and saucer on the coffee table and rose to answer it.

The sheriff strode in, looking dapper in his leather vest. He took his hat off and smoothed his hair.

"Sheriff." I rose to greet him. "What a surprise. What can I do for you?"

"I was wondering if any of you have seen Jack Duncan lately?"

I looked over at Eliza, but then, worried about being transparent in regard to their recent nuptials, I turned back to the sheriff.

"No, I haven't. Have you Cordelia? Eliza?"

"Not for a couple of days," Eliza said. "I've been so busy with Rupert's legal matters I haven't seen much of anyone." Her eyes met mine. "Except Arabella, of course. Mr. Duncan and I are supposed to meet later this evening to discuss some business about the claim. Why do you ask, Sheriff?"

"I was just out at his place, to ask him some more questions for the murder investigation, and he wasn't there. In fact, it looks as if he hasn't been there for a while. Funny thing is, his front door was opened, so I stepped inside and I found bear scat in the house. Everything was torn apart and some of his stores of food had been broken into."

"Oh my goodness!" Eliza jumped to her feet, spilling her tea down the front of her dress. "Do you think he was . . . was attacked?"

"I saw no evidence of that nature," he said. "But . . ."

"Let me help you with that," I said to Eliza, quickly grabbing a couple of the tea towels from the tray.

"Could the bear have dragged him away?" I asked, helping to blot the liquid on Eliza's dress.

"That's not common for Ursidae," Cordelia piped in. "If Mr. Duncan was attacked by a bear—and the only reason any bear in this region would attack is if Mr. Duncan got between him and its food source or its cub—the bear would have left him there."

"Perhaps Mr. Duncan was injured and left the house to go get help?" I ventured.

"Oh dear! Poor Jack!" Eliza wailed.

"Maybe he went to Denver or Addison?" Cordelia suggested. "Perhaps he needed a holiday, or he might have gone on business. He is quite an industrious businessman, and—"

"Ladies!" Mr. Marshall finally cut in. We all stopped what we were doing and gave him our full attention. "I thought he might have been attacked as well, but there was no blood. More likely, the bear got in after Jack left, or was taken."

"Taken? What makes you think he was taken?" I asked.

"None of his horses were missing from his barn."

"Maybe he went fishing. I know he likes to fish," Eliza said. "He could have gone on foot. He also likes to walk into town sometimes. Says it's good for his constitution."

"He's not fishing. All his fishing gear seemed to be there. I checked his shed. And his tackle box was in the study. Looks like that's where he likes to tie his flies."

I left Eliza to finish dabbing up the moisture from her dress and stepped closer to the sheriff, crossing my arms over my chest. I could tell he was avoiding something.

"What aren't you telling us, Sheriff? Why do you think he was taken?"

"Look, I don't want to cause alarm—"

"Please, Sheriff? What is it?" I implored.

He pulled something from his vest pocket and held it out to me. It was a calling card. Drawn on the front of it was a tiny bouquet of flowers—a rose, a lily, and lily of the valley, all tied with a pink bow.

I looked up into Mr. Marshall's eyes. "Just like the one found with Mr. Townsend's body and the one left under my door."

"There's more," he said. "Turn it over."

I slowly turned the card over. Written in bold block letters were the words, *Tell Arabella Pryce that if she doesn't stop asking questions, she's next.*

Chapter Twenty-Three

I sat at the walnut desk in the annex office going through some of the files the former manager had left in the file drawers in search of a carpenter to properly seal up the squirrel holes and the hole punched through the second-floor privy wall.

I found it difficult to concentrate, as I was rather preoccupied with the disappearance of Jack Duncan and the threat to myself. My latest encounter with the Sheriff also consumed my thoughts.

This time, Sheriff Marshall's pleas that I not involve myself further in the case had become quite adamant.

"I don't think you should leave the hotel," he'd said, looking down at me with those faraway indigo eyes. "Here, you are surrounded by people. There is less chance for the killer to—"

"I refuse to live my life in fear, Sheriff. I will go about my business as usual."

His jaw twitched. "Arabella, I'm warning you."

"Against what, pray tell? The killer could very well be a guest at the hotel for all we know."

He set his hands on his hips and looked away from me. I was right, of course, and he knew it.

"You can't protect me every minute of every day," I said.

He turned his gaze back to mine. Those ocean-blue eyes were filled with tumultuous waves of concern and my heart leaped.

"More's the pity," he said quietly. My breath froze in my lungs as our eyes remained locked. Everything in the world dropped away, and there was nothing and no one but him and me.

I sucked in a breath, and I found myself staring at the file drawer, catapulted out of my tender remembrance.

"Arabella, there you are!" Cordelia burst into the room, sending Bijou into a delighted round of barking.

Cordelia was winded, and her cheeks were pink from exertion. "Why is Mr. Johns sitting in front of the door?"

"What? Mr. Johns?" I stepped out into the hallway. He was sitting in a chair, the front legs tipped up and the back of it resting on the wall.

"What is the meaning of this, Mr. Johns?" I asked.

The front legs of the chair hit the floor with a loud *thunk*. He quickly scrambled to his feet.

"The Sheriff told me to keep an eye on you."

I gritted my teeth. Not this again. "He did, did he?"

"Yes, ma'am. He temporarily deputized me." He opened the coat of his bellman's uniform and proudly showed me his badge.

How dare he use one of my employees to be my jailer. Again!

"So I am to be confined?" I asked, trying my best to hold my temper.

"No, ma'am. But I am to accompany you wherever you go."

"Oh, blast it!" I said. This was beyond the pale. I turned and went back into my rooms, slamming the door.

"Oh my goodness. What's wrong?" Cordelia asked.

"It seems the Sheriff has assigned me a protector."

"Well, given the warning on the calling card left at Mr. Duncan's, it's probably not a bad idea, Arabella."

I heaved a sigh, still irritated about the whole thing. Cordelia rested her hands on her hips, trying to catch her breath.

"You look as if you are positively bursting. Have you just returned from Addison?" I asked.

"Yes, and I have news of a very disturbing nature." She pressed her hand against her corset, her breath still coming hard and fast.

"Sit down, sit down," I said, guiding her to the single armchair across from the desk.

"Should I have Kitty brew some tea?" I asked, worried at her flushed appearance.

"Already asked her on my way in. She'll be here shortly."

"What is this disturbing news?"

She took in a deep breath, collecting herself. Just then Kitty entered with a tray with a cozy-covered teapot and a set of teacups.

"Shouldn't Mr. Johns be downstairs?" she asked.

I shook my head. "It's a long story."

"Here's your tea," she said.

She was about to leave when Cordelia stopped her. "Kitty, stay. We might need your help."

"All right. What do you need?"

"I have just returned from Addison. I went there in search of church records to prove that Mr. Townsend had indeed married Helen Digby."

"You didn't believe it, either?" Kitty said with a wry smirk on her face.

We both looked up at her in surprise.

"You doubted her claims?" I asked.

"Something didn't smell right with her. What did you find out?"

Cordelia continued. "As I had mentioned before, Pastor Green was new to the church and didn't know of a marriage between the two. The church secretary was out on an errand, but the pastor directed me to the record book. I searched through it twice and found nothing."

Anyway, as I was about to leave, the secretary returned. When I asked her about Miss Digby and Mr. Townsend, her face clouded over—like she was angry or something. Said she'd never heard of him, but she'd certainly heard of her. Helen Digby had been living at her sister's rooming house!"

"Well, wonders never cease," Kitty said.

"I wonder if the marriage certificate she showed us was a fake," I said.

"If so, it was a very convincing one," Cordelia said.

"Maybe she was after Rupert's money," Kitty said. "Do you think she might be the killer?"

Cordelia pressed her lips together. "I think it's a possibility. I found something else of interest." She then pulled something from her handbag. It was a photograph of a woman and a very tall man. The photo was marred and scratched, and it was difficult to make out their faces, but there was something familiar about the woman. If I wasn't mistaken, she looked very much like Helen Digby.

"Where did you get this?" I asked.

"The secretary at the church told me where the rooming house was. I spoke with her sister, the owner, and she gave it to me. She found this in a small photograph book on the floor of Helen's room after she'd moved out. Said if I happened to run into her in La Plata Springs to tell 'that conniver' she still owes money for room and board."

I leaned back in my chair, shaking my head. Helen had been so convincing, telling me of her life with Rupert—how they'd met, how he'd left her. I suddenly remembered something.

"But she's also named in Rupert's will," I said.

"They could have been lovers," Kitty said.

"Or the will is a fake as well," I added.

Cordelia pulled something else out of her bag: a folded piece of newspaper. She unfolded it and presented it to me. Kitty bent low over my shoulder to view it as well. It was a photograph of a man who looked like the one in the photo with the woman who resembled Helen. He was in prison clothes.

"Arthur Digby," she said. "He was convicted for the murder of Charles Clark . . . in Chicago, Illinois."

"Illinois? Clark?" Kitty said. "That's strange."

"What?" Cordelia asked.

"There was a girl who worked for me some time ago, Marta. She found herself a husband in Addison and they moved to Denver, but she mentioned a woman she used to work with in Evanston, Illinois, I think it was, named Clark. Can't recall her given name."

"What about her?"

Kitty shook her head. "According to Marta, the brothel she was with in Illinois was shut down because of this woman. That's why Marta came out West. Said she'd heard there was opportunity in the mining camps. Anyway, the story was, one of this Clark woman's customers, a wealthy one, ended up shot in her room. But he lived to tell the tale. Said she cleaned out his bank account. Claimed she drugged him to get the account information, then shot him. The police never found the woman."

"Do you think there is a connection here?" I asked her. "Clark is a pretty common surname."

"Oh my goodness!" Cordelia gasped. "That's the case!"

My brow furrowed. "What case?"

"The case I was telling you about. The one in Chicago where a calling card was left at the scene of the crime. That was it! I remember now."

"But the woman I was talking about was in Evanston," Kitty said.

"Evanston is just outside Chicago," I stated. "Do you think our killer is this Clark woman?"

Cordelia sighed. "I don't know."

Kitty's lips pressed down into a frown. "I don't know, either. The name just rang a bell is all. Made me remember the story."

I shook my head, frustrated. This information was interesting, but Charles Clark and the woman who bore the same name may have nothing to do with each other. Although, the calling card was a significant coincidence.

I turned to Cordelia, holding up the article about Arthur Digby. "Where did you get this?"

"It was in the photo book."

"So who is Arthur Digby, and what is his relationship to Helen?" I mused out loud. "Brother? Father? Husband?"

"And is he still in jail?" Kitty asked.

"The only way to find out, is to ask Miss Digby."

"We need to take this information to the sheriff, Arabella," Cordelia said, using a stern, motherly tone. "If she is the killer . . ."

"If she knew about Rupert Townsend's money and his claim in the mine," I said, "then she also knew about his partnership with Mr. Duncan."

"Who is now missing," Kitty added.

"Exactly," I said. "All right. I'll take this information to the sheriff." I stood up.

"What would you like us to do?" Cordelia asked.

"Nothing other than what you'd normally be doing this time of day. I shouldn't be long."

Chapter Twenty-Four

I stepped out the doorway of my rooms to see Mr. Johns in the same position I'd found him before, tipped back in the chair. But this time he was asleep. I thought about sneaking away from him, but as I was going to see the sheriff, I wasn't up for a scolding and decided it best my bodyguard accompany me. I loudly cleared my throat.

Mr. Johns snorted and his eyes flew open. He jumped to his feet a bit unsteadily. "Yes, ma'am?"

"I need to go see the sheriff."

"Yes, ma'am." He placed his hat on his head.

I made my way to the stairs and quickly descended to the third-floor landing. As I turned the corner to go down the next flight, Mr. Johns let out a yelp and came tumbling down after me. He landed with a dull thud on the bottom stair.

"My goodness, Mr. Johns." I rushed over to him. "Are you all right?"

"Yep. Yep," he said, his voice strained. He got himself to his feet and then promptly collapsed.

"You most certainly are not all right." I helped him to sit on the stair.

He winced, sucking air through his teeth. "It's my ankle."

"Stay right here," I said.

I quickly made my way down the stairs to the lobby. Mr. Pettyjohn was perusing some reading material at the registration desk.

"Mr. Pettyjohn, I need your assistance. Mr. Johns has taken a fall and hurt his ankle. Could you please send Clarence to fetch the doctor?"

"Right away, Mrs. Pryce."

"Thank you. Mr. Johns is on the third-floor landing. If you would please check on him after instructing Clarence, I need to run a quick errand of the utmost importance."

"Yes, Mrs. Pryce."

Satisfied that Mr. Johns would be in good hands, I left the hotel.

The afternoon sun penetrated the silk of my jacket, warming me in the crisp autumn air. I hurried down the street, not making eye contact with anyone, lest I be stopped for a chat. I even made sure to turn my head as I passed by Miss Chatterley's newspaper office.

Finally, I reached the sheriff's office. Two horses, both of them saddled, were standing at the hitching rail. One of them was Queenie, the sheriff's horse.

I entered to see Sheriff Marshall taking a tray to a man in one of the cells. Perhaps he was the owner of the horse outside.

"Arabella, what are you doing here? Where is Mr. Johns?" the sheriff asked, a look of alarm on his face.

"He's— Well, he's had a bit of an accident. He was asleep outside my door, and when I told him I had to come see you, he followed me down the stairs but fell and hurt his ankle. He is quite unable to walk on it."

The sheriff shook his head. "I really do need a bona fide deputy," he said under his breath. He fixed his steely-blue gaze on me. "What did you need, Arabella?"

"I have more information for you about—"

He tilted his head toward his prisoner.

"Oh, I see. Is he the . . . ?"

"No." He quickly ushered me away from the cell. "What is it?"

I handed the sheriff the photo.

"What is this?" he asked.

"Look closely at it," I encouraged.

He held the photo closer to his face and squinted. "This looks like the woman who claims to be Rupert's wife—er, his first wife," he said.

"Yes, I believe it is Helen Digby."

"Who is the man?" he asked.

I produced the newspaper article. After perusing it, he sucked a breath through pursed lips. "I'd heard about this murder. Killed the man in his sleep."

I winced. "How awful. Do you suppose Arthur Digby is Helen's husband? Or former husband, rather, before Rupert? If they were indeed married."

"Hard to say. He's obviously some kind of relation." He raised his gaze from the newspaper clipping. "Where did you get this?"

"Cordelia made a trip to Addison. It was given to her by a woman who owns a boarding house there. It was where Miss Digby had been staying."

He exhaled loudly through his nose. "I thought I told you to leave the investigation alone."

"Exactly. Cordelia went. I did not." I gave him a smile. "She also discovered something else of note."

He rolled his shoulders back in an attempt, it seemed, to loosen the tension there. Tension that I was obviously causing. He crossed his arms over his chest. "The suspense is killing me."

"There is no record of Helen's marrying Rupert. Before she went to the rooming house and the library, Cordelia visited St. Alban's Church. The pastor there allowed her to see the record book."

A spark of interest lit up his face. "You don't say? So the marriage certificate is a forgery."

"Quite possibly."

"Which means the will could be a fake as well," he concluded.

"Indeed. Do you know what happened to Arthur Digby?" I asked. "Did he hang?"

He pulled his upper lip between his teeth and ran a hand over his mouth. "He escaped."

The words made my stomach cave in on itself. "Oh . . . If he was married to Helen, what if he knew Helen had married Rupert and he came to enact his revenge? There is something else," I said.

"Of course there is," he said with a sardonic tone that I did not appreciate.

I told him of the story of the Clark woman and the calling card. "Do you think there is a possibility that she might be a relation of the Charles Clark killed by Arthur Digby?" I asked. "And don't you think the calling card is a strange coincidence?"

"That's hard to say. Chicago is a densely populated area. And, yes, the part about the calling card is definitely something to consider."

"What if Helen is this Clark woman?" I asked.

His eyes shifted from the article to mine. "I'll head out to Townsend's house to have a word with Miss Digby."

"I'm coming with you," I said resolutely.

He walked over to his desk chair where his gun belt hung and strapped it onto his hips. "No, you are not."

"But I've brought you this vital information. And information about Mr. Parkhurst, and Mr. Archer, and even information about Cynthia Mayes. Any one of them could be—"

"Go back to the hotel."

I straightened my back. "No."

"Arabella—" He regarded me with those sea-swept eyes, and I mustered my most charming smile.

"But I'll be safe with you." I batted my eyelashes at him, showing absolutely no shame.

Unfortunately, my attempt at feminine wiles was met with a stony expression. It seemed he was immune.

"Oh, come on, Sheriff! I've been involved from the beginning."

"Yes, against my orders."

I could no longer maintain my smile. "Your *orders?* I beg your pardon, no one *orders* me to do or not do anything." I realized I was playing with fire, that there might be consequences of going up against a lawman like this, but his tone, and words, harkened back to my mother and her demands, and it raised my ire.

"So you keep saying. Against my *request*, then. Please, Arabella. It's dangerous."

I knew I would not be able to convince him, hardheaded as he was, so there was no point in my standing here arguing with him.

"Any word on Mr. Duncan yet? Has he returned?"

His jaw flexed. "No. Constance said she saw Duncan get into a carriage down near the General. It was headed out of town."

"Did she see who was driving the carriage?"

"No."

"So maybe he did walk into town, like Eliza said. And then he went to Addison or Denver as Cordelia suggested. If he had planned to go with an associate, that would explain why his horses and carriage were still in his barn."

"Could be." He swiped the keys to the jail cell off his desk and tossed them into a drawer. I glanced over at his prisoner, who was enthusiastically tucking into the food the sheriff had brought him. He paid us no mind.

"But what about the calling card that was left there?"

He shook his head. "I have no idea."

I didn't at all like the fact that Jack Duncan was now missing. Especially because he'd married Eliza and would now have access to her half of the claim.

"What if he killed Rupert?" I said.

"I had the same thought, at first, but he was at the wedding. And he was at the reception as well. There were several eyewitnesses."

"He could have had an accomplice," I added. "Maybe they left town together?"

"I thought about that, too. But why leave everything behind? His ranch, his cattle, his stately home—they are all worth a fortune in and of themselves. Besides, running would just make him look guilty."

I considered his words. It was true that if he had killed Rupert, so far there had been no proof, or even evidence of his guilt. He'd have been better off hedging his bets by sticking around.

"Well, if that's the case, then perhaps whoever was in

the carriage with him was forcing him to leave, holding him at gunpoint?"

"That seems more likely to me. I've wired the Addison and Denver sheriff's offices. Told them about the situation."

"Why didn't you go after him?"

"I've only just found out that he'd gotten into that carriage, Arabella. And he left a few days ago. We can't say for sure that he was abducted. Besides, I have my hands a bit full here with—"

I crossed my arms over my chest. "With keeping an eye on me?"

He shrugged. "With the murder case."

I resisted any further banter. We didn't have time for it.

"But if you think Jack Duncan left of his own volition, why would the calling card have been left at his house?"

"Could be a ruse to cause a distraction, to get me to go after Duncan."

"So, in that case, you think that the person who left the card knew Mr. Duncan was leaving town?" I asked.

"It's possible."

"But what about the house being upended?"

"It was a bear, Arabella. They are full of mischief. The state of the house might not be related to his disappearance, but whoever left that card wanted us to think it was. I believe they wanted me to go after him, to leave town."

"For what purpose?"

He met my gaze with a look of deep concern in his eyes. "Don't you remember what was written on the back of the card?"

"Oh. Me. You think they wanted you to leave so they could get to me."

"Yep."

"So you think that Mr. Duncan left town on some kind

of business and the killer knew this, and then planted the card?"

"I think it's a strong possibility."

"Well, if Mr. Duncan left of his own accord, why would he leave and not tell Eliza?" I wondered out loud.

Mr. Marshall froze momentarily and then slowly closed the desk drawer.

"Why would he tell Eliza? What business is it of hers what the man does or where he goes?"

I immediately realized my indiscretion. "Well . . . they are . . . business partners now. His leaving town might have had something to do with the Cougar claim."

He gave me a dubious look. "Arabella, go back to the hotel. You shouldn't have left in the first place. And you shouldn't be alone."

"But—"

"Go!" He pointed toward the door. He really could be so infuriating.

"Fine!" I huffed. I turned on my heel and walked out the door. He was right, as much as I hated to admit it. I shouldn't be on my own with a killer on my tail. The safest place for me to be was with him, I reasoned, even if he didn't know it. I rounded the corner of the building and waited, hidden from view.

It wasn't long before he came out and walked up to the hitching rail. He spent a moment stroking Queenie's fore-head. He then held something out for her to eat, probably a sweet, and got on. I waited until he was a little ways down the road before I approached the other horse. It was a black horse with four white socks and a blaze down its face.

"Hello there." I looked under the horse's belly to deter-mine its sex. "My fine chap, shall we be friends?"

He blinked his eyes slowly and licked his lips. I untied

the reins from the hitching rail and slung them over his neck one at a time. I had only ridden a horse three times in my life. Once as a child, and then another time doubled up with the sheriff, and a third time on my own on a horse named Bessie from the livery. All three instances culminated in most humiliating scenes with me on my backside on the ground.

Determined not to let the sheriff get too far ahead of me, I lifted my left foot up in an attempt to get it into the stirrup, but the horse was quite tall. After three tries, I got the toe of my boot in, and grabbing on to the horn of the saddle, I strained to pull myself up. I was about to swing my right leg over the horse's rump when he decided to walk off. I lost my balance and found myself face down, slung over the saddle like a sack of potatoes.

"Whoa there, friend," I said, trying to sound confident, but the horse paid me absolutely no mind and continued walking. Luckily, he was following the sheriff's horse.

With some effort I was able to hike my leg up onto its rump but felt myself slipping with each jarring step. Clinging desperately to the saddle horn, I finally managed to get my leg over but felt like a complete imbecile as I could not right myself because of the tangle of my skirts. I must have looked like a jockey who'd had too much Pimm's No. 1 at the jockey club. I tried not to acknowledge the fact that several people in the street had stopped to stare. It would be an absolute miracle if I managed to get out of this town with my reputation intact.

Finally, after a few more seconds of desperate squirming, I was able to sit upright. Unfortunately, my skirt did not accompany my leg, so it was frightfully exposed. A quick glance at one couple on the street, a woman who clearly was aghast at my display and a man who was smiling with delight, flooded my face with heat. She roundly jabbed her spouse in the ribs with her elbow, causing him to let out a grunt of displeasure.

I let out a chuckle at the spectacle I had caused. "Come on, boy," I said to my mount. "Let's go. Save me from myself."

Chapter Twenty-Five

I encouraged the horse with my heels, and he broke into a trot, which was terribly uncomfortable. I was bouncing so violently my hat had shifted down low over my forehead and I could feel the pins in my hair coming loose, but I didn't dare release my hands from the saddle horn, nor the reins, for fear of toppling to the ground. Still, I was not required to steer as my equine conveyance followed his friend.

We turned off the main street and headed toward the foothills where Rupert Townsend's house was located.

It wasn't long before Sheriff Marshall arrived in front of Rupert's house. He dismounted, stepped up to the front door, knocked, and within seconds, he was invited in. I urged my equine friend to trot faster, and I hung on for dear life.

Finally, he came to a stop near Queenie and gave a snicker of affection. The two touched noses. After some difficulty, I managed to get off and, to my delight, landed on my feet this time. Progress! Who needed riding lessons? Not me, by Jove!

I pulled down my jacket, smoothed my skirts, straightened my hat, and then made my way up the five steps to the front door. I knocked.

"Mrs. Pryce," Helen said in surprise when she opened the door.

"Hello, Helen. May I come in?" Without waiting for her response, I swept through the door. Sheriff Marshall was standing at the fireplace next to a winged armchair. I noticed several boxes and crates scattered about.

"What are you doing here?" he growled.

"I've come to pay Miss Digby a visit. To see how she is settling in." I smiled at him, and he rolled his eyes.

"As I said to the sheriff, I really am quite busy," Helen said tersely.

"Are you leaving us?" I asked, scanning the room.

"Possibly. I haven't decided yet. But there's nothing for me here."

"Oh dear. But what about the house?"

"I've thought about selling it, but like I said, I'm not sure."

"Well, I'm sorry to hear that you might leave. Where would you go?"

"Mrs. Pryce," the sheriff cut in, "if you don't mind, we were in the middle of something here."

I gave him a prim smile. "Don't mind me."

The muscles in Mr. Marshall's perfectly square jaw flexed, and he fixed me with a glare.

A baby's cry came from somewhere at the back of the house.

"I'd better . . . get that," Helen said and fled from the room.

The sheriff approached me, his face like thunder. "I warned you, Arabella. Why did you follow me?"

I raised my chin. "You said I shouldn't be alone. Besides, I am part of this investigation whether you like it or not. You must admit I have been useful to you."

He offered an exasperated sigh. "Why do you persist? This doesn't concern you."

"It *does* concern me. Not only is Eliza my friend, but Rupert Townsend was murdered on his way to my hotel, where I was hosting their wedding reception. And now I am in danger."

Helen returned with the baby, who was red-faced from sleep and crying. When she saw me, the little cherub smiled and held out her arms toward me. To say I was surprised at this display of familiarity would be an understatement. I had never had much to do with babies. I had nothing against them, mind you, I just had absolutely no experience with them whatsoever, other than this one when I carried her to the hotel for her distressed mother.

The child nearly leaped out of Helen's grasp. To keep her from falling to the ground, I grabbed hold of her. She gave a chortle of delight as I settled her in my arms.

The sheriff, seeing that Helen was no longer occupied with Clara, commenced with his questions. "Miss Digby, do you know an Arthur Digby?"

Her face froze, and her eyelids blinked rapidly. "No—no, can't say as I do."

Interesting. A lie.

The sheriff and I exchanged a glance. He then produced the photograph I had given him, and he handed it to her.

She pressed her lips together in a grim line.

"This is you?" the sheriff pressed.

"Yes."

"And this is Arthur Digby?" He then pulled the article from his front pocket and held it up to her.

She sighed, handing the photograph back. "Yes."

"Who is he?" Sheriff Marshall asked.

"He . . . he's my brother."

"Why did you lie?" I asked, bouncing the child up and down as she played with my watch necklace, fascinated. The sheriff gave me a sideways glance, but I ignored him.

"He's a murderer," Helen said. "I don't want any association with him. That's why I left Chicago. Didn't think that story would follow me all the way to Colorado."

"Did you know Charles Clark? The man he killed?" the sheriff asked.

"Never heard of him before."

"Miss Digby, may I see your marriage certificate?"

Helen darted a look at me, like I had somehow betrayed a confidence. She then gestured to the boxes scattered about the floor.

"Not sure I can find it at the moment," she said.

"I can wait." The sheriff widened his stance, planting his feet firmly on the floor.

Helen heaved a sigh. "I'll be right back."

She went out of the room, leaving the sheriff and me in an awkward silence. I could practically see steam shooting from his ears. He was not pleased with me in the least, which I supposed I understood but still found a bit hurtful. I had just provided him with vital information to the case.

She returned and handed the document to the sheriff. He gave it a quick once-over. "From what I understand, there is no record of your marriage to Rupert Townsend."

"What?" Her face contorted into an appalled grimace.

She pointed to the certificate. "You have the proof right there. Rupert himself signed it, and so did the pastor."

The sheriff nodded. "That is Rupert's signature . . . or a very good forgery, but there is no record at the church," he persisted.

"How would you know that?" she asked.

"I have a source. A . . . reliable source." His voice strained at the words, and I tried my best to refrain from smiling. At least he thought I was reliable.

"All right," she said, throwing her hands in the air. "It's true. We had that document made up. The pastor at the church wouldn't marry us on account of—well, on account of my past."

"You mean, your association with your brother?" the sheriff asked.

"No . . . *my* past. What I used to do . . . in Chicago. Word had gotten out by some old biddies in Addison about my . . . former profession."

"You were a prostitute," I said, Kitty's story coming to mind.

Helen glared at me. "Yeah, I was, but that was a long time ago."

"And the name Clark doesn't mean anything to you?" I pressed.

"No!" she insisted loudly, making me flinch. The baby whimpered.

"Back to Arthur Digby," the sheriff said, giving me a sideways glance.

"Like I told you," she continued, "when Arthur killed that man, I wanted to leave him—and my former life— behind me. I wanted to start over. Rupert knew about my past, but he didn't care. And so he had that certificate made up. To make me legitimate. So that I could hold my head up high in that town."

"I see," the sheriff said. "But then he left you. Why?"

She closed her eyes as if to shut out the pain. "Some habits die hard," she said quietly.

"You were unfaithful to him." I shifted Clara over to my other hip. The child was growing heavier by the minute, but she was quiet now and seemed content in my arms.

"And the will?" the sheriff asked.

Her eyes widened in alarm. "That's real. I swear it. I saw him write it out before I, well, you know . . ."

"Broke his heart?" I said.

She pressed her lips together. "Yes. I was actually just as surprised as you that he hadn't changed it. I don't know if he just didn't get around to it, or—"

"Or if he was just a decent man who wanted you looked after. He gave Eliza the claim and you everything else," the sheriff finished for her.

"Right," she said under her breath.

Clara suddenly twisted in my arms and reached for the floor. She squirmed and let out a squeal, wanting to be set down. I complied with her wishes, and on her hands and knees, she scuttled away from us into the hallway.

Worried she'd hurt herself with so many boxes around, I went after her, amazed at the speed with which she traveled. She led me to a room that looked like an office. A large desk was positioned in front of a wall of bookshelves that were full to bursting. Rupert must have been a voracious reader.

Not wanting to miss out on the conversation between Sheriff Marshall and Helen, I bent down to scoop the baby up when something to the left of the doorway caught my eyes. It was a pair of green-tinted spectacles. One of the arms was broken off.

Mr. Duncan had been wearing green spectacles just like that the other day. Had he paid Miss Digby a visit? Since he and Rupert had been partners, maybe there had been some kind of business to discuss with Helen in regard to Rupert's estate? Perhaps that's why Mr. Duncan had been heading out of town.

The knot that had suddenly appeared in my stomach told me that something was not quite right here, but I couldn't grasp what it was.

Clara was trying to pull herself up to standing by grasping a cloth that was draped over the table. Fearing she would send the contents of the table crashing on top of her, I quickly grabbed her and picked her up. She was not at all happy with me and started to cry.

I took her back to the parlor to find that the sheriff had placed his hat back on his head. "Thank you for your time, Miss Digby. Let's go, Mrs. Pryce."

"Excuse me?" The hair on the back of my neck prickled at his demanding tone.

"Miss Digby is busy. We mustn't take up any more of her time."

I knew he was furious with me for following him, so I thought it best to do what he said. I wished I had heard the rest of his conversation with Helen, though.

I handed Clara to her. "Good day, Helen." She took the baby and nodded at me.

I let the sheriff usher me out the door. When he saw the two horses standing in front of the porch, he stopped short. "You stole the horse in front of my office?" He looked over at me, his sea-blue eyes suddenly darkening with storm clouds.

"I didn't exactly *steal* him. I *borrowed* him."

"Really, woman, you have some nerve. I have half a mind to arrest you."

"You wouldn't dare," I challenged.

"Don't press me. Now go back to the hotel."

"But shouldn't I ride the horse back to your office?"

He gave me another dubious glare.

"You said I shouldn't be alone," I reminded him again.

Shaking his head, he rolled his jaw. I knew I had pushed him to the very limit, so I thought I would try to smooth things over.

"I apologize, Sheriff. I know I have overstepped my bounds."

"You are being very careless about your own safety, Arabella. It's almost as if you think you are immune to danger—or worse. It smacks of either arrogance or ignorance. I haven't decided which."

I let out a sharp exhale, feeling as if he'd delivered a blow to my stomach. In fact, I was rendered speechless, something that hadn't happened to me in— Well, I don't think I'd ever been rendered speechless. I stood gaping at him, my mouth open, although I found it hard to breathe.

"Get on, then." He nodded toward the horse.

Still unable to utter another word, I obeyed, this time with more ease, but not much more due to the volume of my skirts. If I was to continue this silly pursuit, I would have to secure a riding skirt or some riding pants. And truth be known, now that I had upset the sheriff to the point of his thinking me either full of myself or a complete dolt, I found that it made me feel awful and that his good opinion of me *did* matter to me.

He got up onto his horse, and they walked on, leaving me and my mount behind. I tapped my heels on the horse's sides, and he took up a trot to catch up to Queenie.

"I've been thinking about those riding lessons," I said when we came alongside them, trying to get back in his good books.

"Really." His expression remained stony.

"I'm quite clumsy on a horse, I'm afraid." I figured a little humility might do me good at the moment, much as it galled me to call attention to my failings.

"You got that right."

I thought I detected a crack in his veneer, a hint of a smile, but couldn't be sure. "Maybe after we—or rather, *you* get to the bottom of this murder investigation, I could avail you of your services?"

He pulled Queenie to a halt, which caused my horse to stop, and he looked over at me, probably trying to discern my sincerity on the matter.

"I'm quite serious, Sheriff. I believe I'm ready. And it is a skill that would definitely come in handy living in these parts."

He took a deep breath. "All right. That sounds like a deal."

I smiled, relieved that I had broken the ice. We walked on.

"I saw something interesting at the house," I ventured.

He shook his head. "Of course you did. And you are about to enlighten me?"

"It was a pair of sunshades—green-tinted spectacles. Quite expensive. They are all the rage in New York. Anyway, they were on the floor of Rupert's office."

"And this is interesting how?"

"They were exactly like the pair I saw Mr. Duncan wearing the other day."

He pulled Queenie to a stop again. My horse followed suit. "And?"

"Well, I just thought that it was interesting is all. They were broken, too. Do you suppose Mr. Duncan paid Helen a visit? And if so, why? And if those were his glasses, why were they broken and lying on the floor?"

"This is a harsh climate, Arabella, and the sun is brutal. I'm sure there are others in town who wear the same green-tinted spectacles. Besides, they might have been hers. Or Rupert's.

There was stuff scattered all over that house. She was obviously going through all the things she'd acquired in Rupert's will."

"But have you ever seen Rupert wear sun spectacles before?"

"Can't say that I have."

"I've not seen Helen wear them, either," I said.

"She hasn't been in town that long."

"True." I thought about pursuing this line of thought but didn't want to irritate him further. I shrugged. "I suppose you are right."

"Speaking of the will, do you buy her story?" I asked. "That it's genuine?"

"I'm not sure," he said but didn't elaborate.

We turned down an alleyway to get to the main street, but instead of heading toward his office, Sheriff Marshall was steering Queenie toward the hotel.

"Shouldn't we get the horse back to your hitching post?" I asked. "Does it belong to your prisoner?"

"My prisoner isn't going anywhere anytime soon."

"What is he in for?"

He pulled Queenie to a halt again and looked me squarely in the eye. "Horse thievery."

"Oh." I gulped.

He clucked to Queenie, and we moved on.

He was intent on seeing me back to the hotel safely, which was both lovely and a bit patronizing at the same time. For so many years in my youth, my every move had been controlled by my mother, and any attempt by anyone to rule over me in any way triggered those feelings of entrapment and isolation. Marrying William had allowed me to discover my independence. No longer had I needed to sing for my supper. Thus, a whole new world opened up for me. I was finally mistress of my own life.

I knew the sheriff had no wish to control me, even though he might wish to arrest me. He just wanted me to be safe. Which was part of his job. And if I'm honest, I hoped it was also because he meant what he said that he cared about me. But someone—the killer—had given me an ultimatum, and that simply would not do.

I would not rest until they were found.

Chapter Twenty-Six

After checking in with Mr. Pettyjohn to see how Mr. Johns was faring—he'd been diagnosed with a sprained ankle and taken to his abode in the annex to rest—I went up to my rooms. Cordelia was sitting at the parlor desk working on some correspondence, bless her, and Bijou was fast asleep on her bed under the window.

"You have been gone quite a while," Cordelia said as I took off my hat and straightened my hair. It had come loose with my jolting ride through town. "Did you speak with the sheriff?"

I told her of my adventure and Helen's true marital status.

"She and Mr. Townsend never were married?"

I shook my head. "But he still provided for her, according to the will."

"You don't think the will is a fake?"

"I honestly don't know."

"So, if Helen and Mr. Townsend weren't married, that

means that Eliza's marriage to him is legitimate. That will be of some comfort to her."

"I hope so," I said.

"And Arthur Digby is Helen's brother?" she asked.

Suddenly, Percival appeared on the love seat. Bijou, probably having sensed a shift in the atmosphere, woke up and emitted a low growl.

"Bijou!" Cordelia said. "My goodness, what are you growling at?"

I quickly positioned myself so that Cordelia would have to face me as we spoke. I couldn't risk her turning around in the chair to possibly see my nosey and persistent ghost friend. The chances were low, unless he chose to reveal himself, but still, I didn't want to risk it.

Bijou stood in her bed, staring at Percival who held a scolding finger out to her. Dear Lord, didn't he realize he was provoking her?

"She probably just had a dream that woke her up," I said.

"Silly dog." She chuckled. "You were saying? About Arthur Digby?"

"Yes. Helen claims she came West to avoid the scandal. Said she wanted nothing more to do with him or her former life."

"Understandably so," Cordelia agreed. "Do you think she will stay in La Plata Springs?"

"Hard to say. She was very unclear about the whole matter. She was going through Rupert's things, which I suppose are *her* things if the will is legitimate. She came to town with nothing but that carpetbag. Now, she has a home and an entire household of goods. I would think she would want to stay. It seemed very comfortable there."

"Well, if she does plan to leave, I'm sure she would wait until she knows what happened to Mr. Townsend."

I tapped a finger on my chin, thinking. "She doesn't seem all that interested in the investigation."

"Maybe it's too painful for her?" Cordelia offered. "Sounds like she's been through a lot."

"Yes. Or she feels guilty for driving Rupert away," I said absently.

"Did anything come about regarding the name Clark?"

"No. Helen claims she knew nothing of the man her brother killed."

Cordelia turned to the papers on the desk and began to fold them. "Well, I'd best get these letters to the post office. And Bijou needs a walk. Would you like to come?"

"No, thanks. I think I will check to see if Eliza is in. I'd like to tell her about Helen and that her marriage is legitimate."

"She will be relieved, I'm sure." She stuffed the letters into envelopes and then stood up. I glanced over at Percival and, with a tilt of my head, implored him to make himself scarce. In a blink, he was gone. Bijou barked.

"All right, Bijou," Cordelia said. "I know. You'd like to go outside."

"Do be careful, Cordelia."

She gave me a nod. "Lottie said she needed to go to the post office, too. We are going together. Won't be gone more than a minute!"

"Oh, good." I took the leash from the hook near the door, and Bijou scampered over, excited at the prospect of a walk. I attached the lead to her collar and handed it to Cordelia.

As soon as they left, Percival popped into the mirror.

Pipe smoke swirled about his head, and the room filled with the spicy fragrance.

"So, the plot thickens," he stated.

"Yes, but I'm afraid it hasn't gotten us any closer to finding out who killed Rupert Townsend."

"No. Who do you believe is suspect number one?" he asked. "I suppose the blacksmith is in the clear?"

"Most likely. I feel rather bad for suspecting him. He's always been so kind to me. According to Sheriff Marshall, he doesn't have a ruthless bone in his body."

"Quite unlike Boss Archer." Percival raised an eyebrow.

"Hmm. You do have a point there. Mr. Archer would probably do anything to get what he wants. But why would he risk what he has built in this town?"

He let out a laugh. "The man thinks he is bulletproof, Arabella. He thinks his power will protect him from anything."

"Yes, I would have to agree."

"What about the seamstress?"

"Cynthia Mayes. Right. She did have feelings for Rupert, but if she was to commit a crime of passion, wouldn't she have gone after Eliza?" I reasoned. "Eliza stood in the way of any chance Miss Mayes had with Rupert."

"Perhaps that is her plan," Percival suggested. "Eliza could be next."

"Or me," I said, remembering the warning at my door.

"You must admit, the calling card does have a certain . . . femininity to it."

"You think the killer is a woman?" I asked. I still had my suspicions about Helen, too.

He shrugged.

"But the murder was so violent. Surely, Rupert put up a

fight. Would a woman have the physical power to render him helpless?"

"If she was angry enough, I suppose."

"I wish I could find more evidence," I muttered.

"What about this Arthur Digby?" Percival asked.

"What of him?"

"Didn't the sheriff say he escaped?"

I blinked at him in surprise. "You were in the sheriff's office earlier?"

He gave a brief nod. How strange. I could always seem to feel his presence. How had I missed it? Perhaps I was too focused on imparting the information to the sheriff.

"What if he followed his sister . . . here?"

"Why would he do that?"

"Maybe he knew of the relationship with Townsend, of the will. How close were Miss Digby and her brother? Perhaps they had continued their correspondence."

"She said she wanted nothing to do with him."

"And she's been truthful about everything?" he asked dubiously.

"No. She hasn't. And I must admit, when I thought Arthur Digby was her husband, I'd had the same notion, that he'd come West, perhaps for revenge, against Rupert. But as they aren't married . . . Still, you could be right, Percival. Perhaps Sheriff Marshall might put a Wanted sign up around town. I'll talk with him about it."

"Good idea, dear."

"Well, I'm off to see Eliza. Finally, I have some good news to tell her."

I descended to the third floor and knocked on Eliza's door. There was a great deal of shuffling noises coming from behind it, and it took her a few moments to answer.

"Arabella, how good to see you."

She didn't sound like it was good to see me at all. Her tone was flat, and the normal luminescent quality of her eyes had sharpened. She didn't offer to let me in.

"Hello. I wanted to see how you are getting on and if you've heard from Mr. Duncan. The sheriff said he'd seen him getting into a carriage that was headed out of town."

The tension in her face eased somewhat. "Yes. The sheriff told me as much, and no, I haven't heard from him. I have a feeling he went to visit his lawyer in Denver."

"Oh, I see. And what of his house at the ranch? The sheriff said it was a terrible mess."

"Yes, I am going over there momentarily to straighten up and see how I might like to make the place feel a little like my own. For when I move in, of course."

I stood there, suddenly feeling very awkward. I thought it extremely odd that she didn't invite me in. She was usually so happy to see me.

"Eliza, may I come in? I need to tell you something else, and I'd rather not do it while standing in the hallway."

She responded by opening the door and gesturing to me to come inside. The cold indifference wafting off her was perplexing indeed. I stepped through the doorway and closed the door behind me. She did not offer me a seat, which again, I thought strange. Perhaps my news would cheer her up.

"I've just learned that Rupert was not actually married to Miss Digby. The church in Addison would not marry them on account of . . . well, Miss Digby's past. She was once a prostitute. Rupert had the false marriage certificate made up so that she would be respectable. So, you see, you did not marry a man who was already married."

"So he was living a lie," she stated with that same detached flatness.

"Well, I suppose, but he was trying to do right by Miss Digby. I think that says something about his character."

She huffed. "Indeed." Her gaze drifted from mine and sought out the window.

"Eliza, are you all right?"

She turned back to me with a tight-lipped smile. "Yes, of course. Why do you ask?"

"You seem . . . upset about something."

She closed her eyes and released a sigh. When she opened them, her face had softened a bit and her smile was less strained. Her large eyes blinked with moisture. "I think I may have made a mistake in marrying Jack."

"Oh dear," I said with sympathy, although I had thought she might come to this realization. It all seemed so hurried. "Why do you say that?"

"I believe he married me to get ahold of Rupert's half of the claim."

I pressed my lips together. That thought had crossed my mind, too, but I didn't want to say it to her. What if it wasn't true? What if his intentions were pure?

"But that was a gift. To you. Can he do that?"

The stoniness of her features returned. "He is a man, Arabella. Men can do whatever they please in this world. I believe he has gone to see his lawyer in Denver to find a way to take my claim."

"But— Are you sure?"

"Not entirely," she said. Her face then crumpled with sadness.

"Oh, come now." I put my hands on her shoulders.

248

"You have been through so much recently, no wonder you are at sixes and sevens. Let's sit down." I guided her to the sofa.

"But I have so much to do."

"It can wait, dear. Shall I have Maggie bring us some tea?"

She arranged her skirts to prevent any wrinkling of the fabric. She was wearing yet another dress I had not seen before. It was a beautiful, deep-brown satin affair, very rich, like chocolate, with black brocade trim.

"No. I only have a moment. I must be getting on, and I have some correspondence to finish first."

"Very well," I said. "I will leave you to it, then. But only if I know that you are all right."

She sniffed. "I'm fine." She swiped at a tear that had fallen on her cheek. "I need a handkerchief," she said, about to get up.

"You sit. I'll fetch one. Where are they?"

"In the top drawer of the bureau in the bedroom."

I got up and made my way into the bedroom. I quickly went to the narrow top drawer on the left and pulled it open. Lying inside were a half a dozen folded lace hankies. I took one up, closed the drawer, and then nearly jumped out of my skin as Percival appeared, sitting on the far end of the bureau.

"What are you doing here?" I hissed.

"After listening to you and Cordelia talking—"

I narrowed my eyes at him. "You mean after *eavesdropping*."

He rolled his eyes. "All right. After *eavesdropping* on you two, I remembered something. As I was making my rounds earlier, I spotted something you should know about," he whispered.

"Arabella? Could you find them?" Eliza called from the other room.

"Yes! Coming." I gave Percival a pointed glare. "Later," I whispered to him.

He tilted his head toward a leather valise in the corner of the room. I glanced down at it and embossed in small gold letters on the top of it was *L. Clark.*

I gasped. *Clark.* Like Charles Clark.

"Arabella, never mind about the handkerchief." Eliza was standing in the doorway. Percival vanished. "What have you been doing in here?" she asked, looking around the room.

"Oh, I—I was just—"

I walked over to the window and grasped part of the lace sheer under the curtain in my hand. "I was just checking the drapes. From what I understand, there was a little problem with moths in the spring. They had done some damage in some of the rooms, and . . ." My eyes drifted toward the valise again. "Is that your bag?" I asked.

"Yes," she said.

"Who is L. Clark?"

"Oh. That. I have no idea. I purchased the bag from a shop in Denver. I got a special price for it, as it had belonged to someone else first."

"Ah. I see."

It seemed a very strange coincidence, but then again, Clark was a relatively common name. At least in England. And a good deal of English people had settled in the New World a century ago.

"I really must be going," Eliza said, not bothering to disguise the impatience in her voice.

"My apologies." I handed her the handkerchief. "Are you feeling better?"

She shrugged. "I suppose."

"I'm sure you have nothing to worry about with Mr. Duncan," I said, not knowing at all if that statement was true, but I wanted to comfort her.

"We'll see," she said.

"I'll be going, then." I gave her an air kiss and left with a very unsettled feeling in my belly.

Chapter Twenty-Seven

The conversation I'd just had with Eliza made me wonder if I knew the woman at all. She was so different—not the sweet demure person I had grown so fond of. There was a cold detachment about her that I had not experienced before.

And I could not get the image of that valise out of my mind.

L. Clark.

Her explanation was plausible, but there was something in my gut that told me otherwise. I knew what I had to do.

I hurried down the stairs, dashed through the lobby, and headed across the street toward the post office, which housed the telephone and telegraph exchange.

Once there, I was greeted by Mr. Crawford, the postmaster. He was a rotund specimen with fleshy jowls covered by pork-chop side burns. I was not well acquainted with him but had met him a time or two in the Bella.

"Hello, Mr. Crawford."

"Mrs. Pryce. What can I do for you?"

"I'd like to send a wire to the *Chicago Tribune* please."

"Very well." He took out a notebook and pencil and handed them to me. "Write it there, and I will send it immediately. Do you require a response?"

"Yes."

"I'll let you know as soon as it comes in."

"Thank you so much, Mr. Crawford."

I jotted down my request for information about the murder of Charles Clark. I signed it *Sheriff Clayton Marshall, La Plata Springs, Colorado.*

I handed the notebook back to Mr. Crawford, who quickly perused it but stopped short when he read the signature. He glanced up at me with questioning eyes.

"Oh, did I not mention that the sheriff asked me to do this for him? He's very busy at the moment. You know, with finding Mr. Townsend's killer."

"Does he think there may be a connection with the Charles Clark case in Chicago?" Mr. Crawford asked. "I read about that."

I nodded toward the notebook. "I assume so."

"Then shouldn't I notify him of the response?"

"No," I answered quickly. "I'll take the information and give it to him."

"All right, then. I'll get to it."

I left the office with a stab of guilt piercing my gut at lying to the man, but should Eliza's valise have a connection to the Clark murder case, I wanted to have the proper information before I brought it to the sheriff, lest he scold me again for interfering, or worse yet, lock me up for it. I realized it was quite a long shot, but there had been little to no progress made in the case, and we needed to explore any and all possibilities.

As I crossed the street, Eliza came out of the Arabella

and stood on the entrance steps with the valise in hand. How odd. Was she leaving?

She headed north, walking at a fast clip. I decided to follow her.

Several people greeted me on the street, which was pleasant. It had taken a little time, but I felt like the townsfolk of La Plata Springs were finally warming to me. Or was it me warming to them? In any case, it lifted my spirits.

Eliza suddenly disappeared into a building. It was unmarked and actually looked quite like a house. When I got closer, I could see a small placard on the door. It read, DUNCAN AND ASSOCIATES. Given that Mr. Duncan's home was a little ways from town, it made sense that he would have an office that would provide him closer proximity to the mining office and any business associates.

I considered whether or not I should go in after her. But if she saw me, what would I say? I decided to wait some distance away. I nestled myself in the recessed doorway of an empty building that I had heard was once Archer's Mercantile before Mr. Archer had built a larger space for his store.

From directly across the street I saw Cynthia Mayes. She had stepped out from her shop to examine her window display. There was something large and metal in her right hand that glinted in the sunlight. Was it a pair of scissors? One of the tools of her trade? I thought with some cynicism that it would make a very convenient murder weapon.

I recalled the fatal stab wound that had been inflicted on poor Rupert. The doctor had said the implement had pierced his right lung, which was most likely the cause of death. But if the killer was right-handed, as it appeared Miss Mayes was, why would they reach across his body to stab the right side? Why not go for the left, which would be directly opposite their hand and closer to the heart? I suppose that would make sense if there hadn't been any kind of struggle, if Mr. Townsend had not seen it coming.

She went back into her shop, shutting the door behind her.

Then Eliza came out of Mr. Duncan's building still holding the valise, so I retreated deeper into the narrow doorway until she passed, then followed her again. Her gait was even quicker now, and it took some effort to keep up with her.

She made her way back to the hotel and entered through the large, ornate doorway. What had she been after? Was she checking to see if Mr. Duncan had returned? And why take the valise?

I was just about to cross the street to go back to the hotel, too, when someone called my name. It was Mr. Crawford.

He hurriedly made his way over to me. "I have a response from the *Chicago Tribune* for you," he said, a little out of breath.

"That was fast."

"Yes. Quite efficient they were." He handed me a nest of curled teletype paper.

"Thank you, Mr. Crawford."

"You're welcome. Well, I must get back. Lots to do. Sorry I didn't coil it nicely for you."

I took the featherlight tangle of paper and made my way back to the hotel. Once back up in my rooms, I straightened the long strip.

"Telegraph message?" Cordelia asked. She was sitting at the desk writing something. "Is it from Mr. Blackthorn? I have been awaiting his response."

"No, it's from the *Chicago Tribune*."

"Oh? News about you? Have Mr. Rankin's stories about your life in La Plata Springs reached Chicago?"

Before leaving New York, I had arranged with the editor of the *New York City Times* to publish stories of my good work in the Western frontier. He owed me a favor or two on account of the fact that my husband had been a financial supporter of his paper, and because he had purchased and published a libelous story from writer Atticus Brooks that had insinuated I was a murderer.

"No."

I told her about the valise.

"That is an odd coincidence," she said. "What does the message say?"

"It says here that Arthur Digby was found guilty of the murder and jailed. He escaped in February and is still at large. A calling card was left at the scene of the crime."

"That much we knew."

"Apparently, Mr. Clark left behind two daughters—twins. They, too, have disappeared."

"Do you suppose Arthur Digby killed the daughters?"

"According to this, he is under suspicion of abducting and killing the daughters, but the police have dropped the case."

"Why?" Cordelia asked.

"It doesn't say."

Cordelia, deep in thought, tapped the tip of her writing pen on her letter, making a bit of a mess with the ink.

"The Chicago police are notoriously understaffed for the amount of crime committed there," she said. "Perhaps their trail came to a dead end and they had to move on to other cases."

"Perhaps."

I happened to look down at Bijou, who had settled at

my feet, and saw that one of the strips of paper had fallen to the floor, probably when I had unfurled the first.

"Wait, there's more." I picked it up, and pulling it taut, I read the remainder of the message. "Oh my goodness."

"What? What does it say?" Cordelia hopped up from the chair and came to look over my shoulder and gasped.

"Arthur Digby was married to one of the sisters. Rose Clark." Immediately, I thought of Eliza's valise. But the inscription on it read *L. Clark.* Furthermore, Eliza had said she'd purchased the case used.

"Rose Clark. Another Rose," Cordelia said. "So, Arthur Digby, Helen's brother, is married to Rose Clark, one of Charles Clark's twin daughters. Did Helen make any mention of this Rose Clark?"

"No. Said she had no idea who Charles Clark was."

"But *Rose.*"

"Yes, I know." I scanned the strips again. "Another strange coincidence."

"And there was a calling card left on the body of Mr. Clark, a card very similar to the ones that have been found here."

"Yes. The sheriff even said so," I said. "But I don't think he knew what was on the calling card."

"Neither did I when I recalled the story." She shrugged. "I think you should talk to Helen again. I'll go with you. Has she settled in at Rupert's house?"

"In the process," I said. "If she's not packing."

"Maybe we should go to Sheriff Marshall?"

I shook my head. "No. He's not pleased with me at the moment. Says that I—well, we are in danger because of the killer's warning on the card found at Mr. Duncan's ranch.

"And the one left under our door."

"Right. And this could be nothing, Cordelia. I don't

want to risk his wrath if this means nothing. Helen could very well have been telling the truth, that she knows nothing of Mr. Clark or his daughter Rose."

As I said the words, a strange feeling came over me. It was a sense of knowing—of knowing that I was onto something here. But how could I possibly articulate that to the sheriff? No, I would have to have more before I spoke to him about the case again.

"All right. Get your coat and hat," I said. "Come, Bijou, we are going on an outing."

The urchin raised herself on her hind legs, pawing the air, a huge smile on her sweet little face and her tail wagging happily.

Chapter Twenty-Eight

I had Mr. Pettyjohn summon Mr. Ellis to drive us to Mr. Townsend's home.

We alighted from the carriage and headed for the front porch steps when something in the window caught my eye. There were two women within the house, leaning over something on the parlor sideboard that was positioned against the wall. One of the women was Helen, and the other was . . . Eliza.

"Cordelia, look." I pointed to them.

"Is that Eliza?"

"Yes. What is she doing here?"

"Perhaps it has something to do with Mr. Townsend's estate?"

"We'll see," I said and mounted the steps. I knocked.

It took a few minutes, but Helen came to the door. "Mrs. Pryce. Another visit?"

"Yes. I had some more questions for you."

"It's really not a good time. I'm trying to get Clara down for a nap."

I blinked at her. It certainly hadn't looked like that was what she was doing before.

"It won't take but a minute." I insisted.

"No, really. I am not prepared for company."

She was about to close the door when I said, "It's about a woman named Rose Clark. I believe she is married to your brother?"

Her face paled, and she gave me a pinched smile. Nevertheless, she opened the door. Cordelia, Bijou, and I entered. Eliza was nowhere to be seen.

Helen crossed her arms. "What do you want to know?"

"I told you about the calling card left on Mr. Townsend's body, the one with the rose and lily bouquet?"

"Yes. What of it?"

"Well, it seems that when your brother killed Mr. Charles Clark, he also left a calling card."

The corners of her mouth turned downward, and she narrowed her eyes. "What of it?"

"I also know that your brother has escaped imprisonment in Chicago. Helen, do you think your brother and his wife are here in La Plata Springs?"

She stiffened. From the corner of my eye, I saw Bijou toddle off down the hall.

"I told you. I want nothing to do with my brother. I don't know where he is."

From somewhere in the back of the house, Clara began to cry, and at the sound, Bijou immediately began to bark.

"But you must admit, Helen, the calling card is quite a coincidence," I continued, determined to keep her attention.

She shrugged a shoulder. "Maybe whoever killed Rupert knew about the murder my brother committed in Chicago and copied the idea of the calling card."

"She is quite upset," Cordelia entered from the hallway carrying Clara. Bijou was following behind with a concerned look on her little canine face. I hadn't noticed Cordelia even leaving the room. She held the baby out for Helen to take, but Helen made no move to accept the pitifully wailing child.

A doorway at the back of the parlor suddenly opened, and Eliza stepped through. When she saw us standing there with Helen, her mouth dropped open. "What are you doing here?" She approached us, her hands clenched and her arms held tightly against her waist.

"I could ask you the same question."

"I . . . I came to visit Helen."

Clara immediately stopped crying. She squirmed in Cordelia's arms, holding her little hands out to Eliza. I blinked in surprise. There was a familiarity there that sent a chill down my spine.

Eliza reached for the child, and as she did, the three-quarter-length sleeve of her blouse rose higher above her arm, and I saw something on the inside of her forearm that stopped my heart.

A tattoo of a sprig of lily of the valley.

I swallowed hard, trying my best not to panic. My mind was a jumble of all the information I had gathered. The calling card. Helen and her brother. The murder of Charles Clark and the twin daughters he'd left behind, Rose Clark and . . . L. Clark.

L. Clark.

"You're sisters," I said. "Twin sisters. The daughters of Charles Clark. Rose and . . ."

Helen reached down and lifted her skirt. When she did so, I noticed the comb in her hair. It was a match to the comb found in Rupert Townsend's carriage.

"You—" I started. But before I could finish, she pulled something from her stocking. It was a knife. She lunged for me, holding it up to my face. My stomach caved in on itself, and my mouth went so dry I could scarcely swallow.

Cordelia gasped.

"You just wouldn't stop, would you?" she said, moving the knife to my throat. "Sticking your nose in where it doesn't belong. You're like a dog searching for a bone."

I started to say something, and she pressed the tip of the knife deeper into my neck. I wasn't sure, but I thought I felt a trickle of blood ooze onto my collar.

"Don't you move," she snarled at me. "Either of you, or your pretty face will be carved to bits."

Eliza put Clara on the floor and rushed at Cordelia, pulling her arms behind her. Cordelia pulled away, and I felt the tip of the knife sink in a little deeper.

"Cordelia, don't," I said.

Eliza smiled at me. "Lily Clark. Pleased to meet you."

My heart fell to the pit of my stomach. How could I have been so deceived? Was I so desperate for someone to like me that I had been completely blinded by Eliza's— Lily's—charms? I had always prided myself on being a shrewd judge of character. It was a skill I had developed young, while growing up in the theater, living among all sorts of people with varying morals and values, and with my mother whose character was questionable at best.

"Your tattoo," I said quietly, the pang of disappointment and sadness bleeding an ache through my chest. "It's lily of the valley, not a lily. What does it represent?"

She gave me a sinister smile. "I told you. It was my mother's favorite flower. She was killed. By—"

"Our father," Helen—or rather, Rose—finished for her.

Lily took Cordelia by the arm again. "The lout sat

around at home, ordering her about. When he wasn't at home berating her, he was out drinking, gambling, womanizing. She worked herself to death to keep us fed and a roof over our heads."

Clara began to cry again, and Bijou went over to her and licked her face.

"Who is Arthur Digby?" I asked.

"My beloved," Rose whispered.

"Is he here, in La Plata Springs?" I asked.

"Shut up with your questions and move," she said, circling behind me. I felt the tip of the knife between my shoulder blades.

"What are you doing?" I asked.

"Coming up with a plan," she said. "Bring her, too, Lily."

"Pick up the dog," Lily said to Cordelia. My heart lurched. What would become of my poor, little, defenseless Bijou?

We slowly moved toward the back of the parlor, and when we came to the door that Lily had emerged from, Rose grabbed my arm. "Open the door," she instructed.

I complied. The doorway led to stairs down into a cellar or basement of some kind. A faint light glowed from below.

I descended slowly, my mind spinning, trying to come up with a plan of escape. As I walked, my eyes trying to adjust to the murky dimness, panic took hold of me. They were going to kill us and leave us here in this underground hell to rot.

I blinked, and my vision, having finally adjusted to the minimal light in the room, cleared. I saw a male figure slumped against a pile of large burlap sacks, his head lolled to one side.

"Mr. Duncan!" I cried.

He righted his head. His face was swollen and bruised. He had been beaten. Badly.

Rose shoved me, and I nearly tripped on my skirts. Lily did the same with Cordelia, and then they both backed away from us.

I mustered my strongest voice. "You won't get away with this. As soon as it's clear we're missing, the sheriff will come looking for us."

I'd had command of my voice, but my heart was pounding with such ferocity I felt I could scarcely breathe.

The two women hurried up the stairs and shut the door. The click of a lock filled the silence.

We were trapped.

Chapter Twenty-Nine

Dim light came from a narrow window at the top of the wall. I scanned the room. Rupert had obviously been using the space for storage. There was some old furniture, some trunks, a bucket of coal, and the burlap sacks Mr. Duncan was propped up against. From the lumps and bumps in them, I figured they might contain potatoes or some other ground crop. My inner query was answered when I saw the butt of several carrots to Mr. Duncan's right. There was also a jug next to him.

"Mr. Duncan?" I knelt down next to him. "Did Lily and Rose do this to you?" I found it hard to believe that a woman could deliver this kind of beating, unless they had used some kind of implement.

Blood had crusted under his nose, and his right eye was swollen shut. A purple, half-moon bruise had settled under it. His lower lip was also swollen and split at the corner.

He grunted and tried to sit up straighter but winced and clutched at his ribs. I nodded at Cordelia, and together, we helped him right himself. Bijou toddled up to him and nestled at his side.

"There was a man." His voice was gravelly and strained, as if it hurt him to speak.

"A man? Did you happen to get his name?"

He shook his head.

"I'm guessing the man is Arthur Digby," I said to Cordelia.

"Undoubtedly," she agreed.

"Did he break into your home?" I asked.

He shook his head. "I had walked to my office in town. As I was leaving my office he showed up in a carriage. I didn't recognize the driver. He told me to get in, that Eliza had sent for me and he'd take me to her. She had some kind of surprise for me. We ended up at this house, and when we stepped inside, he hit me on the back of the head with something. When I woke up, I was down here. It wasn't until later, when she showed up, that I realized I'd been had."

I stood up to look at the wound. His hair was matted with blood, and with the dim light in the room, it was difficult to see how big the wound was.

"Let me guess," I said, gently moving the hair away. The wound was still oozing. "Rose and Lily find wealthy men, charm them into marrying them—"

"Or fake the marriage and the will," Cordelia said. "But why did Helen—er, Rose—pretend to be married to Rupert when Lily had already married him?"

"If we knew them as adversaries, it would throw off any suspicion that they were acting as a team," I said. "And, in the end, you were the real catch weren't you Mr. Duncan?"

He glanced up at me and nodded.

"How do you mean?" Cordelia asked.

Mr. Duncan reached toward the back of his head and winced. When he pulled his hand away, it was covered in blood.

"I need to wrap something around his head to staunch the bleeding," I said to Cordelia. She scanned the room and went to one of the trunks. She opened it and pulled out something white. It looked like a man's shirt. She ripped off one of the sleeves and brought it over.

"Nicely done." I smiled at her and then focused my attention on wrapping Mr. Duncan's head.

"You have a lot more wealth than Mr. Townsend, don't you?" I asked him. I hated to be so indelicate about the matter, but the situation certainly stacked up that way.

Mr. Duncan nodded. "Three times what he had."

"But how did they know about you and the claim?" Cordelia asked. "And your partnership with Rupert?"

"When the Cougar started to produce, Constance Chatterley did a story. Sold it to one of the papers in Denver."

"But Rose said she had been living in Addison," Cordelia said.

I nodded. "Probably waiting for Lily to get her hooks into Rupert."

"And once they were married, she had Digby, or her sister, kill him."

When I had the bandage secure, I stood back to survey my handiwork.

"Thank you," Mr. Duncan said, looking a tad brighter. "But when they killed Rupert, they didn't realize that they needed my signature to sign over Rupert's half to Eliza— and that the claim was in Rupert's house safe."

"The copy of the claim we saw had your initials on it," I said. "Not a signature."

Cordelia tilted her head. "Obviously a fake."

He nodded. "Right. But they didn't account for the fact that all mining claims have a special seal from the land office. So, they needed me to sign over the official claim, and I'm the only one, besides Rupert, who knows the combination to that safe."

"So, it was Eliza's—Lily's—idea for the two of you to marry?" I asked.

His jaw tightened, and a look of disgust flitted across his bruised and battered features. "At first, I felt sorry for her. She seemed so distraught about Rupert. And Boss Archer was being such a pest about the claim. I knew he wouldn't let up on her. Her plan seemed to make sense, and I, like a fool, fell for it. She's so beautiful and smart, and I've been . . . well, lonely. I have always wanted to marry, but I'd never met the right woman. I thought we would grow to love each other in time."

He shook his head. "I shouldn't have jumped in so quickly. Only hours after we married, Eliza started pressing me about signing over the claim. She also mentioned my will. Said that since we were sharing the claim, we might as well share everything."

"But you wouldn't sign it over to her," Cordelia stated.

"I was taken aback at her urgent insistence. I mean, we were married. We had a lifetime to get everything square."

I pulled my bottom lip between my teeth. Poor man. He'd been duped, just as Rupert had. But at least he hadn't complied with her demands yet.

He pointed to the jug next to him. "Water. Please hand it to me."

Cordelia picked it up, pulled out the cork, and helped him to drink. He'd been down there for a couple of days. I wondered if they'd fed him at all. At least they'd left him with water.

"I wouldn't put it past them to be working on a forgery of your will as we speak," I said with a modicum of disgust. "Like they did Rupert's. And once that's done, they wouldn't need the claim."

"A forgery of my will wouldn't work," Mr. Duncan said. "I have the original with an attorney in Denver and copies of it with a niece in Utah and a trusted friend in California. Eliza knows this. Rupert didn't have a will. He hadn't written anything down."

"And that's why it would have been easy for them to get away with it." I thought back to the morning Eliza, Helen, and I had come to Rupert's house to look for the copy of the will. Helen had found the strongbox where it, and the fake copy of the Cougar, had been placed.

"Helen planted the strongbox here. And left the key for me to find," I mused.

"And that was the morning after we'd found Clara alone in Helen's room, "Cordelia said. "She came back carrying the carpet bag. She must have used it to bring the strong box here, with the fake documents inside."

Mr. Duncan shifted his weight again and winced. "I told Rupert he should have a will drawn up, especially since he'd come into money. He wanted to take care of his mother. Give her the house and any money that was left should he die. But he never got around to it. It was foolish of him." He leaned his head back onto the burlap sacks. Perspiration coated his face and his lips were turning a ghastly shade of white.

"They are trying to wear me down," he said, his voice trailing off.

"We have to get you out of here," I said. "It doesn't look like you can take much more."

He shook his head.

I glanced up at the window. It was too small for any of us to fit through. And too high up to boot.

Then, an idea struck. I glanced over at Mr. Duncan. Bijou had crawled into his lap. His hand rested on her back.

"I need something to write on." I got up and went to the bucket of coal and took out a small piece.

"Arabella?" Cordelia said. "What are you doing?"

"Ah!" I said, delighted. Sitting on top of one of the trunks was a crumpled-up piece of newspaper. I tore off a small piece and wrote: "Sheriff. Townsend basement." I folded it into a narrow strip.

"Cordelia, help me move one of these trunks under the window."

"Neither one of us can fit through there," she said.

"No. But Bijou can."

"And then what?"

Hearing her name, Bijou left Mr. Duncan's lap and ambled over to me. I slipped the note under her collar, and then folded it around it. "She'll go to the hotel. Hopefully, someone will see this note. At the very least, once they see she is unaccompanied and that we are missing, they'll look for us."

"But that could take hours. Days. They may not get to us . . . in time." Cordelia was always so pragmatic, sometimes to the point of being pessimistic, which rankled on occasion. This being one of those occasions.

"I think it's the only chance we have."

She nodded. "All right."

Together, we dragged one of the trunks over. I climbed on top. Reaching my arms up, my hands barely touched the bottom of the sill, but if I could get the window open, I could lift Bijou and get her out. I scrabbled about trying to find a latch to open it, but there was none.

"I need something to break the window."

Cordelia began searching among the articles lying about. In seconds, she found a baseball bat.

"Perfect!" I said as she handed it to me.

Ducking my head and closing my eyes, I struck the small window with the bat, and shards of glass flew everywhere. I held my breath, hoping that no one upstairs had heard the noise. I held my finger to my lips, signaling to Cordelia to remain quiet. We waited a few long minutes listening for any activity upstairs. It appeared nothing was amiss. I then tapped at the pane until it had all been shattered. Pieces of glass had landed in my hair and on my clothes, and I did my best to shake it off.

"All right, Cordelia. Give Bijou to me."

She lifted Bijou and handed her to me. "Here you go."

Bijou happily licked my cheek. "All right, sweetheart, we don't have time for cuddles right now. You need to find us some help."

I carefully raised her as high as I could. She started to squirm in my hands, and I feared I might drop her. I pushed her up toward the window, and she set her paws on the bottom of the window frame. I hoped I had cleared enough of the glass that she didn't injure her paws. She scrabbled to gain purchase on the ground above us, and with a final shove on her bottom, she was out. She turned around and looked down at me, her head cocked and her tongue out, panting from the exertion.

"Go, Bijou!" I said.

She sat down and cocked her head to the other side, whining. The poor thing was confused and distressed.

"Go home!" I said. "Go on!"

After blinking at me for several seconds, she finally left.

"Did she go?" Cordelia asked.

"Yes." I climbed down from my perch. "I don't know if this will work, but it's our only chance."

"They won't kill me until I give them the combination to the safe, but you two . . ."

"We have the bat," Cordelia said. "We could fight them off."

"What else might we find?" I went to another trunk and began to search its contents. It was only clothing and some blankets. I looked in another, and then in the one I'd used to stand on to reach the window. There was nothing that could be used for self-defense.

"Mr. Duncan." I went over to him. He had slumped farther down the burlap sacks, and his breathing had become labored. "Do you think you could stand? Do you think you could muster the strength to help us fight them off when they come back?"

He let out a breath and then winced. He held his arm out to me in a gesture that I assist him.

"Cordelia, help me get him up."

She went to the other side of him and took hold of his other arm.

"Ready?" I asked.

He gave me a quick nod.

"One, two, three—" We started to pull him up when he let out a growl of agony.

"Stop! Stop!" he cried. We released him, and he sank back down, clutching his sides. He started to cough and gasp for breath.

Cordelia and I shared a glance, and with a tilt of her head she bade me come with her to the other side of the room.

"He probably has some broken ribs," she whispered. "And from his breathing and that coughing, I'm afraid one of those ribs may have punctured his lung. We can't move him."

I bit my lower lip. "Well, then it's up to us. We need to be ready."

She nodded.

"I hope Bijou finds her way to the hotel."

Suddenly, I was engulfed with doubt. What a silly idea.

"We need to store our energy," Cordelia said. She went over to Mr. Duncan and sat down next to him. "Come on, Arabella."

I went over and sat with them.

And then we waited.

Chapter Thirty

A noise coming from the doorway startled me awake. I opened my eyes to the darkened room. A faint glow of moonlight filtered through the broken window.

How long had we been down here?

I glanced over at my companions, and they, too, had fallen asleep. My stomach growled with hunger. We had been down here for hours.

Suddenly, a shaft of light shone down into the room from above, illuminating the staircase.

"Cordelia!" I hissed. "Wake up!" I took hold of the baseball bat and held it behind me.

Mr. Duncan coughed, and Cordelia stirred.

"What is it, Arabella?" she asked, her voice groggy from sleep.

A male figure descended the steps, and following behind were Lily and Rose, both carrying lanterns. Something metal glinted in the man's hands. A knife. I sucked in a breath.

"Well, don't you look cozy," Lily said.

Cordelia and I quickly got to our feet. I kept the bat concealed behind me. The beating of my pulse roared in my ears, and my mind raced with all the possible scenarios of what might take place in the impending struggle. Without Mr. Duncan's help, it would be nearly impossible to fight off all three of them.

"Go for her first," Lily instructed the man, pointing at Cordelia. His features finally came into view. It was indeed Arthur Digby. My heart leaped to my throat.

"Not Cordelia," I said. "Let her go."

Rose gave an amused snort. "And why would we do that? She'd go straight to the sheriff."

"The sheriff is probably already on his way," Cordelia said.

Rose laughed.

"Let them both go," Mr. Duncan said. "I'll give you the combination and sign the claim, and that will be the end of it."

"No!" I shouted. "You can't let them get away with this." I pulled the bat from behind my back and held it in front of me. "Why, Eliz—Lily? Why are you doing this? Don't you have enough money from the other wealthy men you've swindled? Or killed?"

She scoffed. "It will never be enough. Rose and I were left with nothing. Our father was a rich man. He swindled a number of stupid people. But he didn't share his money with us. Kept us in a run-down shack while he lived in a fancy hotel. Until he lost it all. Then he started drinking. Made our mother go out and work. Made us . . . sleep with men for money."

I recalled that Helen had told me she'd been a prostitute. At least that wasn't a lie.

"He killed our mother with slavery. Any money she

made, or we made, went to his card games, booze, and women," Rose said.

"Rich men." Lily snorted. "They are all the same."

"So you're praying upon wealthy men and punishing them for what your father did to you and your mother?" I asked, perplexed at the logic.

She shrugged. "Yes. When I saw Rupert's advertisement in the paper, I thought, how pathetic. But it was then that I'd realized he was the very Rupert Townsend who had made so much money with the Cougar claim."

"What about your friend here? Arthur Digby?"

Rose stepped forward. "You mean my husband? He's different. He saved us from that poor excuse of a father. He's useful. Aren't you, dearest?"

"In more ways than one," he said, moving toward Cordelia. "I don't mind saying that my wife and her sister are the brains and I'm the brawn. It works for us."

I raised the bat above my shoulder and stood in front of her.

"Don't," I warned. My whole body had gone cold with fear. Calling upon my skills, I imagined myself onstage, acting out the part. Onstage, in the world of pretense, anything was possible. Anything at all.

"Come now, Arabella," Lily said. "You don't think you can fight off a big, strong man like Arthur do you?"

I swallowed, trying to keep the vision of myself acting the part of a strong warrior woman. "I'll give it everything I've got."

She laughed. "Oh, I do like you, Arabella. It's too bad you had to go and stick your nose into all of this. We could have been friends. True friends."

Her words were like a dagger to my heart. I had liked her, too. I'd thought I had found someone with whom I shared a mutual connection, a confidant. We had seemed to have so much in common.

How thoroughly I had been deceived.

"You don't know the meaning of the word *friendship*," I said.

Her eyes narrowed, and then she jutted her chin toward Arthur Digby. "We've wasted enough time." Then she nodded toward Cordelia.

Thinking he would go for her, I raised the bat higher in the air, and before I knew it, he kicked me in the stomach. All the air in my lungs came out in a whoosh. I went hurtling backward and fell with a hard thud on the floor. Pain shot up my tailbone and into my back, blurring my vision. I fought to bring oxygen into my lungs again, gasping for breath.

Lily grabbed the bat and stood over me while Arthur Digby had taken hold of Cordelia and held the knife to her throat.

Rose approached Mr. Duncan. "All right, give me the combination and your friends won't get hurt."

"Don't believe her," I said. "They'll kill us anyway."

Mr. Duncan's breathing had become more labored, but he nodded at Rose and motioned with his hand for her to come closer.

"Don't, Mr. Duncan!" I said.

Mr. Duncan opened his mouth to speak and Rose bent down to hear. But instead of talking, he raised his arm and backhanded her across the face. She stumbled and then tripped on her skirts, falling to the floor.

Lily, distracted, turned away from me, and seeing my opportunity, I kicked her soundly in the knee. She howled in pain and lowered the bat.

I scrambled to my feet and then sucked in a breath. The

pain searing my tailbone threatened to bring me to my knees, but I managed to get upright. I took hold of the bat again.

"Stop!" Arthur Digby shouted. He held Cordelia tight across the chest, pressing the knife to her throat. "I'll slice her throat, I swear it."

Lily and Rose both managed to get to their feet.

"Let's try this again." Rose pressed her hand to her jaw and rolled it back and forth. She approached Mr. Duncan once more. "No funny business or Arthur will make a mess of your friend. Understand?"

Suddenly, the sound of a dog barking echoed from upstairs.

Bijou!

She scampered down the stairs, and following her, cast in the luminescent light from above us like an angel from Heaven, was Clayton Marshall. My heart leaped with joy. Bijou ran to me and jumped up on my skirts. I wanted to bend down and shower her with kisses, but I didn't dare lower the bat.

Behind the sheriff were Bob Parkhurst and Archibald Archer.

"Don't come any closer," Arthur Digby warned, taking an even tighter hold on Cordelia. Her eyes, fixed on me, were wide with fear.

Lily and Rose made a move to come for me, but I held the bat across my body, ready to swing at them like they were two leather-covered baseballs. We were at a standoff.

"Let Cordelia go, Digby. It's over," the sheriff said.

Arthur Digby scowled, his face taking on a menacing grimace. "I'll hurt her, or worse."

"There's no way out, Digby, unless you go through the three of us."

Bob Parkhurst and Archibald Archer both stepped forward and drew their guns.

"I don't take kindly to people taking advantage of the folks of La Plata Springs," Mr. Archer said.

"And I don't like being taken for a fool," Bob Parkhurst said, directing his words at Lily.

I couldn't agree more.

"I thought you were dead," she said back, and then glared at Arthur Digby. Obviously, it had been his mistake.

"Well, you thought wrong," Mr. Parkhurst rubbed the back of his head and winced. It was obviously still tender.

"Why did you try to kill Mr. Parkhurst?" I asked her.

Before she could answer, Mr. Parkhurst cut in. "It was something I saw. Something that slipped from her handbag the day I met her at the train station. It was a calling card that said *Martin Beale, Talent Manager.* It meant nothing at the time, nor did her suitcase that, strangely, had the name *L. Clark* on it."

He shook a finger in the air. "Not until I met a guy by the name of Saul Beale who had come through town by stage coach, headed to Denver. He was going there to handle the affairs of his brother, a talent manager who'd been murdered several months ago. Unfortunately, the case had gone cold, but he said he thought a woman by the name of Lillian Clark, a client of his brother's, might have been involved. It wasn't until later that evening that I remembered the suitcase. I was about to go and ask Miss Swindon—I mean, Miss Clark, about it, but then *that guy*"—he pointed to Arthur Digby—"showed up at my livery asking me to make him a double ought horseshoe, and the next thing I know, I'm waking up in Doc Tate's infirmary days later."

I turned to Lily. "You knew he'd spoken to your manager's brother," I guessed. "You were afraid he'd put two and two together."

She shrugged a dainty shoulder. "I saw them, yes. I couldn't have Mr. Parkhurst ruin our plans."

Arthur tightened his grip on Cordelia, and she let out a little squeak.

"Give it up, Digby," the sheriff said. "I've been doing a little research on you and your relationship with Rose and Lily Clark. Don't make them accessory to murder again. They might have a chance to get out early, but if you kill her, you'll all hang for sure."

So he had discovered their true identities as well.

Arthur Digby, taking an even tighter hold on Cordelia started to back up, receding into the darkness. Bijou started barking and ran over to them. Growling, she took a hold of his pant leg with her teeth and pulled.

"Get off!" He struck at her with his foot, loosening her hold, but she went after him again, her little teeth sinking into the fabric of his trousers, growling all the while.

He attempted to strike at Bijou harder this time but lost his balance. In a flash, Cordelia rammed her elbow into his stomach and wriggled out of his grasp.

The sheriff pulled his gun and pointed it at the man. He stepped closer. "It's over, Digby."

He then tilted his head toward the other two men. With their guns still trained on Lily and Rose they each took a sister by the arm and started to lead them upstairs.

Carefully, Sheriff Marshall approached Arthur Digby. "On the ground, face down," he commanded.

The man, his face filled with fury, hesitated.

The sheriff's voice was deep and dangerous. "Do it *now*."

Mr. Digby snarled but lowered himself to the ground.

Taking handcuffs from the back of his belt, the sheriff held them out to me while keeping the gun aimed at Mr. Digby.

"You may have the honors, Arabella," he said with a smile at me.

"Thank you," I said, grinning back at him.

Chapter Thirty-One

ONE WEEK LATER

"That's good, Arabella. Lift the reins and lay them across the horse's neck, guiding him which way to turn," Sheriff Marshall instructed.

I did as he said and smiled as I gently pushed the horse to turn right by using the pressure of the left rein on his neck. Magically, the horse, a fine white mount named Monty, turned to the right.

"I would have thought to use the right rein like this to turn him." I held the right rein out and maneuvered it farther away from the horse's neck.

"That works, too," the sheriff said. "That's called a direct rein. It's more commonly used in English riding. What I asked you to do is to use an indirect rein, which we cowboys prefer."

"This really isn't so hard," I said.

He beamed up at me with those captivating sapphire eyes. "You're a natural, when you're concentrating."

I smirked at him, although I couldn't really argue his point. The only times I had ridden, I had been wholly occupied with other things, not present in the moment. In truth, it hadn't been fair to the horses I had been riding.

"Once you get the hang of it, once you know good communication, your body will take over, and you won't be required to think so much," he said.

"When can I go faster?" I asked, feeling confident now that I was aware I was "a natural."

"Maybe next time," he said. "You need to understand the fundamentals. We don't want any more accidents."

He, of course, was referring to the time I rode with him out to Masterson Grove in search of Clarence Hays, my bellboy at the Arabella. The horse I had been riding had spooked and I'd tumbled out of the saddle, landed on my rump, and painfully twisted my ankle in the stirrup.

"No. We certainly don't," I said. I carefully dismounted and gave Monty a scratch on his withers. "Thank you, Sheriff." I turned to him and looked up into his handsome face.

"You're welcome, Arabella," he said quietly. "But when are you going to start calling me Clay? We're friends, right?"

Our gazes locked, and suddenly my throat went dry.

"I . . . I . . ." I was so lost in those beguiling eyes I couldn't make my voice work. Why did my throat have to betray me at this moment? It was completely ridiculous that I was rendered speechless by his beautiful face, his soothing voice, and those impossibly gorgeous eyes. I had always been a master of my emotions. It was completely essential to my craft. But in Sheriff Marshall—Clay's—presence, it all went out the window.

Determined to get ahold of myself again, I cleared my throat, summoned my skills, and gave him a cordial smile.

"Of course we are friends—" I tried to utter his name but couldn't quite bring myself to do it.

He must have sensed this because he chuckled. "How did you figure out the true identities of Lily and Rose Clark?" he asked, thankfully changing the subject.

"It was a number of things," I said. "Mostly everything I've already told you, but seeing that photograph of Helen —as we knew her then—and Mr. Digby . . . "

"Yes. That's what got me looking into her background." He rested an arm on the top of Monty's neck and ran his fingers through the horse's mane.

"Things got a little stranger when I saw Eliza's—Lily's —suitcase in her room," I continued. "The one Mr. Parkhurst had mentioned, with *L. Clark* embossed on the top." I left out the fact that it was actually Percival who had noticed the suitcase first. "Then I'd heard about the twin Clark girls." A wave of hot guilt engulfed me at having sent that wire to Chicago, pretending to be the sheriff. I would have to tell him. But things were going so wonderfully between us at the moment. I would have to find the right time. "It was then I started to believe Eliza could be a suspect."

"No wonder you became suspicious."

"I didn't put it completely together until we went to Rupert's house to talk with Helen again about Mr. Digby and his wife, Rose. It was kind of a funny coincidence that Mr. Emerson's wife's name was Rose as well."

"It's a popular name," the sheriff said.

"Yes. Helen had never mentioned anything about her brother's wife, which I found odd as he had murdered his wife's father. Anyway, when Cordelia and I got to the house, we saw Eliza through the window, which was also a little strange. As far as I knew, they had been rivals for Rupert's affections and his estate. I decided to give Eliza the benefit of the doubt and assumed she had come to talk with Helen about Rupert's effects. But it was when I saw the tattoo of a lily of the valley on Eliza's arm that I started to put it all together."

He nodded. "The calling card."

"I guess it was some kind of tribute to their mother," I added. "It's quite sad actually, what happened to their mother. And their upbringing was quite sad as well. It made them so embittered. They felt it entitled them to take advantage of rich men."

I was so lost in my recounting of the sisters' scheme that I didn't notice how intently the sheriff was studying my face. Suddenly, I became self-conscious. Another thing that never used to happened to me until I met the sheriff. Irritated at my misbehaving feelings, I straightened my shoulders and looked away from him, busying myself with stroking the horse's neck.

"What is it, Sheriff Marshall? Have I said something daft?" Having mastered my emotions again, I looked back at him, determined not to get lost in those eyes.

"No." He smiled, making my insides feel a jumble. I did my best to ignore it.

"Oh! Did someone get in touch with Rupert's mother?" I asked.

"Yes. I had Sally send a wire. She sometimes helps me with correspondence and other stuff like that. We received a response back from a woman who is taking care of Mrs. Townsend. It seems she's quite ill. Hopefully the proceeds from Rupert's house will help with her care."

"Yes, yes, that would be good," I said.

"What's going to become of the child?" he asked. "Is she still with you?"

I shook my head, my heart suddenly heavy with missing the beautiful little girl.

After her mother and the other criminals were apprehended at Rupert's house and Dr. Tate had come to tend to Mr. Duncan, Cordelia and I had taken little Clara with us to the hotel until the county authorities had come to take her to an orphanage in Las Ciervas, a town about sixty miles due West of here, run by the Sisters of Mercy. I had been worried about her fate, but we had just received good news.

"No, she's not. She's going to a good family in Addison until her mother is released from prison. How long do you reckon she will be incarcerated?"

"That depends on the judge," he said. "If it's Fess Denton, could be ten years or so. He's pretty tough."

I hoped it would be ten years or more so that little Clara could grow up with the care and attention she needed. She would also be raised with three siblings, something I would have loved.

He reached out and lifted my chin with his finger. A tingle went down my spine at his touch.

"You all right?" he asked. "You look downright melancholic."

I looked up into his eyes, and my throat grew tight. "Yes. Yes, I'm fine. I just miss her, that's all. She is such a sweet little girl."

He pulled his hand away and crossed his arms over his chest. "Did you ever think about having children?"

I blinked at the bluntness of his question. "That's rather personal, Mr. Marshall."

He raised his hand in apology. "I'm sorry. I just— Well, my wife wanted to have children."

I sucked in a breath. Constance Chatterley had once

mentioned to me that the sheriff was widowed. I wasn't sure if I should let on that I knew this. He had never offered the information.

"It never happened for us, though," he went on. "I think it broke her heart. She died five years back."

"I'm so sorry," I said.

"Not of a broken heart but influenza. Took her really fast."

"How terrible." I sympathized with his pain, but I was also glad that he'd shared this with me. He was such a closed book most of the time. I felt I should reciprocate.

"I always intended to have children with William, but I was so caught up in my career. I thought I would have plenty of time, but . . ."

"Life is short," he finished for me.

We stood there in silence for a few moments. Monty the horse blew out and then licked his lips.

"Guess the best thing we can do is make the most of the time we have,"

"I guess so," I agreed.

"Oh, I've been meaning to ask you, did you ever find out who put that stone in the oven on the day of the wedding?" he asked, changing the subject, for which I again was grateful.

"No. I haven't really had time to look into it or even really think about it."

"Guess that's a mystery for another day."

I smiled. "Yes, I suppose so."

Another uncomfortable silence ensued.

"Well," he said, breaking the tension, "what do you say, Arabella? Should we have another riding lesson next week?" He gazed down at me, his eyes sparkling with amusement.

I couldn't help but return the smile. "I think that would be lovely . . . Clay."

He laughed, and we walked back to the livery together, Monty trailing behind.

After Monty was back in his stall, munching on some oats, Clay and I parted ways.

I went back to the hotel, feeling like I was walking on air. I hadn't felt so carefree in a very long time. The mounting tasks I had to accomplish at the hotel, along with its financial difficulties, as well as the challenges I faced keeping my theater afloat in my absence, suddenly seemed achievable.

I quickly mounted the stairs, eager to be rid of my coat and hat so that I could get to the business at hand. But before I even entered the room, I could smell Percival's pipe tobacco.

I walked into the parlor to find him sitting in the love seat. There was no sign of Cordelia or Bijou. They must have been out for a walk. I set my hat on the desk and took off my coat, hanging it on the back of my chair.

"Don't you look lovely," he said. "You are positively glowing."

I set my hands on my hips, smiling at him. "Am I?"

"Indeed," he said, his lips turning up in a wry grin. "What have you been up to, Arabella?"

"Up to? I haven't been up to anything at all."

"Then why the glow?"

"Really, Percival. You are such a busybody."

He puffed on his pipe, studying me. "It's just that since you've arrived in our little town, you've been tense, uptight, and dare I say, a bit unhappy. What's changed?"

I shrugged my shoulders. "Nothing's changed, Percival. I've just had a good day. A *very* good day."

vinci-books.com/pryceofgreed

A poisoned guest. A web of family secrets. Can a clairvoyant actress solve the mystery before scandal steals the show?

Tasked with organizing a grand Winter Festival, Arabella Pryce is eager to impress—until a wealthy guest is murdered. Torn between keeping her secrets and aiding the sheriff, she must unmask a killer before her own fate takes a deadly turn.

Turn the page for a free preview…

The Pryce of Greed: Chapter One

TUESDAY, DECEMBER 5, 1885

The Bella Saloon hummed and buzzed with music, dancing, and laughter. It was one of our busier nights as Mr. Archibald Archer was hosting a party. Among the many guests were his sister, Bertha Stewart; her son, Ralph Stewart; and his wife, Mrs. Mary Alice Edwards-Stewart. They had come from California for their yearly visit earlier in the fall.

"My dear Mrs. Pryce, I understand you are responsible for running this year's annual Winter Festival," Mrs. Edwards-Stewart said. An elegant woman, she was striking with golden hair and an intense emerald gaze. Her well-defined cheekbones added a certain grace to her appearance, creating a look that was both striking and refined. Her taste in clothing was on par with mine, and her mink-collared coat and cuffs were of the highest fashion.

I nodded. "Yes. Apparently, the honor of planning the

festival has always fallen on the manager of the Arabella Hotel, and as I have no manager at present, that is me."

"The little children of St. Anne's Orphanage so look forward to the occasion," she said with a demure smile. "It is the bright spot in their year. We are not at all religious, but the family likes to support charitable causes."

I forced a smile. "I have a wonderful committee this year, so we will do our very best for the children." A knot formed in my stomach as I said the words. As an acclaimed actress, I was good at displaying confidence and assurance with my expressions and gestures, even if there was a host of anxious feelings brewing inside me. Focus was required to deliver my gift to others. And, if I do say so myself, I excelled at my art.

"You will do a marvelous job!" Mr. Archer, also known by the rather gauche moniker of Boss, exclaimed. "And you will make Archer & Archer Mining Company proud. Our little Winter Festival is one of the hallmarks of La Plata Springs."

Mr. Archer was a formidable presence in the room and about town. He was the founder and acting Mayor of La Plata Springs and owned of many of the nearby mines. He also owned nearly all the businesses in our bustling community and had a reputation for wanting every last one of them in his control . . . the Arabella included.

He had approached me on numerous occasions about buying the Arabella, and I had been sorely tempted to sell, as there had been, and still were, many problems with the hotel. But my late husband, who had bequeathed it to me, made it very clear that I was to run the hotel for an entire year in order to gain my full inheritance, which was a vast sum. He also expressly demanded I not sell to Mr. Archer. Apparently, they had not got on well. I didn't know the reasons behind the animosity, and I didn't care to. It was true Mr. Archer was ruthless in business, but so far, in the five months I had been in town, I had found him charming and supportive.

Mrs. Stewart, who had an even more daunting air about her than her brother, looked at me with a distinct coolness. I hadn't been acquainted with her for more than a few days, yet it seemed she consistently wore an uncompromising expression on her pale face, her lips tense and thin and her jaw rigid. If she'd let her features relax, she might be attractive. She had a glorious head of light-brown hair highlighted throughout with silver streaks, which she wore in a loose top knot.

The man standing next to her, a Dr. Cornelius S. Briggs, remained quiet but seemed attentive to the conversation. I wondered at his relationship with Mrs. Stewart. Was he a paramour or merely her doctor who traveled with her? No one had offered up the information, and it would be rude to ask.

"It's important that La Plata Springs be seen as a town that is inviting to tourists," she said. "Along with the railroad and the mines, not to mention the neighboring Indian communities, the township must convey to the public at large that this is a fashionable place to visit."

The blood drained from my head as I read into her words the prospect of failure in my duties as the organizer of the Winter Festival. Failure was something I could not endure. I always had, and would now, do everything in my power to succeed.

"Oh, Mother." Ralph Stewart chuckled. "You are putting too much pressure on this lovely woman. Everyone always has a good time at the festival, especially the children."

Just then, Bijou, my little Havanese dog, scampered up to us and danced on her hind legs, begging for attention. Her paws and long ears were sodden from the snow outside.

Mr. Stewart bent down to tousle Bijou's head, which she delighted in. He was a devastatingly handsome man in his early thirties, whose looks rivaled that of a Greek Adonis. He had a head of thick brown curls, dreamy dark eyes, and full sensual lips. Not that I took particular notice, of course, I told myself as my pulse quickened at the tenderness he showed Bijou.

"I'm so sorry," I said. "Bijou, sit!"

With a pitiful look in her little button eyes, she obeyed, embarrassed to be scolded in front of the guests.

"There you are!" Cordelia, my assistant, companion, and best friend, rushed up to us and picked up the dog. "Bijou would not be deterred from joining the party," she said, quite breathless from her sojourn outside. Her complexion was rosy from the cold and her sable eyelashes wet with moisture. Droplets of melted snow shimmered on the coil of thick, reddish-blond braid at the crown of her head. The shoulders of her dress were damp, too.

For such an intelligent woman, I wondered at the fact she had not worn a coat to take the dog outside, but she could, at times, get a bit lost in her own musings and did not often think outside of them. She did, however, have the wherewithal to bring a towel for Bijou, and she wrapped her up in it.

"I took her outside to do her business," she explained. "I had hoped the fresh air would distract her from the party but to no avail. She wants to be with the guests. Besides, it was just too wet for her to be out there for long."

I glanced at the large windows near the street entrance

of the saloon. The snow was now coming down in sheets, blanketing the ground.

"Very well, Cordelia. I'll take her."

"All right," she said with a shiver and handed the dog over to me. "I'll be right back. I'd like to change my dress."

"Yes, please do. We can't have you catching cold." I turned to the group. "Again, I apologize for the dog. She can be a little overenthusiastic at times."

Mr. Stewart reached out to pat Bijou's head again. "She is no bother, Mrs. Pryce. She is as charming as you are."

"Don't be such a sycophant, Ralph," his mother chided.

He dropped his gaze away from mine and pulled his hand back, giving me a slight bow. My eyes traveled to his wife, who regarded me with a prim smile.

Breaking the odd tension, Mr. Archer clapped his hands. "I must thank you again for tonight's party," he said. "You have once more organized a lovely gala. I knew I could count on you."

By "once more," he was referring to a wedding reception I had hosted a few months ago. Unfortunately, however, the groom was unable to attend as he had been murdered that very day.

Mr. Archer turned his attention to the group. "Did you know that in addition to Mrs. Pryce's beauty, and her accomplishments on the stage, and her social grace"—I balked at the word *grace* as, in truth, I had a tendency toward clumsiness. Some might even say I was accident prone, as the handsome sheriff in town, Mr. Clayton Marshall, had noted on several occasions—"that Mrs. Pryce is quite the detective? She has solved several mysteries since her arrival. We are so lucky to have her here."

I smiled at the praise of my sleuthing skills, though it

was a bit thick. From the sternness of her countenance, Mrs. Stewart seemed to agree.

I had only been prompted to solve said mysteries to either save my own neck or to support a friend. I had no wish to solve another murder—should another befall us, God forbid—ever again.

"Oh." I batted a dismissive hand in the air. "You are too kind, Mr. Archer. I am no detective. Just a concerned citizen," I demurred.

As to his other compliments, I will admit that in addition to my panache on the stage, I did excel at entertaining. One did not spend a good deal of one's life in New York society without mastering such skills. The city's elite clamored to be invited to one of my parties at our Fifth Avenue mansion.

How I longed to get back to that life, but I was here, fulfilling my duties at the hotel. So, I would make the best of it, despite the somewhat crude amenities of the limited kitchen and lack of an accomplished chef. But Lottie, our new cook, did have her own set of skills, and they were improving by the week.

Though flattered by his words and the confidence he'd placed in me for the welcome reception for his sister, I was a bit surprised Mr. Archer insisted his family stay at the Arabella and not his hotel, the General, just three doors down, for the weekend of the festival. He was determined to make his hotel a rival to mine.

"If you don't mind my saying," I said to the group, "and don't get me wrong, I certainly appreciate the business, but I had assumed you all would have stayed at Mr. Archer's hotel this weekend or continued to stay on at his ranch."

"Well," Mr. Archer said, tilting his head toward the window, "we decided to leave the ranch for a few days as we were concerned the weather might prevent us from attending the party, and—"

"I prefer staying in town, anyway," Mrs. Stewart cut in.

Mr. Stewart chuckled at his mother. "Mother is a city dweller through and through, and she does love her creature comforts," he explained. "We have been at Uncle Archibald's house for several weeks now, and we felt we were wearing out our welcome."

"Bah!" Mr. Archer said. "Nonsense. You are always welcome. But as I was saying, Mrs. Pryce, we were concerned the weather might impinge on our attending the festival. As to the General—"

"It is substandard in amenities," Mrs. Stewart said, interrupting him once again. She glared at him with such fierceness it made me flinch. Mr. Archer cleared his throat, obviously uncomfortable with his sister's blunt assessment of his hotel.

In that instant I felt sorry for the man, though I had to agree. However, I never would have said as much to Mr. Archer's face. The General was nothing compared to the Arabella. Mine was the best hotel for miles, and it rivaled any luxury accommodation in Denver. Mr. Archer's hotel was simple in its offerings, with rudimentary furnishings and without food service or the niceties of a fine hotel. It served primarily as a rooming house for the miners in Mr. Archer's employ.

Mr. Archer cleared his throat again and then addressed me with a restrained smile. "The Arabella is a much more suitable lodging," he finished. "And I figured you could use the business."

I blinked at the tone of condescension in his voice and bit back a retort. He wasn't wrong about my needing the business, but how rude to say so in front of everyone!

Mrs. Stewart scoffed. Perhaps she, too, thought his comment uncalled for.

Uncomfortable with the tension in the air, I was about to change the subject but was diverted when a sudden wave of icy coolness permeated the room and the distinct smell of pipe tobacco tickled my nose. A zing of anxiety coursed through my body that the others might sense the presence of yet one more guest, uninvited as he was: Mr. Percival Blank, the Arabella's resident ghost.

Grab your copy…
vinci-books.com/pryceofgreed

The Pryce of Greed: Chapter Two

Much to my annoyance, which also verged on fear, Percival stood between Mr. Archer and Mrs. Stewart with his hands behind his back and a ridiculous smile on his transparent face. Bijou, who sometimes read my emotions better than even I did, barked. She usually barked or growled when he appeared, and I often wondered whether she could see him or merely sensed his presence.

"Hush, girl," I said, lowering her to the floor.

"So, Mrs. Pryce," Dr. Briggs resumed the conversation, obviously just as uncomfortable as I was with the strain between Mr. Archer and his sister, for which I was grateful. However, at the moment, I found myself tongue-tied at Percival's sudden appearance. "Tell me about this detective business," he continued. "I find it quite fascinating."

Snapping out of my paralysis, I shook my head and looked at him. He was every bit the distinguished gentleman, with an intelligent demeanor and inquisitive gray eyes. "As I said, I'm no detective. I just lend a hand when necessary."

I glanced at Percival who raised his eyebrows at me. My involvement in the investigation of La Plata Springs' most recent murder had been vexing to Sheriff Marshall. He claimed he was concerned for my safety, which I don't doubt, but I had believed I'd had good reason to pursue such a task, as I was helping a friend. But that was finished, and now I could concentrate on matters of the hotel.

Mrs. Stewart crossed her arms, clutching them to her sides. "My goodness, I suddenly feel quite a draft in here," she said with a shiver and a look of utter distaste.

"Do you?" I asked, giving her a smile. "I'm quite warm."

Despite the chill that always accompanied Percival, I was overcome with heat. This particular ability to see spiritual entities had caused me a good deal of trouble, and I daresay trauma, as a child. It had instilled in me the perpetual fear that should someone learn of my abilities or witness me interacting with a person who was not visible to anyone else, I would succumb to the fate of some of my distant relatives who had been accused of witchcraft, or insanity, and had ended up in an asylum because of it.

I knew not everyone had the potential to see Percival, only those who shared my sensitivities, and so far, no one in the town seemed to do so. Should he choose to, my ghostly friend could still make himself visible, but it required a good deal of effort on his part. Especially if the viewer had a natural resistance to that phenomenon. However, there were other ways he could make himself known, as he was doing now with the frigidity of the air.

"It *is* a bit cold in here," Mrs. Edwards-Stewart concurred with her mother-in-law.

"Very well." I nodded toward the fireplace on the south wall of the saloon. "I will have Clarence stoke the fire. I'll go fetch him." I glared at Percival and gave a discreet tilt of my head toward the door that led to the hotel lobby. "The drafts in here can be quite bothersome!" I added.

With Bijou on my heels, I pushed my way through the lead and glass door and entered the lobby. A wave of cool air followed, sending a shiver up my spine. I hustled my way to another door, which was positioned behind the reception area, and entered into a narrow hallway that led to the hotel's annex.

Once through it, I whirled around to find Percival standing there with that pensive and Byronic expression he often wore on his translucent face. Bijou barked again, and I shushed her.

"What are you doing, Percival?" I asked in a loud whisper.

He lifted a shoulder in a shrug. "I don't know why you worry so. I mean no harm."

"Yes, I know you mean no harm, but—"

"I just wanted to join the party. It's been some time since I've seen the Stewarts. I see young Ralph has finally settled with a wife. He's always been quite the ladies' man."

"I don't have time to talk with you, Percival. I must get back to my guests."

"Very well." He sighed with a forlorn expression on his face. "Are you banishing me to our rooms?"

I rolled my eyes at him. "They are *my* rooms, and of course not. Do as you wish. Just stay away . . . please?"

"If you insist," he said reluctantly.

When I entered the Bella once again, I was affronted with loud, arguing voices. Bijou scuttled over to Kitty Carlisle, the manager of the Bella, who shared a glance with me at the commotion. One of the saloon girls picked up the little dog and held her protectively to her chest.

A man with his back to me was confronting Ralph Stewart. "I know you did it!" the man said, his voice thick with a Mexican accent. The room had gone silent and all eyes were on the small group.

"Here now, Mr. Valdez," Mr. Archer said, stepping in.

The man rounded on him. "You are the cause of it all!"

I rushed over to them. "Excuse me, is there a problem here?"

The man straightened his coat. He had a proud face, with deep-set coal eyes, heavy brows, and an equally heavy, if not impressive, mustache that trailed to his chin. He wore a thick gold chain with a pendant around his neck. It looked to be a religious medal of some sort.

"This man"—he pointed a finger at Mr. Stewart— "killed my brother!"

Mrs. Edwards-Stewart narrowed her eyes at him. "How dare you—"

The elder Mrs. Stewart remained silent, but her expression was hard as granite.

"Now, now, Valdez." Mr. Archer laid a hand on his shoulder. "Let's finish this business at another time, shall we? We are upsetting the guests."

The man shook off his hand. "This isn't over, *señor!*"

He gave me a quick nod and then stormed over to the bar.

"My goodness." I glanced over at Mr. Stewart, whose eyes, glinting with rage, followed him.

Killed his brother?

There had been an Enrique Valdez who had been a guest of the hotel a year ago and was found dead in his room. Could it be the same man this Mr. Valdez had been referring to? I had not yet arrived in La Plata Springs at the time of Enrique Valdez's death, but from what I had learned, there had been no visible evidence of murder, and according to Mr. Archer, there had been no doctor to examine the body. It was assumed he'd died from drink or natural causes.

Mr. Archer let out an uncomfortable chuckle. "It's of no issue, Mrs. Pryce. A minor . . . family matter."

I glanced over at the bar. Mr. Valdez had ordered a beer and sat perched on one of the barstools, his gazed fixed on Ralph Stewart.

Ignoring him, Mr. Stewart's features rearranged themselves to reassume his charming countenance. He graced me with that dazzling smile of his as his startling and powerful gaze settled upon mine. "A trifle, Mrs. Pryce. Do not worry yourself over it. Though, I must say, you are quite captivating with the glow of concern on your adorable face."

"Oh— I" Despite my shock and utter confusion at Mr. Valdez's accusation of murder, I found myself blushing at Mr. Stewart's boldness, especially since his wife was standing right next to him. "I-I'm fine," I said. "As long as everything is all right here."

"Your solicitude is admirable," he said, his voice like butter and his eyes holding me hostage.

"Ralph." A stern voice echoed behind me, shattering the tension in the air. Sheriff Clayton Marshall strode up to us. His stormy blue eyes settled on me, and a hint of a smile turned up his lips. It vanished as fast as it had appeared when he refocused his attention on Mr. Stewart.

Grab your copy…
vinci-books.com/pryceofgreed

About the Author

Kari Bovée is an award-winning author of historical mysteries, weaving suspense and unforgettable characters into captivating tales. Her enthusiasm for storytelling began in early childhood, as illustrated by a note sent to her parents from her third-grade teacher praising her talent for writing. This passion flourished during her pursuit of a Bachelor of Arts in English Literature at the University of San Diego. There, she customized her studies to include independent projects in short story writing, playwriting, novel writing, and even a debut as a theater director.

Her acclaimed Annie Oakley Mystery Series, Grace Michelle Mysteries, and The Pryce of Murder Series have earned recognition in national and international writing competitions. Her awards include the Chanticleer International Goethe Grand Prize for *Peccadillo at the Palace* (2020) and the New Mexico/Arizona Hillerman Award for *Girl with a Gun* (2019).

Before turning to fiction, Kari worked as a technical writer, educator, and consultant, but storytelling has always been her true passion. She and her husband, Kevin, spend their time between their horse property in the beautiful Land of Enchantment, New Mexico, their home on the sunny shores of Hawaii, and their travels to inspiring destinations.